I0678527

Gordon A. Long

Praise for the "World of Change" Series

"...from this point I couldn't put the book down until the last page. It is engaging, terrifying, suspenseful, and surprising."
- Books and Pals Reviews

"The author's imagination has created a great universe and left me wanting to know what happens to Aleria in the next book in the series.
Highly recommended."
- Amazon Reviewer

"Out of Mischief is definitely a fun read, and I would recommend it for young adults and grown-ups alike"
- Amazon Reviewer

"The book's strength is the depth of character of its protagonists and antagonists."
- Amazon Reviewer

"I always find myself easily drawn into the complex worlds Mr. Long creates...I would happily recommend this novel to readers of fantasy, adventure, and romance."
- Cas Peace, author of the "Artisans of Albia" Saga

Gordon A. Long

Into Trouble

Gordon A. Long

AIRBORN PRESS
Delta, 2014

Gordon A. Long

Into Trouble

Published by
AIRBORN PRESS
4958 10A Ave, Delta, B. C.
V4M 1X8
Canada

ISBN - 978-0-9921243-4-2

Printed by Kindle

Cover:
Design by Dusty Hagerud and Gordon A. Long
Model Josie Buter
Photography by Gordon A. Long

Back cover painting "Road Through an Oak Forest,"1646-47 by Jacob Isacksz van Ruisdael

Gordon A. Long

Thanks

To Elizabeth Hull for her ideas and her editing
Dusty and Josie for their artistic assistance

CONTENTS

Gordon A. Long

"*Actions that are justified require little scrutiny. Actions spurred by emotion, unaffected by reason, require reflection. Thus, in a future situation of the sort, you will act on different principles and be more pleased at the outcome.*"

- Master Ogima

1. Answer to a Challenge

Aleria looked up the street ahead, where brightly dressed young women gathered towards the Grand Portico of their old school. She noted that many had armed escorts. *Hmm. Must be worse than I thought.* Then she looked at her companion, striding along as if she were going somewhere important. "Tell me again. Why are we attending this event?"

Mito grinned over at her. "We are going to the Fall Reunion to reaffirm our ties with our class and our loyalty to the principles of the Young Ladies' Academy. It's traditional."

Aleria nodded with as straight a face as she could manage. "And since neither of us, as I recall, had such a warm or rewarding stay at the Young Ladies' Academy, nor did we form close ties with many of our classmates, nor do we have much use for traditions — especially outmoded ones — the question remains. Why?"

Mito shrugged. "I'm not sure. We should show up to the Graduate Ladies' Tea, anyway. Whether we go to the Fealty Ceremony tonight is another thing."

"The Twins won't be there."

"Let's just see how the Tea goes, shall we?"

Aleria grinned at her friend. "Maybe you just wanted an excuse to get dressed up."

"I am not dressed up! Not any more than I should be."

Aleria regarded Mito's warm-hued autumn dress, its skirt emblazoned with falling-leaf patterns that Aleria knew her friend embroidered herself. "You look pretty good. Some of these swordsmen are pretty well turned out. I wonder if any of them are eligible bachelors."

Mito reddened. "That is not why I'm going." She turned to regard Aleria. "You certainly didn't overdress."

"I have a dress on. It isn't too short; it isn't too long. It is an appropriate colour for the season: medium brown. I have quite dainty shoes on, with even a little bit of heel." She turned to regard her reflection in a shop window. "They wouldn't be much good in a fight, but for afternoon tea, they'll do."

"Oh, you'll do, I suppose. But..."

1

Gordon A. Long

Something in her friend's face alerted Aleria and she turned. A nondescript young man stood there. He was dressed in a workman's smock and he hadn't shaved lately. The sour odour of an unwashed body enveloped them. His shoulders were hunched, and he held out his hand to Mito.

"You ladies got a coin for a poor lad, down on his luck?"

Mito glanced around in confusion. "No...I...I'm not carrying any..."

The lad leaned in. "Then what about that necklace? It looks like it's worth a bit. I'll take that."

Mito's uncertainty disappeared, and she backed up against the nearest shop wall. "You will do no such thing." Aleria could see the fingers of her right hand bunching up the hem of her skirt at her thigh, just the level where a hideaway dagger would hang.

"And who's gonna stop me? C'mon, lady. You don't need that, 'n' I do."

"And if I won't give it to you?"

He loomed over her. "I need some money. I ain't et for two days. You don't want me to get rough, now, do you?

Mito looked over at her. "What are we going to do with this person, Aleria?"

The boy's face changed. "Aleria?" He glanced at her, then looked again. "Aleria...oh."

"Yes, Aleria. I know you, don't I? You're Geran's buddy. I see you down at the Raven once in a while...Miedio. What do you think you're doing?"

"Um...well, they told me there was a lotta girls meetin' here today, and I really need some money...so I thought..."

"You didn't think too much. Do you know what trouble you're in?"

"Yeah...look, Aleria, please don't tell Geran, hey?"

"And why shouldn't I tell Geran?"

"He told me he'd lend me some money, but I said I was fine, and he warned me about doin' somethin' like this."

"But you were too proud to take his money. You'd rather rob some defenceless girl."

"Yeah, but they ain't so defenceless. They all had men with 'em, today. I ain't seen so many swords on one street in all the time I bin in the city."

"And we're going to see a lot more in the future, mostly because of people like you. Now the question again. What are we going to do with you?"

"I didn't do nothin'. I didn't!"

"Only because we stopped you. What do you need money for?"

"I'm gonna get throwed outa my room, and I ain't et proper for weeks."

"And why is that?"

"I can't find any work. I tried, Aleria, I really did. But nobody needs men right now, and I ain't got a trade to speak of."

Aleria looked at Mito, who shrugged. She dug in her reticule. "All right. Here's a crown. Use it for what you need. Do you know where the Dalmyn Cartage yard is?"

"Yeah. Yeah, I know that."

"Be there tomorrow first thing the gate opens. I'll find something for you. And no more of this thieving, Miedio. Got it?"

"Yeah, Aleria, I got it. I didn't want to rob no one. I just didn't know where to go."

"I suppose. Away you go now."

"Yeah, thanks Aleria." He turned to Mito. "I'm sorry, Miss. I hope I didn't scare you too much."

"You didn't scare me. Now git." She flicked her fingers in a shooing motion.

Clutching the coin with both fists, the lad scurried away.

The two friends looked at each other, and Aleria threw up her hands. "I've been saying for months that there's something wrong. That kid would work if he could. There just isn't anything for him. And it's not as if the economy is down. The harvests were fine this year. Our cartage trade is booming."

She shook her head. "They taught us in Politics and History class that our Enlightened Monarchy here in Galesia was the best government in the world. Better than the anarchy they have over in Ferboden since they had their Citizen's Revolution or whatever they called it."

"Better than the wondrous Domaland, which is run by an oligarchy of businessmen, I gather." Mito shuddered.

"Exactly. But here we are with revolutions every other year, and beggars and thieves roaming the streets of the capital city. What's wrong with us?"

"I don't know. I guess you'll have to fix it, won't you?"

She favoured her friend with a look of scorn. "Sure thing. Right after I find the fabled iron mines in the Eastern Shield." She shrugged. "Well, at least we can find a place for Miedio. If he can work at all."

"I wish it was that easy to find a place for me."

Aleria regarded her friend. "Are you serious?"

"I don't want to talk about it now. Let's go to the Tea."

"Fine with me."

They turned and continued down the street, but Aleria's mind was no longer on the upcoming celebration.

* * *

Aleria looked around the reception room. Beautiful panelling, beautiful dresses, beautiful young women circulating in meaningless eddies. "I have no idea what any of these people have been doing."

"You'll have something to talk about, then. I'm sure they're all interested in what you're doing."

She snorted. "As if I was a sideshow at the circus, maybe."

Mito glanced at Aleria's hip. "At least you didn't wear your sword."

Aleria swished her dress. "It impedes the flow of the fabric when I move."

"Oh, my. Evidence of fashion sense. The girl is growing normal."

"I am, however, still wearing the hideout you gave me."

"I wasn't expecting a complete transformation." Mito edged closer and dropped her voice. "I'm wearing one, too." She touched her right leg.

"I know." Aleria frowned. "And aren't you glad you were."

Mito grinned. "I hardly needed it, bastioned behind your fearsome reputation."

A new voice broke in from behind them. "Aleria and Mito, as usual. What bastions are you two talking about? Is life still all swords and battles?"

They turned to discover Plendinta, who was dressed as if a battle were the last thing on her agenda. "As it happens, Mito had just mentioned the street robberies."

The other girl shuddered. "Yes, horrible, isn't it? My brother had to escort me. He wasn't too pleased. How did you two get here?"

Aleria glanced at Mito, shrugged. "We walked."

Plendinta grinned. "Of course, nobody is going to bother you, are they?"

Aleria shook her head. "I don't know. The main assets a person needs on the street these days are sharp eyes and ears. By the time you have to fight, it's too late. You could be in the middle of a riot in an instant."

"It's certainly time they did something about those awful people!"

Aleria shrugged again. "Not a day to be talking politics. What have you been doing to keep out of trouble?"

"I'm a working girl these days." Plendinta indicated her pleated skirt and tailored jacket. Her hair was twisted up in a neat swirl behind her head.

Mito looked her up and down. "I wondered at the new look. It suits you."

"Thank you."

"What are you working at?"

Plendinta's look became wary. "We don't all have the leisure to do what we want, Aleria. My father's office manager left suddenly, and I was the only one available to fill in." Her face brightened. "It turns out I'm rather good at organizing people."

Aleria laughed. "I could have told you that years ago. Good for you." She looked the other girl up and down, then frowned and shook her head.

"What's wrong?" Plendinta tried to look at her own clothing.

"I couldn't wear a skirt that tight at the yard. I have to get up into wagon beds and climb piles of goods. And I wear walking boots because of the mud. I don't think they'd match."

Plendinta's smile returned. "No, I can't see you in a business outfit." She nodded, as if confirming a thought. "So you're working, too."

"Five and a half days a week. Invoicing and accounts payable."

"You always were good at Math. You like it?"

"Not much, but it's the price you pay for being in the middle of the action. I may have to run the business some day, and I need to be familiar with everything."

They nodded to each other in mutual respect, then Plendinta turned to glance around at the crowd. "Well, I've got a lot of people to talk to."

"You're chair of the planning committee, aren't you?"

The other girl grinned. "Organizing people. My skill."

Aleria raised a hand, and Plendinta scurried off through the growing crowd, making brief stops to talk to various people.

"She seems happy." She glanced over at Mito. "You don't. What's the problem?"

Mito's lip twisted, more of a grimace than a smile. "I know some of the girls will be horrified that Plendinta is working. They will find it much more comfortable when I tell them what I've been doing, which isn't much. But I'd take her place any day."

"Hmm. Well, if you're not enjoying the tea, we can leave."

Mito straightened her back. "I have nothing to be ashamed of, and jealousy is unbecoming a lady. We stay."

Aleria slapped her friend on the back, propelling her toward a nearby group. "That's the spirit. Let's find out if the punch is more interesting than the tea was."

They circulated through the crowd, and Aleria was gratified by the respect she received. "At least nobody has looked at me as if I were a sideshow."

"Try not to act like one and you'll be fine."

"This constant jabber is beginning to pall. Can we find somewhere quiet to sit down?"

"The Seniors' Room is probably empty."

"Fine idea." They started down the hallway.

Aleria looked around as if seeing the school for the first time. "You know, this is no place for me."

"You've been acting the perfect lady."

"I can cope. But think about it. All the other girls came with armed escorts; we walked here alone without a second thought. You frightened off a bandit – not much of one, I admit, but nonetheless a bandit – merely by mentioning my name. What place do I have at a lady's tea?"

Mito had no answer, and they were walking silently, each immersed in her own thoughts, as they entered the Seniors' Sitting Room. The group of girls who stood chatting and looking out the big bay window had certainly not noticed them.

"...I should hope she isn't! After the way her family acted, I'm surprised she was even allowed to attend the Academy, let alone reaffirm her Fealty in public."

Aleria froze, her hand on Mito's arm, aghast at the stricken look on her friend's face.

A voice chimed in. "What do you mean, Envelune?"

The other girl smirked. "You know the story. Her uncle bamboozled a whole bunch of people into investing in some project or other and then he let the venture fail and ruined everyone."

Aleria had never thought much of Envelune. She was a round-cheeked girl with protruding lips and a vacant smile that some of the boys thought pretty. That smile froze on her face as she turned to realize who was behind her.

"Oh. Aleria..." Her pudgy hand flew to her mouth in a predictable, helpless, gesture that infuriated Aleria even more. She stepped forward, her fists clenched. The other girl seemed to shrink, and her cowardice brought a sneer to Aleria's lip. She stared for a moment, deciding which piece to take off first...

A grip on her arm spun her around. "No, Aleria!"

"What do you mean, 'no?' This apple-brain has just impugned your honour and the honour of your family, and you think..."

Mito's grip firmed with unexpected strength. "My honour. My way."

"Your..." She was stunned by her friend's intensity, and that short pause was enough for Mito to slip in front of her.

"You should hope I'm not what, Envelune?"

The round blue eyes shifted right, then left, received no support. "Why, nothing, Mito. I didn't really mean..."

"But it sounded like you meant it, Envelune."

"Oh, no, it was just something I heard. I didn't mean to..."

"I see." Mito's voice stayed soft. "You didn't really mean it. Maybe you just now realize you shouldn't have said it out loud."

The girl nodded vehemently.

"And when you said it out loud, and you heard what it sounded like?"

The girl swallowed, winced, an ugly screwing-up of her face.

"What did it make you sound like?"

"It...sounded quite horrible."

"And when you realized that I had heard it?"

A tear started in the corner of her eye, pulling a dark trail of makeup down the soft cheek, "Oh, Mito, I just feel dreadful. I don't know how I can ever..."

Mito laid a gentle hand on the girl's round arm. "Perhaps you can, Envelune. If you really want to help me, the next time you hear someone say something like that, you can suggest that they check the facts before they spread malicious gossip. Can you do that?"

Envelune gulped again and nodded until it seemed she would injure her neck.

"Thank you, Envelune. That will help me a lot. And it will make you feel so much better, as well."

Envelune stared for another moment into Mito's calm face, and then the tears began to stream. "Oh, Mito, I'm...so..." The "sorry" was drowned in a wail of anguish, and the girl rushed from the room.

Mito glanced around at the stunned faces. "And what were we discussing that I'm not going to do?"

Only Plendinta had the starch to answer. "Attend the Fealty Ceremony tonight. Of course you're coming. Envelune is such a ninny sometimes."

"You shouldn't let her go on like that. It isn't good for her."

Plendinta glanced at Mito, then took a more careful look. "No...no, I can see that it might not be." Then her face lost its thoughtfulness. "But you are coming?"

Mito smiled. "We had been discussing it, but we hadn't decided. The Twins have some other affair they have to go to, and they want Aleria and me to keep them company."

"Mito, please come." Plendinta turned to Aleria. "Tell the Dennals they have to come, too. It just won't be right with all of you missing."

Aleria refrained from rubbing her forearm where Mito's grasp had left a definite welt. "That's very kind of you to say, Plendinta. We'll talk to the others and see what we can organize."

She gave the group a pleasant smile, then she and Mito made a graceful departure.

They had only rounded the corner when Aleria whirled. "Mito! Whatever..." Then she saw her friend's face: completely white. Her left hand shaking despite its firm clutch on her right arm.

"Mito, are you all right?"

The girl smiled, but her lip trembled. "Oh, yes, I'm fine. I...just need to sit down."

"Come over..."

The other's spine stiffened. "No! Not here. I can handle it!"

"I think we've made our ladylike appearance at the Tea. Let us make a discreet departure."

"I'm with you on that idea."

With pressed lips, Mito strode into the street, her arms tight to her body as if holding herself together by their strength alone. Aleria stepped alongside, shooting nervous glances at her friend's set visage.

As they made their way along the sidewalk she was relieved to see the colour come back to Mito's face and the stiffness leave her body. Soon they were walking at a more normal pace. Aleria felt it was time to speak. "You hurt me."

Mito's eyes flew wide. "Hurt you?"

"Yes, hurt me. Look. You grabbed my arm so hard, you left marks. How am I going to explain that to my mother?"

Mito glanced down with disdain. "Wear a long sleeve. You'll survive."

Aleria snorted. "I'll survive. I'm not sure that Envelune will. Poor, silly little cow."

"What do you mean?"

"I mean she would have been much better off if you'd have let me at her."

"I doubt it. You looked as if you were going to hit her."

"I probably was. Then she could have got mad; it would have been all my fault, and she would have been the poor victim, a role she plays beautifully. You, on the other hand, pinned her down like a mouse in the dissecting lab and stripped her bare. And it sounded like you were being so nice, there's absolutely nothing she can find to take offense at."

"Oh."

"Oh." She mimicked her friend's tone. "Not that she didn't deserve it, mind you."

"I thought I had good reason."

"Of course you did. What she said…"

"That's not why, Aleria. I did it to save her."

"Save her? …you mean…?"

Mito nodded. "I have seen you angry, Aleria, but rarely that angry. I really thought you might injure her."

"Was I ever going to injure her. What she said was so…so mindlessly cruel. So unfair!"

"Yes, it was, but I didn't want you to get into trouble because of me. I can fight my own battles."

"Obviously. It was a masterpiece. I am impressed."

"You're just saying that."

"No, I'm not. You were absolutely heartless. You laid it out so she has to take the full responsibility for her actions, and no one can do anything for her."

"I suppose that's good, isn't it?"

"It is if she can handle it. Do you know what it's going to be like from now on?"

Mito grimaced. "I don't know."

"She's going to be so sickly sweet to you you're not going to be able to handle it."

Mito's lip made a twitch that might have been a smile. "Which I deserve since I was so cruel to her." She glanced sideways. "At least in your twisted interpretation."

Aleria shook her head. "I may have a twisted mind, but I don't think any of them will ever be able to look at you the same again."

Mito frowned. "Come on, Aleria..."

"I mean it. They've never seen you like that before. I've never seen you like that before. What's going on?"

Mito shrugged. "I don't think anything is going on. I'm the same old me I always was. I have often wanted to defend myself, but I have never been placed in a position where I thought it advisable. Because of the way you were feeling, I knew I had to act, and I acted as I thought was correct."

Aleria nodded. "Oh, that was correct, all right. No one could fault you on your deportment." She chuckled. "Only on your benevolence. Poor Envelune."

"Poor Envelune! What about me?"

"I'm getting less and less worried about you." She shook her head once more as they moved on. "'A masterpiece, a true masterpiece."

She looked over at her friend. "Do you think we should go to the ceremony?"

Mito shrugged. "I don't know. Not many people bother with that sort of thing any more. I think the Twins are just making up an excuse not to go. How about you?"

"I don't know either. I had thought I would go before the Twins came up with their plan. Mother always says that even if they don't mean that much to us, those ceremonies mean a lot to other people."

Mito walked a few paces, then nodded. "I'm changing my mind about the whole thing."

"You are?"

"Yes. You and I don't think the Fealty Ceremony has a whole lot of relevance in today's world. It's obvious that Envelune thinks it does."

They had reached Mito's lodgings and stood a moment in the doorway. "And what she thinks should make a difference to us?"

"Maybe it should to me."

Aleria shook her head. "Now, you're really not making sense. You just cheerfully tied her up in the most beautiful bow-knot, and now you're worried about what she thinks?"

Mito frowned a moment. "If that kind of people think it important to keep me away, then I should go."

11

Aleria laughed. "Aha! That sounds like my kind of thinking."

"No, no," Mito sighed. "I'm not just being contrary like you. It's what your mother said. Some of the smaller-minded people set great store by those ceremonies. If I don't show up, some of them might take it as a snub. I don't want to give anyone an excuse to start gossip about me."

Aleria snorted. "You're going to let that sort dictate what you do?"

Mito shrugged. "I have all my life. Why change now?" Then she looked up at Aleria and grinned. "Besides, I've had my fun. I don't mind paying a little for it."

Aleria slapped her friend on the shoulder. "I'm glad you had fun." She peered a bit closer. "Are you all right, now?"

"Yes...you go on home. I'll see you tomorrow."

She looked down at her friend's face, still paler than usual. "What are you doing for the rest of the afternoon?"

"A whole lot of nothing. What else?"

"I'll just come up for an hour or so. We can send a note to the Twins, twisting their arms to come tonight. All right with you?"

"Certainly," Mito gave her a suspicious stare. "If you really want to."

Aleria put on her most casual grin. "I don't want to, but it's that or be polite to several ladies who are coming to see my mother about the Street Children's Charity Tea."

"Aha! An ulterior motive!" Mito turned to the door, pulling out her key.

"Exactly. And I can tell you how Envelune looked with her mascara running down her face!"

They trailed their laughter up the stairway behind them.

2. Teamsters!

Aleria took the package that the teamster offered, regarding him a moment before glancing around the wagon yard, then tucking the precious information under her arm.

"Was anyone different around?"

"What do you mean, my Lady?"

"Please don't call me, 'my Lady' around the yard, Jiame. It's too formal."

"Oh...uh..."

"Call me Ma'am."

"Yes, Ma'am."

"When you picked up the package. Did you notice anyone hanging around where they shouldn't be, that sort of thing."

He frowned, but then his brow cleared. "Oh. You mean like the bandit lookouts we was taught to keep an eye for."

"Yes. That's it. Anything like that?"

"Gee, I dunno, Ma'am. I never thought to check, in this close to the city. We aren't expecting...?"

"No, not any more than normal. I just wondered."

"No, nobody like that, Ma'am."

"Anything else unusual?"

"Anything like what, Ma'am?"

She didn't let out the huge sigh that threatened to rise up from the centre of her being. "I wouldn't know until you told me, Jiame. Just...anything out of the ordinary that you noticed."

"No, nothin' like that, Ma'am."

Aleria repressed the urge to look around again. She had talked long enough, out here in the open. "That's fine, then. Thanks for the delivery. Tell your friend in Hymnos that it got here in good condition."

"I will, Ma'am."

"And keep your eyes open. Everywhere, every road, no matter how safe you think it might be. Dalmyn has lost five wagons and had three men wounded this year, and these packages are even more important than bandits. Remember the rule; 'Dalmyn business is nobody else's.' Keep sharp. That's what a good carter does."

"Oh, yes, Ma'am. I will. I sure will do that, Ma'am."

She nodded, he bowed, and away he went. With a certain amount of relief, she couldn't help but notice. Taking another quick glance around the yard, she went back into the office. She glared at the package for a moment. Wouldn't she love to open it!

As if that was likely to happen. Raif and whoever he worked with up in the Castle – who she wasn't supposed to know – with their "required knowledge" attitude.

Then she shrugged and dropped it in her totebag. She had other things to think about. That circular riposte was ready. She was sure it was ready. But was it ready to try against an opponent who was honestly fighting back?

She looked at the clock. *Damn. I'm supposed to be meeting Mito for a training session.* She slipped off her ink cuffs and hurried into her office for her equipment bag.

* * *

Mito picked herself up off the floor again. "You are so smooth. I never even saw that coming!"

Aleria grinned. "I've practiced that throw about a thousand times against men twice as heavy as you."

"That's five times for me. Nine hundred and some-odd to go. My turn to throw you, now."

"Whatever you say."

There was a brief tussle, and nothing happened.

"What's wrong?"

"I'm not making it easy for you. You have to get me off balance first. Then the throw works. If you don't, then you're off balance, and I throw you."

"All right."

"There. That was much better." Aleria picked herself up. "It's polite in practice to let your partner down a bit easier, though."

"Oh! Did I hurt you?"

"Yes, but not much. That's the most important lesson in training. The pain doesn't matter, as long as you did the move right."

Mito's hands fell to her sides. "You certainly are a different person than you were last year."

"I am?"

"Yes. You seem so sure of things."

"Huh! 'Seem' is the right term."

"Why? What's wrong? Aren't you doing what you wanted to do?"

"Yes, but I'm not sure it's working. I mean, what am I doing? What is a young lady of the Ranked classes doing, learning to be a fighter of some sort? What good is all this?"

Mito shrugged. "I don't know. It was your idea. I thought you liked it. Are you going to quit?"

"No, no. I do enjoy it. I just wonder if it's good for anything."

Mito shook her head. "You haven't changed in that respect, have you? You've never been sure where you fit."

"That's it. There isn't a place for me, anywhere."

"You've got two choices, then, haven't you?"

"Two?"

"Yes. If you don't fit in with society..."

"Then I change myself so I fit in. That's about my only choice."

"Or you change society."

"Some chance of that."

Mito's grin came back. "More chance than of changing you."

"Did you say you wanted to practice getting thrown a few more times?"

Mito shrugged her fighting smock into position and put a fierce scowl on her face. "Let's just see you try it."

"That's a good technique." Aleria dropped to a crouch. "It's difficult to attack you when I'm choking with laughter."

Some time later, after a particularly hard throw, Aleria reached down to help Mito up. "I think it's time to quit."

"But I'm just getting it!"

"You're just getting thrashed. Isn't it time to give up?"

"You said you wanted a good practice."

"Not that good. You'll have bruises all over!"

Mito rolled her shoulders. "I suppose I will. I don't mind. I don't often get the chance to do this. We should practise together more often. I get the feeling that I'm accomplishing something."

15

Aleria grinned. "It sounds like I'm a bad influence. Not very ladylike."

"Then we'll just keep it between ourselves, shall we? Now show me that throw you just used on me. I was flying through the air before I knew what happened."

Aleria took a moment to realize that her friend was serious, then complied without comment. But it got her thinking. *If she can take it, I should be able to. I've been working that riposte for a year. I think I have it. If I don't, I'll just have to give it up. Now, who would be the best opponent...? Roeble Cloet is the best swordsman of the lot, I suppose...*

* * *

She went to sword practice early the next day to prepare herself for the challenge. When she was thoroughly warmed up, she approached her victim.

"Roeble?"

"Yes, Aleria?" He looked up from the weights he was lifting, sweat beading his forehead.

She glanced at the number of steels on the bar. "Impressive. I couldn't lift two of those."

He stood. "You didn't come over here to toss compliments around. What's going on?"

She grinned. "Nothing in particular, but I need a partner for an exercise. You fight with either hand, don't you?"

"I'm not as good with my left, but I'm competent."

"If you're fishing for a compliment, I didn't come over here for that, remember?"

"I'll get a sword."

Soon they were squared off. "What do you want?"

"Just some light sparring, not too fast. I'm trying to work something out."

He shrugged and reached out to touch her blade.

As they sparred, she kept her line a bit lower than she should, knowing that he would respond by attacking into the gap. Sure enough, soon it came, the perfect lunge in the fourth quadrant. With a surge of joy, she felt her reactions take over; there was a quick slither of steel on steel and the merchant's sword clattered across the floor. Silence descended on the training hall. She stood, her head high, aware of attention sliding towards her.

"What was that?"

She grinned.

He walked over and picked up his weapon, and she could see his sword weaving as he ran through his memory of the last pass. He glared at her. "You did it!"

She nodded.

"You made it work!" He frowned. "But my sword was not out of line. My sword is never out of line that way."

"It wasn't to start with."

"Then how did you make it work?"

"I practiced."

He shrugged. "I'm impressed, but you spent all winter working on one move that might work against five out of a hundred fighters, and only if they make a mistake."

"It isn't so much your sword being out of line as my sword being out of line. When you try to follow it..."

"Still. How many left-handers do you meet?"

"Roebel, take your sword in your right hand." She was aware of the movement in the training hall, as work stopped and fighters gravitated towards them.

"My right."

She nodded and stood in *guarde.* He followed her.

"Now attack in third."

"Third?...oh, yes. Of course."

He moved his sword up and around, lunging in towards her shoulder at about half speed. She parried with her tip, then ran her sword down against his, easing the pressure until he had pushed his hand far enough to the side, then flicking her wrist in that special way that flattened her blade alongside his. Then she swept around and upwards, and again his sword flew, scattering the onlookers.

"You did it against my right hand."

"I did. It works equally well, I think."

A new voice came, calm and low. "It does."

Roeble looked up to see Master Ogima standing there. He dropped both hands in disgust. "And that is the lesson."

A small smile may have quirked the corner of the Master's mouth. "And that is the lesson."

"Show me again." The stocky merchant strode to his sword, picked it up. In his right hand.

All right. I'm not so good with this side. She gritted her teeth and tried to relax her shoulders.

With a brief salute, he attacked. Hard. Aleria had a moment's panic, but then she realized that he was alternating lunges in fourth and third quadrants, giving her an opportunity to show what she knew. But he wasn't giving her any breaks.

She picked up her intensity, moving to the attack whenever she could, keeping him honest with the odd quick pattern that she knew she did better than anyone of his size and weight. Finally the moment came when she had enticed his sword into the perfect position, and again she twisted it away. This time he was ready and managed to hold onto his weapon, although it was so far out of line that her sword point touched his breast and was away again before he could recover.

This time there was applause. She looked up, startled. In the heat of the moment, she had forgotten the audience. Guilt flooded through her, and she turned and bowed to Master Ogima, presenting her sword hilt in mute apology for disturbing the class.

To her surprise, he smiled and waved it away, then turned to the rest of his pupils, "And that is the lesson for today." He looked around at his students. "And what is the next lesson?"

Roeble grinned. "I know that one. To do it without thinking."

"Correct. You can be killed thrice in the time it takes to think about what to do next. The move must come when it is the right time, without thought. That shouldn't take more than another five years."

He turned to the rest. "But enough of this. There is no easy lesson here. Aleria has developed an attack that most of you could not manage and many of you would never find use for. Do not waste your time trying to duplicate it."

The others turned back to their practice, some grinning. She turned to the Battle Arts Master. "Are you suggesting that I wasted my time?"

Ogima nodded towards Roeble and walked away. The merchant flexed his wrist as if it were sore, shook his head and sheathed his sword. Without a word, he slapped her shoulder and returned to the exercise she had interrupted.

Her heart singing, she went back to work.

3. A Tougher Challenge

It was good that her training was going so well, because she was discovering that the spying business was, basically, boring. She felt like an errand-girl: taking messages back and forth, never knowing what they contained. She was surprised at how difficult it was, not being able to share her problems with Mito. Finally, one day, her desperation drove her to try an oblique approach.

She strode the length of Mito' parlour, then returned and stopped in front of her friend. "Do you have any idea how dumb carters are?"

Mito glanced up from the blouse she was embroidering. "My father is a carter."

Aleria shot her friend an irritated glance. "You want to stretch it, so is mine. You know what I'm talking about."

"Maybe. Are you sure it's real?"

"You mean they play dumb? Why?"

Mito went on with her work.

"You mean they have to deal with somebody like me, someone they don't usually deal with, and they hide behind it?"

"The thought had entered my mind."

"So what do I do about it? I wear the same work smock that all the women wear. I don't use big words. I just talk to them, like anybody else does."

"Just like anybody else."

"Mito, don't repeat what I say. You know it drives me crazy. What do you mean?" Aleria, glancing quickly, thought she caught a smile at the corner of the other girl's mouth "You like that, don't you? You like getting me all riled up."

Mito's hands fell to her lap. "Well, I don't do it on purpose, but when it happens, I can't help but be entertained."

Aleria threw a cushion that her friend ducked with the ease of long practice. She went back to pacing the room. This was easy in Mito's sparsely furnished apartment. "I just can't seem to get them to talk to me. Naturally, you know."

"Why is this so important?"

"I work with them. They come into the yard, and sometimes they have business in the office, and if I'm there, I deal with it. But if I try to talk to them - you know, just make conversation - they go all closed up and say the stupidest things, and I can't get anywhere at all with them."

"Why would you want to?"

This was getting a bit too close to the mark, and Aleria knew she would have to turn the conversation away.

"I don't know. It's just that...I've never had the chance before. I knew they were there, you know, but I never had reason to say more than two words to anyone like that. And now I find I can't. It's very frustrating."

"Aha! The lady who can do anything she wants finds out she can't."

"Well, don't sound so pleased about it."

"Oh, stop pouting. If you really want to solve the problem, don't complain to me. Put your mind to it. You're supposed to be a thinker."

Aleria regarded her friend more closely. Mito's head was once again bowed over her work. Had that been a slight edge to her voice? "I wasn't complaining. At least I wasn't trying to. I was asking for advice. You're so good at talking to people."

"You mean I'm so good at talking to the lower classes."

"Mito, are you looking for a row? You're taking everything I say the wrong way."

"Maybe you're saying it the wrong way."

"What do you mean? I am...wait a minute!" She stood in front of her friend, demanding her attention. "You're upset. Don't bother to deny it. You're definitely edgy. What is going on? No, don't dig back into your knitting; you know it won't work. What's wrong?"

"I am not knitting."

"You're not acting like yourself, either." She sat beside her friend, removing the blouse from her hands and laying it aside. "Come on. Confess. You in love?"

"I am not! What a stupid question."

"All right, all right, you're not in love. So what is it?"

"Oh, nothing. Nothing specific. Just things in general."

"What? I don't see you having any problems right now."

21

Gordon A. Long

"You mean like you have? Like not being able to deal with carters? I wish I did."

"You wish you had problems? Are you out of your mind?"

"I wish I had your kind of problems. The kind you can work on, the kind you can solve."

Aleria looked into her friend's eyes a moment, then dropped her hands, stood, and went back to pacing.

"Fine. Let's get it out in the open. I'm rich and you're poor. We never talk about it, in case it creates some kind of a rift between us. Well, if something that stupid is going to cause a problem after all the years we've been friends, then I guess it had better start, before we delude ourselves any more.

"I'm rich. I can do what I want. You're poor, and you can't. There's nothing for you to do but hang around the city and try to marry some rich man twice your age and live a rotten life because you have to do it to support your family.

"So I've said it. There it is. Are we still friends?"

Turning to face her friend again, she was relieved to see Mito's slow smile forming.

"Right to the point as usual, Aleria. I couldn't have put it better myself." Then her face became serious again. "If I could only do something! If I could get work!"

"Get work? You can't just go out and offer yourself as a lady's maid, you know."

Mito shrugged. "Don't think I haven't figured that out. You're lucky. You've got a position."

Aleria threw up her hands. "But I don't really have a position. I know it looks like it, but I don't. I just go down to Father's main wagonyard and help out. I've been doing it for most of my life. I've sort of made myself a little niche. People depend on me for certain things because I've always done them. But it's not a position. I'm just the Lord's daughter messing about, and I'm sure all the men in the yard know it."

Mito tilted her head to one side. "I doubt if that's the truth. I'm sure you're quite useful, and I'm sure they appreciate it. It must be nice for them to have someone young and female around."

"You may be right, but that's not what we're talking about. We're talking about you. You need a position? That's it?"

Mito's shoulders slumped. "I'm just so bored. Not as if I can't entertain myself. That's not the problem. I just feel so useless. There's nothing I can do to make my lot in life better. I just sit here, waiting, and soon I'm going to have to go home. They can't afford to keep me here forever.

"And you're so caught up in what you're doing, but of course you can't talk about it that much, because I don't know anything about what's going on, so I just have to watch from the side." Mito's hands clenched in her lap.

"...and think that maybe our school friendship is going to slip away, now that we have our new lives."

Mito shrugged miserably. "Maybe. I don't know."

"I suppose it's possible." Aleria stopped in front of her friend, grabbed her hands, and hauled her to her feet. "So what are you going to do about it? Sit there and mope? I'm going to give you back your own advice. Think about it. Put that intelligent mind of yours to work. What are we going to do about this?"

Mito smiled slightly. "I guess I deserve that." Then her brows furrowed, and she looked at the taller girl for a moment, as if calculating. Finally she spoke. "I'll be honest with you, even if it's a risk. I do have a problem. If I try too hard, it might seem like I'm clinging to you, because you're rich."

Aleria nodded seriously. "It's always best to get these things out in the open. That's what Mother says. Otherwise they fester and spoil relationships. Let's get one thing straight. You're my friend, and I love you, and I don't want to see you go. I'd miss you a great deal. I depend on you. Ask Father. He's always saying he doesn't know what he'd do without you to keep me in balance."

"Oh, he's just joking."

"He's not, and I'm well aware of the fact. Anyway, I don't want you to leave. On the other hand, I doubt if you want to get into some kind of a 'paid companion' sort of position. I can't see our relationship staying anywhere near the same if we did that. So what do we do? Come on, girl. We've got to find you something to do that gives you enough money to live here until you get married to some dashingly handsome and rich son of the higher nobility, and we can work from there. And incidentally, something to do that's interesting enough that your brain doesn't atrophy through lack of use."

"Sounds like a tall order."

"Don't worry. There's no rush. We'll think of something." She stopped moving around and faced her friend. "You know how I said I wished I had your problem? I'd like to restate that. We both have the same problem."

"I suppose." Mito nodded twice. "We are both looking for a place, and our society doesn't seem to have one for us."

Aleria frowned. "And there's a good chance that you're going to solve your problem sooner I'll be solving mine."

"That could be true, now that I think of it."

Aleria picked up her reticule and slipped the strap on her wrist. "I've got to go home, now. I have to get up in the morning. If I don't show up at the yard at the same time as the men it doesn't show a good example."

Mito grinned. "I just can't picture you going to work at the same time as the men. By choice! That's just like Early Practice, last year. I didn't think you'd make it then, even when you had to go."

"You see? Working for a living isn't all it's cracked up to be. I'm going to find you a position, and then you'll be sorry for making fun of me."

They laughed and bantered as she slung on her cloak and moved down the stairs to the street. Now that she was finished school, Mito had moved into a pleasant little suite of rooms over a shop in one of the nicer quarters of the upper city. It was an easy walk from the Dalmyn mansion, so Aleria didn't need the coach to bring her back and forth. It was nearing dusk as she set out, but there was little for a girl to worry about in this area of town, especially one with her training. However, remembering her lessons about not inviting trouble, she kept her eyes open and her hideaway dagger loose in its sheath.

As she paced along, she greeted the odd shopkeeper or errand boy that she passed, but her mind was on other things. The spying business was just the niche for Mito. After all, she would probably be more successful than Aleria herself was at pumping information from the louts who carefully but not subtly slipped those tight grease-cloth packages into her hands. Sometimes she

24

wondered if they even knew what they were carrying. Probably not, in some cases. She would have to start figuring out which were the intelligent ones, and which were just messengers. *Have to keep a list in my head, write nothing down. Then if Mito starts to help, I could tell her, introduce her to them. Yes, I'm going to have to talk to Father.*

She found the opportunity after supper the next day.

"Father?"

"What is it, dear?" His head was still buried in his papers.

She winked at her mother, sitting with a book in the other easy chair. "Mother, tell him to listen to me."

His head came up and he made a point of looking at her. "I answered you already, dear."

She grinned at him. "Of course you did. Now, are you paying attention this time?"

With a sheepish grin, he gave the letter he had been reading one more reluctant glance and put it down.

"Thank you. This is serious." She sat forward a bit. "Mito has a problem."

"Oh?" She knew that would get his attention.

"Yes. The same old one."

"Ah. Poor girl with a name but no husband."

"That's right. And the name's not that strong either."

"And you want me to get her a husband? Wouldn't your mother be better at that?"

She grinned. "No, no, that's not why I'm asking. We're trying to find her something to do so that she can stay in town until she gets a husband."

He thought a moment. "She can always stay here, if that's what you want. I'm sure your mother..." He glanced at his wife, as if tossing the responsibility to her.

"Father, thank you very much, but you know how that would work out."

"I'm glad you realize it. So why are you asking me?"

She tossed her head, side to side. "I don't know. I thought maybe if you put your mind to it..."

He grinned. "You never ask me unless you have something already planned. What do you want me to do?"

She rolled her eyes. "This time I don't have anything planned. She needs a position, but I know there aren't many places for women in the business. I didn't think you could hire her. I did think maybe you might come up with something."

"Can she drive a team?"

"Father! Be serious!"

Her mother put down her book. "You may be approaching this the wrong way."

"Oh?" She couldn't keep the surprise out of her voice.

"Yes. What's your real objective?"

"I told you. To find something to keep Mito..."

Her mother shook her head. "No, it isn't. What's Mito's real objective?"

"Oh, I see. To get married. Hopefully to someone rich enough to help her family out."

Her mother sat back and peered at her daughter. "That sounds quite mercenary. Not the Mito I know."

Aleria shrugged, her hands wide. "She doesn't like it either, but what else can she do? Her family made a huge sacrifice to keep her in the Ladies' Academy all those years. She's one main hope for them. If she could marry well enough, they might even get a foothold back in the city. They might regain the power of their name."

Her father crossed his arms. "So the real problem is her family name, which suffered a few years ago because of some poor political choices and some bad business luck. I remember, now. A failed scheme of some sort. A sawmill, wasn't it?"

"That's right. Her uncle, who is the head of the family, put his name on the line in order to raise money for the project. The idea was to use the cataract at Hymnos for a millwheel to cut lumber. They thought they could cut the Shaeldit timber, then only have to move cut lumber by road to the markets.

"Yes, I remember. It sounded like a good idea, but their wheel was faulty and a flood damaged it."

"That's right. If they'd had more money, they could have bought better steel. If they had more influence in court, they might have got permits for better Mechanicals. If their name had carried the right clout, it could have succeeded. But they didn't have enough of anything. To make it worse, they were using some kind of new construction technique to get around the lack of steel, which nobody seemed to notice until the problems arose. Then all the old fogeys were pointing fingers and saying 'Mechanical, Mechanical, evil, evil!' So they had to sell their town properties and move out to Hymnos. They're using the remains of the mill to grind wheat and running the cartage business that we deal with. It's a good operation, but too small to support a Ranked family, and their name is tainted, so they can't raise money to expand. You know how that works."

"So that's the real problem."

"Yes, father, but I'm not naive enough to think we're going to solve something that her family has been working on for fifteen years. We're concentrating on the problem we can do something about."

Her mother cut in, "Which is...?"

"To get Mito something...no. To get Mito married."

Her mother nodded. "So why don't we get to work on that?"

She stared at her mother a moment. "Really?"

Her mother smiled. "Why not? If it's something you want to do."

"But what do we do?"

Her father laughed. "You put you problem in the hands of an expert. And that's not me." He rose, sliding his papers into a leather case by the chair. "You two go ahead and plan the capture of some poor victim. I don't want to listen to how it's done. It might remove the final illusions I cling to about my own courtship, all those years ago." He wandered out of the room chuckling.

His wife grinned. "Well, I think you can safely say that your father ducked out of this one."

"I think he did. So what are we mere women going to do?"

Her mother leaned back, her hands clasped around one knee. "I suppose we do the usual."

"What's the usual?"

"You know. The social whirl. Parties, outings, appropriate invitations, that sort of thing."

"Mother, you know how I hate that!"

"Yes, I do. Did you ever think it might have a purpose?"

Gordon A. Long

"I suppose."

"That's right. How does Mito feel about it?"

"Just like I...no, I suppose she doesn't, does she? I always thought she put up with it because we had to, but now that I think about it she never complained. Not that she ever complains, mind you. But she would have let me know."

"Well, then, I suppose we'll just have to ask her. There's no sense in making a lot of plans if Mito isn't included. Why don't you invite her around tomorrow afternoon and we can talk. I'll be home from that luncheon at the Aevoli around mid-afternoon."

Her mother thought a moment. "That will be a good time, as it happens. I can drop a few hints, ask a few pointed questions, see what the flow of the current brings."

"Mother! Gossiping again."

"That's right, dear. As long as it's useful gossip." Her mother smiled, patted her cheek and rose. "Now, I have some work to do in the kitchen, and you have to be up early if you're going down to the yard in the morning with your father as usual."

"I certainly am. Thank you very much, Mother. I know you're going to be a great help."

"Anything for a friend of yours."

"I know. I have so few."

"You have as many as you want, dear." With that enigmatic remark, her mother strolled out towards the rear of the house. Deep in thought, Aleria made her way to her rooms, to spend a restless night.

4. An Unwelcome Visit

The middle of the next morning Aleria was involved in a search for some lost papers when she noticed that silence had descended over the office. Looking up, she realized that Raif was in the doorway, and the clerks were all looking at him, unsure of what to do. They didn't know who he was, but anyone dressed in a top hat, spats and gloves at this time of day wasn't a customer. Puzzled, she put the box she was carrying on an empty shelf and stepped forward.

"What brings you around a real workplace?" She could feel the office pick up its pace again. "Aren't you afraid someone will give you some honest labour to do?"

He returned her smile. "Many have tried, none have succeeded. So this is where you toil."

"When I'm not being interrupted by the idle classes. May I assume you're here on business?" She wondered what could be so important to bring him down. She led him into her father's workroom, closed the door, and turned to frown at him. "Should you be here?"

He nodded. "I don't see any problem. I just came down for a visit. I don't think it will do any harm for me to be seen around here sometimes. I needed to talk with you. Can anybody hear us?"

"I don't think so, but I wouldn't say anything too loud. Anybody could be at the door. With the noise from the yard, who would hear them?"

"All right. I just wanted to know if you got any reports from Taine in the last few days."

"Taine? No. I gave you everything three days ago at Lady anSharate's garden tea."

He rose and began to pace the room. "I was hoping for something since. I sent a man out there to look around and I haven't heard anything from him."

"Is something wrong?"

"Nothing overt, or we wouldn't be the ones working on it. But there is a possible problem." He glanced at the door. "Speaking in general terms, there might be a new situation of the kind we have already experienced, but much more serious, because it's much less obvious. That's all I would like to say at the moment. If you haven't any more information, then I'd better go."

"That's all?"

He turned, his hand on the door handle. "What do you mean?"

She raised her hands in exasperation. "You come down here, risking the secrecy of our relationship, just to find out if there's been a message? And there isn't, and you leave? Why did you come? You could have sent a letter. You could have figured out a way to invite me somewhere. But you came yourself. Why?"

He seemed taken aback for a moment. "I just came to see if there was a message, that's all."

"I don't understand. You've got me all worried about this, and now you just walk out? Couldn't you give me a little more?"

"You said anybody could be at the door. I'd better not."

"Right. Well, thank you very much." She walked closer, dropped her voice. "Next time, when you're sitting up there in your castle with all your guards, will you think before you come running down here for no reason? I'm the one in danger if anyone suspects me. Next time, just think, will you?"

He leaned close as well. "We have someone out there, and he's disappeared. Do you know what that could mean?"

"Disappeared?"

"That's right. I sent him undercover and he's just dropped off the map. No contact for weeks. Do you know what that might mean?"

"I...I see. He's out there...alone?" Images rushed into her head, unbidden.

"That's right."

"What can we do?"

"That's the problem. Nothing. Just let me know immediately if anything shows up."

She pulled her thoughts back to the present. "That still doesn't excuse you coming down here. All you've done is make me worry. Next time, can you please wait until you have something to say, or something for me to do, before you risk my cover as well?"

She pulled the door open before he could answer, and stepped into the hall in front of him. She smiled sweetly over her shoulder as she walked away, chatting pleasantly, and he had no choice but to follow. "Thank you for coming, Lord Canah. I'm sure my father will be pleased to hear the news. Do drop by again, whenever you're in the area."

He turned in the doorway, about to say something, but glanced at the rest of the room, full of over-industrious clerks, and changed his mind. "No difficulty at all, Miss Dalmyn. I hope to see you at my father's next reception. Perhaps we can speak further then." He turned on the heel of his shiny black boots and left, striding more rapidly than usual, his cane stabbing the sidewalk as he went.

She turned back into the room, where no one would meet her eye. Through the anger, a small thought came to her that this wasn't such a bad thing. They probably thought she was having some sort of a lovers' quarrel with the young lord who had come to see her. But what a stupid thing to do! *He's going to get a piece of my mind at the Duke's reception next week.*

Then a thought entered her mind, slipping in unbidden. *If there's a rebellion starting, someone has to go out there. Someone we trust. Someone who knows what's going on.* The old images rushed in on her, and she gritted her teeth. *Not me. I've done my duty for the king, and that's it. I don't have to. Nobody's making me. Raif will forbid it outright.*

She felt better at that thought. Raif would never ask her to go into that sort of danger. *But who to send?*

* * *

Aleria strode into the kitchen.

"Mother, have you been pulling strings?"

Her mother didn't pause in rolling the pastry. "You know me, dear. I'm always pulling strings. Which one just gave you a tug?"

Aleria sighed in exasperation, waving the parchment envelope she had just unsealed. "I'm sure you know what I'm talking about. I just received my invitation to Duke anCanah's next reception and Mito's been invited too. Who do you know on the Duke's staff?"

"As it happens, no one. Your father arranged that."

31

"Father?"

"Yes. He is not without social graces, however we may despair of him. Isn't this what we talked about?"

"Oh, most definitely. It will be good for her family to have her seen in the Duke's company."

"Your father did mention that aspect."

She smiled at her mother. "I suppose you did the right thing when you married him."

Her mother used the back of her wrist to rub at a bit of flour on her forehead and only smudged it. "I'm usually of that mind, myself."

"I see it didn't keep you from a life of drudgery in the kitchen, though." Aleria nibbled a strip of raw pastry off the corner of the cutting board. "It needs more sugar."

Her mother gestured with the rolling pin. "It does not. If you won't wait till it's cooked, what do you expect?"

Aleria licked her fingers absently. "I hope I get a chance to talk to Raif. Alone. Just for a moment."

"That sounds ominous."

"Do you know what he did? He came down and visited me at the Yard. I haven't been able to get a straight word out of the clerks since. They keep giggling like a bunch of girls when I go by."

"Why did he come to the Yard? You aren't supposed to be spreading that part of your relationship around, are you?"

"That's what I told him. I don't know why he had to come. He was worried about something, and instead of thinking, he just rushed down. I don't know what's going on, but he must be really worried. I hope so. Otherwise, he's going to get a real piece of my mind next week."

Her mother grinned. "I suspect he's getting used to that."

"What?"

But her mother had already picked up the tray of pastries and was giving the cook detailed instructions as to where and for how long they were to be left to settle. Aleria shrugged and turned away, planning what she was going to say when she got Lord Thoughtless in a corner.

The reception didn't go quite the way she had planned it. She started out showing him a cold shoulder, but Raif was so nice to

Mito that she couldn't stay angry. In fact he was so pleasant to Mito and so polite to Aleria herself that she had suspicions that he was trying to make a point of some sort. However, her friend sparkled under his attention, said all the right things at exactly the right times, and generally had a marvellous afternoon. It was only after Mito was involved in a discussion with three or four thoroughly eligible young men that she thought she could haul Raif away for a moment.

They walked out in the garden, but away from the trees, where no one could get close to them without being seen. She was all prepared to dress him down, but to her surprise, he beat her to the start.

"I'm sorry, Aleria. Maybe I shouldn't have come down there the other day, but I was getting worried. But that's been solved, now."

Her relief took the last of the anger from her. "He's safe?"

"Oh, he's safe, all right."

She glanced at him. "Raif, what is happening in Taine?"

He looked at her strangely for a moment, and she wondered if he was about to refuse to tell her. Finally he sighed. "I suppose I owe you something. Have you heard of Lord Fauvé?"

She puzzled through for a moment. "The name rings a bell. I should know, but I can't remember. Who is he?"

"I'm not surprised that you don't know him. He wouldn't be memorable at all, if he hadn't killed another student when he was here at school. The whole thing was hushed up as a training accident, but I don't think there was much doubt that it was a duel. They'd had words, there was a girl involved - there always is, isn't there - and then the other man is dead from a sword thrust."

She stared up at him. "Leaving aside your comment about women being responsible for all your problems, what has this Lord Fauvé done now?"

He grinned. "Sorry. I didn't mean it quite that way. You could take it as a comment on the gullibility of young men too, you know."

He became serious. "Fauvé hasn't done anything wrong. In fact he's been scrupulously clean in all his dealings. I'm just suspicious, that's all."

"Then what hasn't he done?"

33

"It's not like that. What is happening is that he's having bandit problems. Big bandit problems."

She thought a moment. "Oh. And he needs a larger force of men to chase these bandits down."

He nodded. "He's been increasing his payroll of mercenaries. The problem is, it seems he really has been having bandit problems. His neighbours, too."

"But their problems could be him."

"That's what I wonder."

"And what does the overall area look like?"

"Well, I can't take you in and show you, but it's quite revealing when you place all the bandit raids on one map."

She nodded. "You don't need to show me. Pinpoint the centre: right in the middle of Lord Fauvé's domain."

He nodded glumly. "But so far, he's been clean. He's even asking the king for financial support, in order to clear up the problem. The difficult is, the king might have to send it, unless we can show that it's a hoax."

She looked at him, astonished. "You mean he's been asking the king for money to raise his army for a rebellion? That's...that's..." she shrugged, "...that's pretty impressive, actually. But what's the problem? So he's got fifteen men-at-arms and a few mercenaries. It's hardly enough for a rebellion."

"He has twenty local men, and the same number of mercenaries. That he admits to. He also has a redoubt in the mountains near the border, he says in case the bandits come from Domaland, and he rotates the mercenaries back and forth, so no one can get an accurate count."

"Forty or fifty is bad, but still not enough to cause trouble."

"But what if he had an equal number of bandits? Now we're up to a hundred. Then what if he had support in Domaland? There is a pass through the mountains from his demesne."

"Why would Domaland support him?"

"The Oligarchs are businessmen. They have no use for our monarchy and its restrictions on Mechanicals. If they could get a toehold here with a little independent domain that allowed their traders free rein to sell all the Mechanicals anybody wanted? How do you think the merchants here would react? This isn't a bunch of bullies and disaffected farm hands like Slathe's lot was. This is a serious political threat to the realm."

"I see. And Fauvé is planning all this?"

"He might be. He might not be. That's the problem. I sent one of our pedlars in there three weeks ago and heard once from him. Nothing since. I sent another after him with instructions to look for the first and do nothing else."

"And...?"

"He reported in yesterday. He found the first one, all right. Up at the manor house, comfortable as a fox in his new den."

"Fauvé bought him?"

"Looks like it."

"But the second one got back?"

"Yes. He had no problems, but he was very careful and he wasn't asking any questions about anything sensitive."

"What now?"

Raif shrugged. "We need more information, but we need to get it a different way. It's the backside of the country out there, and they know every stranger that shows up."

"I agree. You know, I have a friend in Taine."

"You do?"

"Yes. A merchant's son I met on the road, just before I met you."

"Oh. A merchant's son. And he's a friend, you say?"

She regarded him through narrowed eyes. "Yes. Is there anything wrong with that? In fact, I got a letter from him just the other day, saying he might be coming to the Capital. Do you want to meet him?"

He held his hands up. "No, no, I don't think so. In fact, if he's going to help us there should be as much distance between him and me as possible. Do you trust him?"

"Of course! I wouldn't have mentioned him, otherwise."

"You met him on the road. How much time did you have to get to know him that well?"

She could feel her cheeks getting hot. "Enough time to know I trust him. That should be enough."

"It should?" She could see the colour rising in his face. "This is a serious situation, Aleria. We can't run a..." he looked around,

35

lowered his voice, "a...business like this one, trusting anyone we meet on the road for a few hours."

He paused to look at her, placed a hand gently on her shoulder. "There are men's lives at stake. You know what it's like to be out there. Think carefully before you recommend him."

She shook his hand away, but then his words got through to her. A shudder ran over her body, and she took a moment to calm herself. "I will think carefully. I won't rush into anything. Shall I invite him to visit, and sound him out? I promise I won't let him know anything until I talk to you."

He stared at her for a moment, then nodded, satisfied. "Yes. That sounds like a good idea if you're very careful. You might get quite a bit of information without him even knowing, if you do it right."

She tossed her head. "Don't worry. I'll pump him to the bottom of the well and he won't even know what he told me."

He glanced at her as if to see if she was joking, then nodded, apparently satisfied. "I shouldn't monopolize your time. Lady anTrus might need your support."

"Thank you for inviting her. I'm sure she's enjoying herself."

"I hope she is. I also hope her family gets over their troubles."

"You know about that?"

He grinned at her surprise. "Father briefed me on the guests as he always does. There seems to be some question as to whether her family weren't victims in that scandal, not the perpetrators."

"Oh?" She could think of nothing to say. *How does he know this when I don't?*

"Oh, yes. They needed to import better Mechanicals from Domaland to make the mill stand up to the higher volume of water in the spring, but there is suspicion that a competitor used some very underhanded tricks to get their permit denied. There was some talk about it at the time, but nothing was done. Father now thinks there should at least have been an inquiry, but now it's too late. So he did some checking, and his suspicions are confirmed to his satisfaction. Otherwise we could never have invited her. Sends the wrong message, you know."

"Yes, I suppose it does."

"Anyway, she seems a very pleasant sort. Can't think why she puts up with you."

She glanced up. "That had better be a smile."

"Point proven. There she is. Let's go see how she's doing."

They were approaching the group of young people. "And the other matter?"

"Do as you think best. I have to trust you, Aleria. We have to trust each other or we can't function."

She nodded, then put on a smile to greet the others.

Going home in the carriage, Mito's rare, quiet smile seemed stuck in place. Aleria couldn't help but grin. "Had a good time?"

"I suppose so."

"You lie. You had a great time."

"Oh, all right. I did. I met some very nice people, and I had a great time. How about you?"

"Don't worry about me. Tell me all about it. Who did you meet?"

Mito reddened. "Aleria, I am not going to do it that way. I will not go out and approach every man I meet as a prospective husband. I will not tear every one of them apart the moment I leave, analysing their financial status, their prospects, their family's acreage. That's...that's odious. If I had to do that, I'd go home and take whatever Fate had in store for me."

Aleria nodded. "Good for you. And if it will make you feel any better, you did a service for your family." She told her friend about her conversation with Raif.

Mito was astonished. "I knew that. I mean, I knew that we always considered ourselves to have been honest. But I always thought that was just how everybody talks. After all, nobody goes on about how dishonest they were, do they?"

"Well, it turns out others feel the same way as you do, because Raif told me that his father could never have invited you otherwise."

"And me just being seen there helps?"

"Oh, yes. You already know that, too, Mito. Remember those girls in our class who took note of every little detail? Who was meeting whom, who was invited, who was not? It turns out that kind of thing can be important for practical reasons. If I were thinking of dealing with your uncle and I saw you visiting at the duke's home, I'd feel more comfortable with the situation, wouldn't I?"

37

Mito shook her head. "I guess I have something to learn about politics."

Aleria laughed. "I guess we all have something to learn."

Mito suddenly became serious, as she often did. "How about you? Did you have a good time?" She paused to look in her friend's face. "I was watching you and Raif when we first came in. Why were you so angry with him?"

Aleria stared at her friend in consternation. "Was it that obvious?"

Mito laid a calming hand on her arm. "I don't think so. I know you pretty well, remember?"

"Oh, good. Yes, I was angry, a bit. He was being obtuse as usual."

Mito waited a moment, and Aleria knew it was time to tell her more, but she couldn't.

"Whatever do you see in him, Aleria? I mean, you always seem to be mad at him. You aren't...well...you wouldn't be seeing him for...political reasons, would you?"

Aleria felt the shock of discovery, then relief that her friend had figured out the spying. Then, as quickly, she realized the truth. *No, she means something else completely.* "Oh! You mean marry him? To further my father's political ambitions? Mito, I hope you know both my father and myself a bit better than that!"

"Well, I'm sorry, but you have to realize how it looks. You two spend a lot of time together, and I know you don't get along, and..."

Aleria sighed inwardly. "No, it's not that, Mito. At least, there's no chance of a marriage. It's just that my father and the Duke are spending a lot of time together due to business and political projects, and for the reasons we discussed earlier, it looks better if our families meet sometimes." It wasn't quite a lie, and she moved on quickly. "My mother has been exchanging recipes with Lady anCanah, you know."

Mito laughed. "If your mother is giving up her recipes, I know it's serious."

"Right! She'd give up her daughter first, any day!"

5. A Welcome Visitor

It was good to see Shen again. He had been in the city for two days before he called on her, which she thought was very circumspect of him. It was a pleasant morning, and she and Mito were in the garden, pretending to weed the flowerbeds but really just enjoying the sunshine. At least Aleria was. Mito had gathered a presentable pile of weeds beside her when the maid announced Shen. Aleria got up and went to kiss him, both cheeks, then a third for friendship.

"It's so good to see you again. You look so impressive, all dressed up!"

He glanced at Mito, then back at her, and grinned. "I thought you liked me pretty well the other way."

She felt herself begin to redden, and shot him a wicked glance. "I'd like you to meet my friend Mito anDrus. She's a polite person, and you'll have to curb your natural impulses around her."

He bowed over Mito's hand formally, as if to show off his court manners. "Drus? From the carting business over Hymnos way?"

"That's right. How would you know of us?"

He shrugged. "We always know who's around when we might need them. Sometimes the big outfits - mentioning no names, because we're being polite today - give us trouble, and we like to have some backup."

Mito grinned, and Aleria could see her getting in on the game. "Well, if you ever have trouble with whoever it is moves your goods down our way and you're looking for someone more reliable, you know where to come."

Aleria gave a long-suffering sigh. "If you two are going to talk business, I suppose that means I'll have to leave."

Shen took her arm with a flourish. "Oh, no, my Lady. I'm sure there are more important things to talk of. How is the lawn for croquet, this year?"

Aleria smiled up at him. "Coming along nicely, thank you. But what a good idea! Mito, where is the croquet equipment? I think I might have use for a mallet quite soon."

The talk ran on in this vein for a while, and all of them enjoyed themselves. The twins showed up later in the morning. Aleria couldn't help but notice how Shen glowed in the attention of four young women, and was glad for him. Her fears of him being an embarrassment were unfounded.

There was an informal gathering at the Sailor's Delight on Feast-day afternoons, and she was happier still when Hana suggested that they take Shen along to meet some of their usual friends. He agreed with enthusiasm, and they parted, all looking forward to meeting again.

"Well, what do you think?"

"I think I pulled a lot more weeds than you did."

"Mito, I'm going to throw this whole pile, small as it is, in your hair if you don't answer."

"I did. You just weren't listening."

"I was listening. You made a comment about my weeding."

"Very appropriately, too, I think"

"Are you trying to be obtuse?"

Mito gave her usual sweet smile. "No, just trying to be subtle."

Aleria studied her friend's face for a moment. *So we're still playing that game, are we?* "You meant that I was preoccupied before he came. You think I was worried."

"And?"

"I guess maybe I was, a little. So, now that the worst is over, what do you think?"

Mito did her the courtesy of answering seriously. "Well, from what you said, I wasn't expecting someone quite so polished. He certainly is witty."

"Yes, I didn't remember that about him, actually."

"What did you remember?"

Aleria found her face getting warm, tried to think of a cutting reply.

Mito giggled. "All right, we won't go into that. The Twins seemed to like him."

"Yes, and they're fussy, too. I'm pleased. To be honest, I was worried a bit. It was so difficult to remember what he was really like, and to try to predict how he would fit in, the Capital being such a different situation from where I met him.

"You mean with his clothes on."

Her head swivelled around abruptly. "Mito! I am astounded!"

"Well, you two started it. I was just keeping up the repartee."

"Well, if you don't mind, we'll just bury that subject, shall we?"

Mito took a moment, then nodded. "I thought so. You'll be dropping that part of the relationship, I suppose."

Aleria nodded. "I didn't know until I saw him here, with all of you. Then it just struck me that it wouldn't be right."

"I hope you let him in on the secret."

"A good point. I think he could tell, but I'll square it with him the first chance I get."

"Like you squared it with Kalmein the night of the graduation?"

Aleria realized she was blushing again. "Mito! You know I don't like to be reminded of that!"

Her friend shrugged, but Aleria could see the stubborn set of her shoulders. "I wouldn't bring it up if I didn't think it was important."

"All right. I deserve to have that mentioned, but I squared that with Kalmein a few months ago..."

"Better late than never, I suppose."

"...and I guarantee I won't make that mistake this time. Why did you bring it up? Do you like him?"

It was Mito's turn to redden. "I told you. I won't discuss young men like that."

Aleria grinned. "Right. Let's see how the Sailor's Delight goes, shall we?"

* * *

As Aleria entered the main lounge at the Sailor's that Feast-day afternoon, she could see a good number of their friends were already there. Sarit had brought a girl from next year's class. Good. Another outsider would make it easier for Shen. She had suggested that he show up a bit later. She wanted a chance to prepare them, and herself. She realized that she wanted this to go well. Very well.

Noticing someone useful to talk to, she went over to where Sarit's group was sitting in one of the big corner booths and made small talk. When there was a gap in the conversation, she turned to Nalt. "Been out to that nice summer place in Taine lately?"

"No, why do you ask?"

"Oh, I've got a friend from that region who's in town this week. Name of Shen Waring. He could be dropping in later this afternoon, and you might have something to talk about. The muddy roads, or something."

He smiled, "Well, I'm sorry to disappoint you, but we've been staying out of that area. Too many bandits."

"Bandits?"

The smile disappeared from his face. "Yes, seriously. There have been attacks on outlying farms and merchant travellers. One of the local landowners has been trying to get up some funds for some policing."

She tried to keep her voice casual. "Oh? Who's that?"

He shrugged. "I don't know. Better ask your friend. As I said, we've been staying away."

"I hope he does something, whoever he is. My father runs a line of freight wagons out that way."

The boy didn't pick up on this invitation, so she turned away, to see Shen hesitating in the doorway.

She raised her voice, just enough to carry. "Shen, over here!"

A grin lit his face, and he started towards her. She went to meet him, tucking her hand under his arm. "Come over and meet some friends of mine. Nalt, here, has a beautiful summer retreat on some lake near Taine, and he's afraid to go there because of bandits or something. Tell him he's silly."

Shen shook hands all round, then nodded to Nalt. "There have been some problems, but I wouldn't worry, if I were you."

Aleria saw a chance to boost Shen's reputation. "Do you still travel all over the region by yourself?"

He nodded and grinned. "Sure, but I'm pretty small stuff. Like I told you, I don't carry anything too valuable, and I talk real fast. Remember those mercenaries I told you about?"

She nodded but shot him a meaningful glance. He knew exactly what she meant, but the gleam in his eye told her that he'd keep her in suspense for a while longer.

Hana sat up a bit. "What mercenaries? You never said anything about meeting mercenaries, Aleria!"

She turned away from his look. "I never met any mercenaries. Shen did."

"And...?"

She nodded to him. "Go ahead, Shen. It's a good story."

He turned to the others. "I was camped just off the road, and it was already dark. All by myself, in a little tent behind a tree. These mercenaries, about a dozen of them, came marching up, thought they'd camp there that night. Remember the rebellion? They were headed out to sign up with the rebels. I was fine until one of them stumbled over me in the dark, looking for firewood. You know how mercenaries are: rough fellows, and they don't like to be surprised. Took a bit of talking to persuade him that I hadn't snuck up on him in my tent."

He grinned as the group laughed, and again Aleria sighed inwardly. Her friend could handle this bunch. Talk turned to the recent unrest, and her interest perked up.

"So you don't think there's going to be any trouble?" Nalt sounded more than a bit concerned.

Shen grinned. "I'd enjoy my summer place, if I were you. Take along a few friends if you want, but don't let a bunch of scum like that spoil your summer."

Aleria found the opening she had been looking for. "But aren't the local lords doing something about the bandits?"

Shen shook his head. "Lord Fauvé has some ideas but doesn't have the finances to handle it. He's hired as many guards as he can afford, but the other landowners are pretty backwards. They only think far enough to protect their own borders and let every man look to his own business."

"So how is this Lord Fauvé handling it?"

Shen shrugged. "I don't know, really." He grinned. "I guess I'll have to ask."

Aleria tried to keep her face calm. "You mean you know him?"

Shen's eyes rested on her for a moment longer than they needed to, and she realized what her question implied. "Certainly. Out in the sticks where I come from, the nobility have to find their company where they can. There's plenty of room on their social calendars for someone with a bit of education," he grinned, "and a lot of native wit."

She picked up the ball gratefully. "Well, you certainly have the wit. I can't see how the education helped you much."

He responded with his own witty insult, and the conversation drifted into less political topics. Aleria faded into the background, wondering how she could have turned the conversation back to Lord Fauvé without seeming too interested. *And what to do about bringing Shen in on the plan. What if Raif is right?*

"You're thinking a lot, Aleria." It was Hana, in a quiet aside.

She smiled at her friend. "True. Things to think about."

"You in love?"

"Why do people always ask that? Don't they think a young woman can have anything more interesting on her mind than men?"

Gita picked up the thread of the conversation from the other side of the table. "You mean there is something more interesting? What?"

They were interrupted by a sudden change in the sound of the room. It wasn't so much a silence as a dip in harshness, and then the noise resumed, but muted. Interested, Aleria scanned the area near the door. Three men had just entered. It wasn't so much their size, their dress, or their military bearing. It was an air of confidence that said 'Exalted' as much as if they had worn uniform. One of them was Raif.

They made no fuss, but took table in the bar area, conversed with a waiter, and sat back, looking around in interest.

"What are they doing here?"

"Gita, will you take your fingernails out of my arm. Raif and his friends are allowed in here, I think."

Hana shook her head. "They've never been here before, I guarantee it. Look how they're staring around. I'll bet he's checking up on you, Aleria."

Aleria shrugged. "Don't be silly. How would he even know I was here? Supposing he had any reason to check up on me. Which he doesn't." She had been watching, however, and when his head turned in her direction she tossed her hair a bit, just enough movement to catch his eye. He raised a hand and smiled, and she nodded in return, then returned to her friends.

"What was that all about?"

"Oh, Gita, it was about nothing. He knows I'm here, now, and I know he is. He'll come over and say hello in a while. He has to, just for good manners. If he has any other reason, that's his opening. If not, then he'll go back to his friends. Why make a big thing about it?"

Gita insisted on looking inscrutable, and Aleria kicked her under the table and concentrated on Fania's conversation with Shen and the others.

Sure enough, a while later a silence fell on her group, and she looked up to see Raif smiling down at her. She rose and extended her hand. "Hello, Lord anCanah. Good to see you again."

He nodded and touched her hand. "I don't recall it being quite so formal in the Sailor's Delight when I used to come here in my student days. Hello, Mito. How's the design for that badge coming?"

"Slowly. I've tried several styles, but nothing I like yet."

"I suspect you're too hard on yourself. Any of those sketches you showed me looked like they would do admirably. However, take your time. I know better than to hurry you. Rush an artist and all you get is a job of work." He turned to the Twins. "And here we have the Indomitable Dennal Duo." He bowed slightly. "I must remind myself to be especially polite."

Hana inclined her head regally. "So far, you do your upbringing justice, my Lord."

Raif grinned at the group. "These ladies have seen fit to question my etiquette on several occasions and have designated themselves my social watchdogs. My poor mother is ecstatic, needless to say." He nodded formally to Gita. "I believe it would be acceptable at this moment to request the acquaintance of your companions."

In a jovial imitation of proper etiquette, the Twins introduced everyone. When Shen's origins came up, Raif exhibited only polite interest, but Aleria, watching from the sidelines, could read a new tension in his body.

"Ah, Waring Weavers. A reliable company. Perhaps under-utilised by my family's interests in that area. How are your people dealing with the bandits?"

Shen shook his head. "I don't think the bandits are quite as serious as everyone at the Capital thinks. However, we have been trying to convoy so we can hire a few guards. It's hard for a small business to afford that."

Gordon A. Long

Raif nodded. "Perhaps I can put a word in, see if we can make some sort of arrangement."

Shen nodded as if this sort of break came his way on a daily basis. Raif turned the conversation to trivialities, and soon, with a casual farewell to Aleria, he rejoined his friends.

Immediately, as she knew they would, the Twins pounced.

"Mito! What was that about?"

'What badge? What are you designing?"

Mito, for once, seemed flustered. "It's only a badge I'm designing for him. He saw some of my embroidery and asked me for a few sketches. You can't do it right with just sketches, though, so I've been basting up some samples. As you heard me say, they aren't coming out very well, so I'm not making much progress."

"You're babbling, Mito."

"What kind of badge?"

Aleria sometimes felt that the twins were a little too enthusiastic, and for once, it didn't look like Mito was going to defend herself. "There is only one badge a young Lord is ever looking for. His Personal Signature. From what I gather, the ones who care take a lot of time and look at a lot of designs before they choose. I suspect Raif just wants Mito to give him some ideas. Right, Mito?"

To her surprise, her friend wasn't completely relieved by this rescue. Her head came up. "Actually, he led me to believe he will be using my design. He was very impressed with my sketches. He says he's tired of all the old stodgy 'coat of arms in gold' ones, and has some specific ideas himself. We talked it through and I was able to sketch out what he was talking about."

Aleria nodded. "You always were an attentive listener. What a good way to put it to use!" She couldn't have been happier. This chance to make a serious contribution to the Canah family could do Mito and her family no harm, and to have Raif openly offer to boost Shen's family business!

The afternoon wore on, and the talk ranged, as it always did, from the serious to the frivolous and back again. Shen carried his end admirably, and she stopped worrying about feeding him opportunities to shine.

46

Given the chance to listen, she began to get the impression that Shen didn't have much interest in politics at all. As long as the bandits weren't bothering his shipments, they weren't important. As long as Lord Fauvé's mercenaries were protecting his business, he was happy to have them there. She filed that in the back of her head for further thought.

The party wound down as people began leaving to prepare for their evening's entertainment. Shen was one of the last to leave - Aleria made sure it was not with her - and soon she and Mito were ensconced in Aleria's sitting room, dressed in their house robes, reviewing the afternoon.

"So, what do you think of Shen, now?"

"He handles himself as well as any of them. Being educated in the country certainly hasn't spoiled his wit."

"His family seem to have quite a bit of money."

"Aleria!"

"I know, I know, I'm not allowed to talk about him like that."

"That's right. You are not. I mean it!"

"I just want you to know, that if it happened that you were interested in him..."

"I'm not interested in him, Aleria."

"...don't let me get in the way, Mito. I'm not in competition or anything."

"You're not in the way, Aleria."

"That's good. If you like him..."

Mito dropped her hands in her lap with a loud sigh. "All right, Aleria. I know you're not going to let it drop until I tell you."

"That's right. I'm not." She looked at her friend in anticipation. "What do you have to tell me?"

Mito looked sideways at her. "Well...I don't want to upset you, but you know what you used to say about the boys in our class?"

"You mean that they were nice enough, but they were only boys?"

"Right."

"So what?...oh."

"I'm sorry Aleria. I know he means something to you, but...that type just doesn't interest me," she stared at her friend, "even if he were rich."

"...I see." Aleria was surprised at the small pang of disappointment this pronouncement gave her. She made a bright smile. "Then I won't be doing any matchmaking in that direction, will I?"

"Aleria, don't go all brittle on me. You had to hear it."

She tried to relax her shoulders, smile naturally. "I know. I got what I deserved that time. No, the reason I'm disappointed is that, when you said it aloud, I realized that I agree. He is a very nice boy, and I like him a lot. Period."

Mito shook her head glumly. "Another chance at romance, doffed at the dance."

Aleria frowned theatrically. "Another spud that's a dud, mired in the mud."

They glanced at each other for the timing, moaned in unison, "Poor us."

Aleria grinned. "Tragic, ain't it?"

Mito shrugged. "I guess we'll find a way to survive."

"We've managed so far. Chin up, girl. The next knight in shining armour is just around the next corner."

Mito clutched the front of her robe. "He better not be! I'm not dressed!" Then she sobered. "What are you going to do now?"

"What? With Shen? Nothing. He can't help but notice how I'm treating him."

"I don't know. Sometimes boys can be very dense. You said you were going to talk to him."

"I haven't had the chance. He's pretty perceptive where people are concerned. Part of why he's a successful merchant, I guess. Don't worry; he knows."

"Well, make sure he does. That sort of thing can be really messy. You've never been caught up in one."

"Neither have you."

"No, but I've watched the other girls doing it for years. They always seem to muddle it up."

"Maybe, but also you never hear about the ones that don't mess up. They aren't worth the gossip."

"True. I hope this is one of those."

"I'll be careful. This visit has probably been good for him, too. He has to have seen how things are around here."

"Probably."

"You are such a worrier, Mito. Come on. I've got a new book that you just have to read. It will take your mind off your troubles."

"Is it another one about pirates? That last one was far too bloodthirsty for me."

"No pirates, but a really tragic three-way love affair."

"Why do you read that sort of junk? You always just laugh at it afterwards."

"I know. But it's fun to pretend while you're reading, isn't it?"

"I suppose."

They walked back into the bedroom, chatting merrily. As they went, Aleria couldn't help but think that things were getting better.

6. Honesty Pays

Aleria was about to breeze into the day lounge when she realized that her mother had a visitor. It would be a friend, or Mother would have used the more formal salon. Still, she slowed and made a decorous entrance, then stopped dead.

"Mito! You said you had a meeting."

Her friend smiled as she placed her teacup on the tray. "I did."

"Oh. Finish early?"

"No."

"What?" She took in the scene. The dainty cups, the inlaid trolley. Her mother dressed for receiving.

"Just what is going on here?"

Her mother levelled her one of those looks.

"Oh. Pardon me for intruding." She turned to leave.

"No, Aleria, don't go. We're almost finished. Please join us."

She turned, unsure how to handle this invitation. The temptation to storm out fought with curiosity. *Just what is going on, here?* She sat down, composed herself into a look she had learned in Comportment class. Out of the corner of her eye, she could see Mito repressing a grin. She focused on her mother.

After a brief moment, Liniema turned to Mito again. "You understand the situation thoroughly?"

Mito pondered a moment. "You're sure he doesn't know?"

"Almost positive."

"And he really should."

"We are agreed on that point."

Mito nodded. "We are. I can create a meeting with him in the next two days. I will find a way to let him know."

Leniema nodded as if sealing a bargain. Then she smiled. "I believe that's it, then." She turned to Aleria. "Business over. I'd like to stay and chat, but I have some other details to attend to. If you've just come back from practice, I'm sure you could use a snack." She indicated the half-empty tray on the trolley as she rose.

As her mother left, Aleria slipped over to her mother's chair and loaded a plate some of the more nutritious dainties. Then she sat back and regarded her friend with mock severity. It was Mito's turn to assume the "polite interest" pose.

Aleria munched for a while, swallowed. "You're going to tell me, so let's jump to that point and save time and energy of an argument."

"Suits me."

"So?"

Mito leaned back. "Well, you know how I was worried about getting a position so that I could afford to stay in the city?"

"I could hardly forget."

"I decided I was going about it the wrong way. A person of my social status would do herself a disservice by stepping down to a position with a wage."

"We discussed that."

"I decided to concentrate on what a woman of my status is supposed to be doing."

"And how did you figure that out?"

Mito gave the grin that made her look about twelve years old. "I went to the expert."

"My mother."

"Exactly. Women like your mother don't sit around at tea parties and gossip about nothing. I know she never sets foot in the wagonyard, but she has influence. She has a position in your father's business, but she deals in facts, not goods."

"I never looked at it that way, but you're right. How can you do that?"

"I realized that I needed to do the same for my family." The dark-haired girl leaned forward eagerly, her eyes bright. "I needed to make a place for myself in the capital so I could further the family's interests here."

"You've already been doing that, by socializing with the Canah family."

"Yes, but that was just the start. I had to make a reputation as a useful person to know."

"How could you do that?"

"That was the problem. Your mother and I discussed it. We looked at my assets. Finally we settled on the strongest and most useful one."

"Your looks?"

Mito looked with longing at a throwable cushion nearby, but Aleria felt safe in this formal setting.

"All right. I was joking. What did you decide on?"

"Honesty. I have spent so much of my life being scrupulously honest, afraid to make the slightest error because of my family's tarnished reputation."

Aleria nodded. "That's true. You did have that reputation at school. I don't see how that helps much. Honesty is a bit of a hindrance in diplomacy."

"Quite the opposite. A person with a reputation for honesty can be very useful. Especially if she has information."

"Has my mother been feeding you information?"

Mito nodded, leaned forward. "It's amazing how many times it is important to get a certain fact to a certain person, and for that person to believe it without question. There is also a great deal of skill involved in the presentation of the fact, so that it is received in the right way. I find I'm quite good at it."

"Subtle and sympathetic."

"That's part of it. Being known as a protégé of Lady Liniema Dalmyn rather helps."

"And I gather you are successful?"

Mito rocked her hand back and forth. "Hard to say. I don't think I've made a fool of myself, anyway. I certainly haven't made any money at it."

"How would you make money at something like that? I mean, without being seen as a complete mercenary."

"I don't expect to. I expect to gain a reputation for honesty, and make friends and contacts."

"And that reputation will connect with the Trus name!"

"Right! After all, I'm the only family member in the capital. Whatever positive steps I can take will have effect out of proportion to my position in the family."

"But this is going to take time. How are you going to support yourself?"

"That's the part of the success I can't pin down. The family business is improving. My uncle has been able to expand his operations. I know part of that's because of me, because he has been interchanging wagon routes with your father. Because of that fact alone, my uncle has decided it's worthwhile having me stay here. I think he also understands the rest of what I'm doing. He was really pleased to hear about the social contacts I've been making. I haven't been able to send him any paying business yet, but everything helps, you know?"

Aleria sat back. "So all this time, while I've been thinking how much help I am to my father by messing about in his office, you've been quietly solving your family's reputation and financial situation single-handedly."

Mito blushed. "Not single-handedly. I'm sure it was just time. We've spent our sentence in purgatory, and people are willing to forgive and forget."

"And at the exact right time, there you are, providing exactly the right boost to the family reputation."

"It seems to be working."

Aleria jumped to her feet. "Well, this calls for a celebration."

"What?"

"A celebration. We must honour your success!"

"No, Aleria. You don't go out and celebrate something like this. You keep it quiet and subtle."

Aleria laughed. "I don't mean to tell anybody what we're celebrating. Let's just go out and have a good time."

"Oh. I suppose..."

"You suppose right. I'll send a note around to the Twins, and we can go out to that restaurant over by the old ramparts."

"And I can pay!"

"No you won't."

"Yes, I will. I'm an agent of my family and I have an allowance for entertaining. I'll put you down as 'prospective customers,' so it won't be me paying, it will be the Drus family business." She became serious. "It isn't cheating. Your family is in cartage, and the twins' father pretty well owns the river transport. When I tell my uncle who I'm dining with, he'll be pleased as punch."

"All right. Let's get moving!"

"You already are."

* * *

53

So Aleria was not too surprised the following month, when Roeble approached her after barehand practice. He was about forty, the elder son of a prominent merchant family, and the man responsible for the caravans they sent into foreign lands. He only came to practice when his work brought him home, but when he trained, he trained hard. Aleria didn't know him well, but she honoured his skill and his mental strength.

"Can I walk with you, Aleria?"

"Certainly. You don't usually go my direction, though."

"I wanted to talk with you. We could go for a drink, if you like."

She regarded him a moment. "There's a tea-shop just up the street." She paused and grinned. "And The Falcon opposite. Whichever you prefer."

He grinned as he ushered her toward the teashop. "Can't be taking a young lady to a tavern. My wife would never approve."

She nodded and led the way inside. They ordered and made small talk about training while the drinks came. Once the server left them alone, Roeble became serious. "I need an opinion on something, Aleria, and Master Ogima told me to talk to you."

"I can't imagine why."

"I don't know why, either. It has to do with the Drus family. Do you know of them?"

"Oh. Yes, I do."

"Good. Here's my problem. I've been having some dealings with their agent in the capital. A young woman named Mito. A niece, I believe. Seems young for such a responsible position. They might be perfect for a business venture I have in mind, but I don't know anything about them. What can you tell me?"

Aleria considered a moment. *How do I approach this? First and foremost is Mito's reputation for honesty.* "You understand they had some trouble, years ago."

"Yes, I know about that." He grinned. "Pardon me for saying so, but I think that whole situation was blown out of proportion by the family's social status. Believe me, all businesspeople have enterprises that go wrong."

Aleria shrugged. "If you use your social standing as a business tool, then you have to take the social consequences when the business has a problem."

54

He nodded slowly. "Good point. However, from what I've heard, anDrus did the best he could in the circumstances, and that was fifteen years ago. I've asked around, and there hasn't been a whiff of scandal associated with him since. What I want to know is, can I believe what this Mito says? What kind of person is she?"

Again, Aleria thought a moment before she spoke. "It's only fair to tell you that she is a friend of mine. I'm biased towards her. However, I hope you will believe me that her honesty is her strongest asset and she isn't likely to compromise that under any circumstances.

"In fact, if it came to a choice between her honour and the good of the family business, I think she would choose to be honest. That's probably more than I should be telling you."

He laughed. "Aleria, many members of the Ranking Classes are in business, just like your father. One factor that we merchants always take into account when dealing with them is that their honour is more important than their business. That was what destroyed the Drus fortune, years ago. They insisted on taking the responsibility while their business partners ducked out and went elsewhere. You haven't told me anything new about anDrus or your friend Mito. I just need to know if she and her family follow the usual pattern."

"I can't speak for her uncle or the family business, but I know that they have been very careful with their reputation for the last fifteen years. If Mito tells you anything, it will be as true as she can determine. That, I would count my life on."

He took a sip of his drink. "High praise."

She grinned. "I've had many years of dealing with her honesty. It hasn't always been an asset, as you might guess."

He smiled in return. "Now, that sounds more like the Aleria I know from practice."

"That was me, all right. Before that, I was making sure I spoke as Mito would have me speak. I have no right to compromise her honesty. Besides, she'd kill me if I didn't!"

The merchant seemed even more satisfied. He set down his empty tea glass, wiped his lips. "May I ask another question?"

"Why not?"

"Well, it's a bit personal. You train very hard. To the extreme, at times."

"Is that a question?"

"I suppose."

"If you want to know why, I don't mind telling you. I was caught up in Slathe's rebellion last year. I spent two weeks trapped in his army and I have not slept well since. I have determined that I will never be so helpless again."

"I see."

She grinned. "Plus, as my friends would tell you, I sometimes overdo things."

She looked at him a moment. "So why do you train so hard?"

He shrugged. "Same reason. I travel in dangerous places and I want to be able to protect myself."

"But you hire guards."

"Nobody can protect you like yourself. Besides, there's a second aspect to it. Confidence."

"What do you mean?"

"When you are physically confident of your ability to protect yourself, people can tell. Especially the kind of people who deal in violence. If you look like a victim, they can sense it and they will take advantage of it. If you have confidence they are more careful."

"I think I see what you mean."

He smiled. "And then there's the third aspect. My wife."

She raised her eyebrows. "Your wife? Is she that hard on you?"

"No," he laughed. "It keeps her from worrying. She knows I train hard and that I can handle myself, so she worries less when I'm on the road. Oh, I know she still worries. But it gives her something positive to think about."

Aleria nodded bitterly. "I know all about worrying when you can't do anything about it. I hate that."

He sobered as well. "True. But I have to go. It's my life."

"Couldn't you send someone else?"

"I could." He shook his head. "But it wouldn't be the same. I have to be there, to know what the situation is, how the prices change and why, how the people talk, how they respond. You have to be there. You can't count on second-hand information, not when your livelihood depends on it."

"I couldn't agree more." She finished her own drink.

He stood. "Well, I mustn't keep you any longer, Aleria. Thank you for being honest about your friend. I will take it all into consideration."

7. Just A Small Slip

Aleria looked once more at the tattered messages strewn over the table in Mito's sitting room. "You'd better put that mess away. I don't want Mito coming back from Hymnos and finding one of those lying around."

"It was good of her to let us use her apartment to meet."

She shrugged. "I don't like it, Raife. I didn't lie to her, but she isn't stupid. We need to find a better place for this."

He grinned. "That's the spy business."

"On the subject of spying, what are we going to do about these? The information is just not clear, and I didn't get anything from the drivers to make any difference."

"That's pretty normal, considering our sources."

"So we need better information."

"What about your contact out there? I assume it's Shen, the lad I met."

She shook her head. *How do I put this so Shen doesn't sound too bad?* "Circumstances...just aren't right for that."

He nodded. "I'm sure you gave it a lot of thought. It has to be your decision."

"Then we're agreed. Someone has to go out there. Someone we trust."

Raif nodded. "There's something going on, and we need an eye on the scene. I should go."

"You can't do it. Too many people know you. We need someone they don't know."

"Then who can we send?"

"I've thought about it. A lot. I don't like it, but I think it has to be me."

He turned slowly to her. "What?"

"Me. I know what we need to know. Nobody knows me. Nobody would suspect a girl."

"You're not going out there."

It was the answer she had expected, but she was stunned by the finality in his voice. "Pardon me?"

"Have you gone completely out of your mind?" His voice rose. "Is your memory so short that you don't remember what happened last time?"

"This isn't the same, Raif. It isn't the same at all."

He shook his head vehemently. "You think it will be different because you're travelling normal routes with commercial transport. Believe me, a group like Slathe's can turn up in a dangerously short time. Especially if they're being supported, as we suspect," he leaned forward anxiously, "and an atrocity with a prominent victim might give Fauvé the incident he needs to swing the support of the King."

She tried to smile, to break the intensity of his stare. "I'm hardly a prominent person."

"But your father is. Your mother is."

"Are you telling me that the situation is so bad that the roads of the kingdom aren't safe for travellers using public transport?"

He made a helpless gesture. Then his eyes shot straight to her. "Why is it so important to you to go out there?"

"Because I'm the right person. All right, I'll be honest. It's also my chance to do something. I can actually be of use, instead of hanging around here playing at helping. I told you, I don't like it either, but I'm the best person."

He shook his head again. "That's not good enough, Aleria. I think you're letting your personal desires get ahead of your common sense."

"My...personal desires?"

"You don't have to go chasing out to ... to see the Waring boy."

"Chasing out to see..." She stared at him. *How can he be so aggressively stupid?*

"Yes. If you send for him, he'll come back. Maybe his family should come to the capital, anyway, meet your family, all that sort of thing. The formalities are important, you know."

"Formalities?"

"I know you don't care for formalities much, Aleria, but have some consideration for Shen's family."

"Formalities? I'm not exactly marrying the man!"

"You're not?" He managed to make it sound like there was something wrong with that.

"No, I'm not. And if I was, what's that to you? He's a very nice person. He is not a 'boy' as you so rudely label him. He's a very responsible young man, and he's very important in his father's business," *How dare he look at me like that!*

"And I slept with him!"

"Did you?"

"Yes, I did. He was kind, and gentle, and considerate, and he treated me like a lady. And I enjoyed it."

"I suppose you did."

His face seemed pale, but showed no emotion. Somehow, this wasn't the reaction that she had wanted, that she had expected.

"I can sleep with whoever I want to!"

"I'm sure you can."

That didn't come out right, either. "Not that I do. Sleep with anyone, I mean."

"That's up to you."

"He's the only one, and it was only once!"

His piercing blue eyes turned to her. "Why are you telling me this?"

"Because...because I didn't want you getting the wrong...because I don't really...because it matters!"

He looked down at her as he swept the messages into his satchel. "I can't really think why."

Then he was striding from the room. Her outstretched hand dropped slowly, uselessly to her side. For a moment she stood there, then realized that her mouth was open. She turned, lowered herself to a chair. *What the hell got into me? Why did I say all that? He just seemed so smug, so self-assured in his superiority. How could he think of Shen like that? Shen is a pleasant person. He was gentle. Kind. Funny. I like him. Why shouldn't I? Just because his family is in trade. So is mine. So is Raif's.*

"Oh shit." She slumped in her seat, barely aware of having spoken aloud. *I am immutably, decisively, and irrevocably an idiot.* She sat there, unaware for a long while that the light was fading from the room, that a damp chill was seeping in through the open window. Finally she shivered, shook her head and stood. She looked around the room. He had stood there. She had stood here.

How had he looked? How had she seemed to him? Like a stupid git, bragging about her conquest. Like a child. A spoiled child.

She shook herself again. She remembered an expression of her father's. *When you act like a fool, hope it's only friends that notice.* Some chance of that.

"Well, Aleria, you've put your foot in a pile this time. The question is, how are you going to clean it off?"

She reached over and closed the window, staring at her reflection in the dark glass for a moment.

The only way to redeem herself was to prove that she was capable. She had to go out there and discover what was going on. Who was this Fauvé? She lit a lamp and strode to the bookshelf. *Mito must have a copy of the Rankings in here somewhere.* It took a while to find him, but there he was: only Esteemed, but legitimate, none the less. No extra honours, no battle records. Several recent acquisitions of land, but nothing impressive. Petty nobility with big aspirations. She wondered who would know anything about him. Besides Shen.

Once again, a pang of anger shot through her. *How could I have been so stupid?* Raif just seemed to bring it out in her.

With a start, she realized that she had forgotten to go to barehanded practice. It was the first session she had missed in weeks. Damn! She gathered her belongings, checked that everything was exactly as she had found it, made certain to lock the door and started home.

When she entered the family room, her mother looked up from her sewing. "Have you been having any trouble at your practices?"

"Trouble?" A pang of guilt for the missed session shot through her. "What do you mean?"

"Master Ogima has asked to speak with us. He didn't say why."

"He never mentioned it to me. When?"

"He will be here this evening. He said it would only take a moment." Her mother looked at her. "Are you sure there's nothing wrong? You look out of sorts."

Aleria grinned wryly. "Nothing to do with practice, Mother."

"Oh. Another battle with Raif?"

"Why do you say that?"

Her mother smiled. "Because that's the only thing I know that can put you into that sort of mood, these days."

"I'm glad I'm so predictable."

"What did he do this time?"

"Nothing except be his usual infuriating self. No, this one was all me."

"All you?"

"All me. I lost my temper and said some very stupid things." She raised her hands in the air. "He just gets this idiotic look on his face. Like he knows he's right, and how could I be so stupid as to miss it."

"And then..."

"...And then I proved him right." She plopped down on a chair, her shoulders slumped.

"Well, that's a change."

Aleria's head came up. "What is?"

"You admitting that you're wrong and he's right."

"Oh, no. It isn't that simple."

Her mother smiled. "Still, it sounds like improvement, to me."

"Well, thank you, mother. I'm glad somebody's happy."

Her mother thought a moment. "I just wonder whether Master Ogima is happy."

"I couldn't say. I've never heard of him doing this before."

Aleria puzzled it over during the evening meal. She was at a complete loss as to why he would want to talk to her parents. *I made very clear to him that my training is my own choice, and nothing to do with them.* Finally she put it aside. *I'll know soon enough.*

It was interesting, despite her anxiety, to see what the Master looked like in street clothing. He seemed slimmer, better groomed than she expected. His hair, which often escaped from his brow-band, was smoothed down, and his semi-formal jacket fitted his broad shoulders neatly, slimming them. He bowed to her mother in full respect for her heritage.

"Come in, Master Ogima. Would you like tea?"

Aleria resisted the impulse to roll her eyes. There were going to be no quick answers at this meeting. All the formalities would be observed.

"The hospitality of anDalmyn is not to be set aside."

Leniema's gracious smile ushered the Master to a chair. The social chatter was beginning to grate on Aleria's nerves when her father came in. Immediately another round of pleasantries started, interrupted by the delivery of the teacart with a selection of light pastries.

Aleria refused these, but she did accept a cup of the special green tea her mother saved for important visitors.

Only after everyone had enquired about everyone else's health and wellbeing and everyone had a cup filled could the business of the meeting be broached. There was a slight pause, then Master Ogima sat straighter and spoke in more formal tones.

"I have asked to meet with all of you in order to discuss an important matter."

They all nodded.

"It has to do with Aleria's training."

Three more nods. Aleria pressed back a giggle that bubbled in the back of her throat, threatening to express itself no matter what she did.

"How has she been doing?"

The master turned to her father, his voice relaxing slightly. "Very well. She has a strong spirit. She has a great deal of talent, and works very hard…"

There was another pause. *Here it comes.*

"Too hard."

"In what way?"

Ogima opened his hands, turned them palms up. "It is not easy to explain. In the Masters' classes, it is expected that the students push themselves to their utmost, and all of them do. Some work harder than others. Roeble Cloet, for example. You know the name?"

Her father nodded. "Merchant family. Roeble is the eldest son."

"Right. Roeble leads his family trading caravans all over the world. He is often in dangerous situations. He trains hard, because he needs the skills he is learning."

"And because it keeps his wife from worrying so much when he's away."

Master Ogima raised his eyebrows.

63

"He told me."

"Understandable." He turned to her parents. "I bring up this man as an example of a good reason for training hard."

"But Aleria?"

"From the beginning, I was concerned with the reason for her training. We spoke of it before she started. Training to cope with fear is a natural response and leads to good training. But Aleria is not training to cope with natural fear. It is different from fear. Fear is a natural response to real danger. With Aleria, the danger is not real. Terror is perhaps a better word. So when Roeble trains hard and then goes into dangerous situations, perhaps actually uses his training, he justifies his work.

"Aleria trains hard, but never gets to use her skills. This leaves her with an unsatisfied feeling. May I ask, have the nightmares stopped?"

Aleria shook her head.

"I had hoped they would, but I am not surprised that they have not. She is unsatisfied, and the fear remains. Her only solution is to train harder. But still she remains unsatisfied. Hold out your arm, Aleria."

She complied. He took a pinch of skin. "See how close to the surface the muscles are? Like a soldier after months in the field. Have you been eating well?"

"Very well, Master Ogima. I watch my food intake very carefully."

"And do you reject many foods? These pastries, for example?"

"They have no decent nutrition."

He ate one. "But they taste good."

"The taste doesn't matter. The food value does."

Ogima merely turned his glance towards her parents.

"I have seen this behaviour before. I had a student who trained himself to the point of collapse, from which it took him a year to recover."

"Are you saying I have to stop training?"

He considered her a moment. "And if you did. What would happen then?"

Stop training? Stop... Panic clutched at her throat. "I...I don't know. I don't know what I'd do..."

"Exactly. If you stopped training, this problem would still exist, and the symptoms would come out in another, perhaps a more destructive, way."

Her father had been silent through all of this. Finally he spoke. "Then what is your solution?"

The older man shook his head. "I think there is no solution under my control. This problem existed before she started training. It existed even before the unfortunate events which brought it to our notice."

Aleria stopped herself from jumping up. "What do you mean?"

The Master gave her one of his looks, and she sat back. She knew what he meant.

"I do not come with solutions ready-made. I merely come with information which I think all must consider."

"But surely you have suggestions."

"On the surface, it is simple. The problem is training without justification."

"So the solution is for Aleria to find uses for her training?" Her mother sounded shocked.

"Are you suggesting I hire out as a mercenary? A caravan guard?"

He smiled a bit. "No, that would be extreme. But I know that if there is no outlet for your hard-won skills, you will not find the peace you seek."

The Master rose. "That is all I have to say. I have presumed on your hospitality long enough. I find it lives up to all expectations," here he smiled at Liniema, but immediately sobered, "and I hope that, with serious thought, a solution to the problem can be found."

Her parents rose as well, and both escorted him to the outer door: a sign of respect. Aleria was too preoccupied to respond. When her parents returned, she realized that she was sitting in the same position, staring at nothing.

Her father sat beside her, close but not touching. "This was not news to us."

"It wasn't?"

Her mother shook her head sadly. "Aleria, you have been treading this line most of your life. This is little different from discussions we have had with several school officials over the years. 'Aleria is pushing too hard. Aleria seems driven to excel. Aleria is going to hurt herself if she doesn't relax a bit.' You know; you were at some of the meetings."

"You left out, 'Aleria is going to hurt someone else,' Mother."

"That one, too."

Her father sighed. "Well, Aleria, you've done it again."

"Done what?"

He shook his head. "You have a talent for arranging things so that you get to do what you want, but for the wrong reasons."

"I don't understand."

Her father took her hand. "You realize the level of concern about the situation in Taine, and what Lord Fauvé is up to. We need information."

"And we can't depend on second-hand information." She leaned toward him. "We need to send someone out there, and it can't just be a hired agent. It has to be someone we can fully trust."

"Exactly. Raif anCanah is determined to be the one, and his father absolutely forbids it. As it happens, I agree. There is no sense in sending an agent as obvious as Raif."

"I know. I told him that today."

Liniema had been listening to this conversation, her face growing paler. "Kensel, you don't mean to suggest..."

Her father shrugged helplessly. "She is the perfect one for the task. She can go out there and visit with the Waring family, even do enough business with them to make it look good, and get a feel for what's going on. Once word gets around that she is there, Fauvé is bound to invite her for a visit, and if she's careful, she can learn a lot without a great deal of risk. We have absolutely no indication that he mistreats anyone.

"You heard what Master Ogima said. She needs to find useful occupation for her training. She at least needs to be in a situation where it might be needed, even if she doesn't actually do any fighting. This problem is in her imagination. She needs to deal with reality, and she isn't going to do that sitting around in Kingsport working in the freight office."

He reached across and took his wife's hand. "We need to let her go."

"But what if...?"

"If it happens, then it happens. That's what letting her go means." He turned to his daughter. "Aleria, there is something which you need to know."

"What?"

"Your mother and I have discussed this many times, since you were old enough that we could understand your personality. All parents worry about their children, but we...felt we had more justification for our worry. We have always been afraid that one of your...incidents, you might call them, would go wrong, and you would be killed. It has almost happened already, once. We thought that having discussed it, and being prepared, it might help when the time came."

"And did it?"

"Who can tell? It was very difficult. It is difficult for any parent. Raif's parents were going through the same thing. Except for one detail."

"I know. Raif was there serving his king and the realm. I was there on a stupid prank. If he died, he died a hero. I would have died an idiot."

Her parents were silent.

"So what do you conclude from this?"

Kensel glanced at his wife, as if asking permission, before he spoke. "I think that if we don't give you the chance to do something useful..."

"...I'll do something stupid again." She sat there a moment. "You know, I should be angry at that. I should be all hurt and pouty that you would think of me that way."

She looked at her father, then turned to her mother. "But I know myself too well."

Liniema rested her hand on her daughter's arm. "And you're growing up."

Aleria tried to grin. "So maybe there's hope for me."

"We see a faint possibility."

"Well, if it helps you any, I'm not jumping for joy about this. In fact, I'm scared, Father. I know it's a tough and dangerous task, and I'm not going in there with any idea of glory. I'll go in, get the information, and get out. I'll keep my head down and take no chances."

"Unless…"

"That's right. Unless it's necessary. Don't worry. My self-preservation instinct is pretty healthy."

Her mother forced a smile. "We hope so."

8. Love Letters

She received another invitation, under the anCanah seal, to a social outing. No surprise; despite their argument, Raif would want to talk to her about the trip. The notes they had been sending back and forth were just not enough, and too likely to get into other hands. Face to face it would have to be, and she wasn't looking forward to the meeting.

She wondered how they would get time alone together, but Raif managed it beautifully. He had invited a bunch of enthusiastic riders, and the duke had some new stock they were all anxious to inspect. Aleria had already been to the stables so she bowed out. Raif offered to keep her company. As usual, if a couple wanted some time alone the rest were quick to realize it, and they trooped off without comment.

Raif led her to his office, a small, crowded room just off his personal suite. The ornate tiled fireplace was partially hidden by two large freestanding cupboards. Books lined one wall, and a map of the realm covered the opposite one. Various pins and marks on the map indicated whatever they were supposed to. She looked a moment, but could figure no pattern.

He arranged a comfortable chair for her and sat opposite. "They'll be gone for a while."

She grinned. "And they think they've set us up for an amorous tête-à-tête. If they only knew it was something much less romantic."

He shrugged. "Some of them would think it was more romantic. At least more interesting. I think we should be quite circumspect about this."

"I couldn't agree more." She sat back, folded her hands in her lap. "So."

"So." He nodded. There was an uncomfortable pause.

"There's something I have to say." She shifted in her chair. "It's about the other day."

"Our little argument?"

"Yes." She took a deep breath. "I was way out of line, and I said some stupid things. I have no excuse. It was just that…" she waved a hand vaguely.

"...that I was behaving in my usual obtuse way."

She glanced at him, surprised to see a slight smile. "Well, you were!"

"I'm sorry, Aleria. It's just that sometimes you astound me. If I'm not saying anything, it's because I can't think of anything appropriate."

She rolled her eyes. "And I interpret it as condemning my actions."

He shrugged. "Well, sometimes..."

"Sometimes you are." She laughed. "And sometimes you're right. Anyway, the upshot of the whole thing is that if I want to visit Shen, there are a lot of easier and safer ways to see him. I'm going out there on a serious mission, and I have no illusions about how dangerous it is."

"And you've got your way, so you can afford to be generous."

She pinned him with a glare. "Don't push your luck, Raif. I apologized once because I thought it was justified. I'm not about to make a habit of it."

He held up his hands in mute defence and she nodded, satisfied. "Now, what is this meeting about?"

"It's mainly about communication." He hitched forward in his chair, all business. "I hate to say it, but I'm going to have to agree on the idea you mentioned in that note. Nobody is going to bother with the love letters of a silly girl."

"Compliments all over, today."

He grinned slightly. "You don't expect me to cave in completely, do you?"

"Fair enough. Oh, I thought of one other thing. I won't be able to send them to you."

"Why not?"

"Raif..."

"Oh. Your cover story. The daughter of a junior branch of a mere Elite house can't be writing love letters to a duke's son. How shall we manage that?"

"Well, I hate to suggest it..."

"...but you already have the answer figured out. I'm just not going to like it."

70

"Not at all. I happen to know someone trustworthy, whom I can send letters to naturally, and she can bring them to you. The problem is that she doesn't know anything about all this, and I won't ask her to take part without telling her. She has a right to know what she's involved in, what she's risking."

"She." He grinned. "You're talking about Mito. That's a marvellous idea. I can't think of anyone more trustworthy: she's a good friend of yours, she's creating my badge, and I have all sorts of reasons to meet with her."

"You don't think that telling her is a problem? It's business of the Realm. Maybe we should clear it with your father."

"My father doesn't have anything to do with this. I have someone in the Palace I should discuss it with, though."

"Someone in the Palace? Who?"

"You are not required to know." He raised a hand to forestall her outburst. "No, Aleria, this isn't me being stubborn. It's one of those things about the spying business. Nobody ever gives you information you don't need. For example, I don't see it as any problem telling Mito what we're doing, but we don't have to tell her everything. We just tell her that you're sending me important information, but you can't send it straight, and she can help. She'll understand. But I agree that she does have to know that she's not just passing love letters."

"Fine. You talk to your superior officer and let me know. Then Mito and I can arrange the details."

"No, I think I should be the one to tell her."

She thought about that. "I see. You'll make sure you only tell her what she's supposed to know. Since I don't know what that is, because I'm not supposed to know, then you have to tell her yourself. Sounds like a fine way to keep control of the situation."

"You are so cynical."

"Cynical, but not wrong. I'm not complaining, just making sure you know that I know."

"Fine. Now, about the code."

"If nobody's going to bother with love letters of a silly girl, why do we need a code?"

"You know I'm not happy with this whole plan, with you out there, fully exposed. We're playing safe."

"Oh, all right. We'll make up a very simple code. Just some key words that signal 'danger' and 'what I say is the opposite of what I mean' and some things like that. I don't know what. We'll figure it out."

"I think we need something a bit more versatile than that, Aleria."

"I've read the spy novels, too, Raif. I am not about to carry a secret codebook with me, which anyone could discover and then know for sure that I'm not what I seem to be. Let's keep it simple."

"What if it's too simple, and I discover once you're gone that there is something I want to say and I can't say it? What if there's some misunderstanding and I get the wrong message from you completely?"

She laughed. "Have you ever read a love letter? You won't get the wrong message. Look, it's simple. We're writing about Fauvé's plans, right? So instead, we write about love. Anything I say about love means his plans. If I sound in love, it means we were right. If I'm unsure, it means I'm not finding anything. If I start talking about loving someone else...'

"I know. It means it's someone else, not him. I don't know, Aleria. It sounds easy when we're sitting here, face to face."

"You're trying to keep too much control of the situation, Raif. You want a complete code so you can give me explicit orders I have to follow."

"I have already lost one agent out there, and it's not a pleasant feeling. You'll pardon me if I want to keep some control, especially since it's you on the front line, and I don't want anything to go wrong."

"Why Raif, I think that's a compliment."

He frowned. "Huh. Do the Royal Army a favour, will you, Aleria?"

"The Army?"

"Yes. Don't ever join up."

"What?"

"You don't get it, and I suspect you never will. I'm supposed to be running this operation. I answer to my superior officer, and he expects the people who work under me to answer to me in a similar way."

"Well, he'd better learn that the spying business doesn't work like that, hadn't he?"

Raif shook his head glumly. "Some hope." He looked her straight in the face. "I know you think this is all because I didn't get to go myself."

She shrugged. "Maybe there's a bit of that in it."

"Yes, well, maybe there is. But I've been out there, and I know what it's like, and I don't like sending you."

"And I don't like you not trusting me to use the proper precautions to take care of myself. So there we have it."

"I suppose."

Unspoken was the fact that he didn't like her going out to where Shen was. He didn't know that she had come to an understanding with Shen about their friendship. *Well, he said it himself. He doesn't need the information, so he isn't getting it.*

"It was a bit of trouble getting you out the last time. I don't want to have to do it again."

There was a brief pause. She realized that it was the first time in a long while they had mentioned their original meeting. She also realized that it didn't bother her. She let him know with a smile. "All right. Let's figure out a code."

She pulled the paper towards her. "You realize that I'm going to get back at you by making my love letters especially mushy."

"I can't wait."

Their time together was interrupted by the sound of returning voices. They didn't want to be seen in the private part of the house, so they had to leave it at that. "We'll talk again before you leave."

"Maybe. If not," she laughed, "I'll send you a letter."

He frowned, but then the others spotted them and crowded around, cheerfully discussing the merits of the new horses.

9. Working Girl

Aleria refused to feel sorry for herself, but it seemed like that blister hadn't healed properly. She wished she had taken better care of her body the first week. She had been so proud of her ability to endure pain over long periods of time that she had ignored the message it was sending her; damage was being done.

She squirmed on the wagon seat, shifting her weight away from the sore spot, but the sweat still stung. Trying to take her mind off the discomfort, she regarded the horses as she had been taught to do. The team was pulling disgustingly well. She had chosen a good pair: docile and evenly matched.

She had been driving horses all her life, but nothing like the length of this trip, and she hadn't been prepared for the grinding monotony of the road, alone on the wagon seat, the other drivers lost in their own thoughts ahead and behind.

"Come on, there, Maude. Let's take a run at that hill." She flicked the reins, and the horses' heads came up a fraction. "Let's have some speed, there, Topsy. Hup, now!"

She tried not to play favourites, but she really liked the off horse better. Maude was shorter and stockier than her mate, and the white blaze on her nose and the longer white hairs that covered her hooves gave her a handsome air. Topsy, the darker of the two, was older and sometimes too smart for comfort. When you picked up a hoof to check it, she would lean on you. If you got a twist in the harness, she wasn't shy about nipping your arm.

Both of them were placid, friendly beasts, though. A child could run under Maude's belly without a twitch from her huge hooves. One had in the last village, to Aleria's dismay, the hilarity of the other drivers and the terror of the child's mother. Maude had swung her head around to regard the tiny interloper for a moment, then snorted derisively.

At her urging, the team picked up their pace, and the loaded wagon rolled sedately up the small incline. As she cleared the top the rest of the train stretched out in front of her. To her relief, she could also see buildings in the distance. Mopping her brow with a sweaty forearm she turned to the driver behind her.

"Bersac ahead."

"Well, don't stop to gawk at it. It ain't that pretty. You never seen a town before?"

She grinned and urged her horses the last few, slow, steps over the rise. Her fellow-teamsters were a good lot. They were used to women driving – smaller loads, two-horse teams, or deadheading empty wagons – so they accepted her easily.

As she had made her way further from the capital she had modified her story. These men all knew she was related somehow to the anDalmyn family, an edge of safety she didn't want to give up, but this far from the main depot none of them had seen her before, especially in anything but teamster's clothes. She had been on the road for two weeks, working her way towards Taine in slow stages. By the time she arrived some time next week, she could choose her level of anonymity.

Shen knew she was coming, but she had refrained from firming up a date. She wondered if perhaps this secrecy was childish. Playing at spies. However, it did give her a degree of freedom so that she could run the game her own way. Better send a messenger ahead tonight, though. Manners were manners.

Five wagons ahead and one behind. That pretty well placed her in the hierarchy: a long way back in the dust. Fortunately it had rained the night before, cooling the air and settling the road surface.

She squirmed on the hard plank again. No teamster worth his wages, woman or not, would ever be caught with padding on the seat. She didn't even want to risk extra cloth under her skirt. Better to tough it out. Sooner or later, her butt would toughen up.

She passed the time by composing in her head what she would send to Raif. All she had to do was encode a letter saying basically nothing, because there was nothing to say. The roads seemed safe, there was no gossip of bandits, and she was nowhere near Taine yet. Still, knowing how important it was to have regular contact, she sent a dutiful missive with every Dalmyn wagon they met.

And received a lot of good-natured joshing from the other drivers for it, which she took with good grace. At least her cover seemed to be working.

Bersac was too small to have a Dalmyn depot, so they camped on the common, circling their wagons loosely and picketing the horses close by. Another night of boring inn food, hard beds and smelly functionaries. *At least there's room in the wagon for my own bed linen.* She shouldered her pack and followed the others inside.

* * *

Despite a slight flutter of nerves, she was relieved to see Taine slide up out of the mist of a rainy day a week later. It was a medium-sized town by provincial standards, with nothing to recommend or condemn it. A lot of varnished porticos and tiled roofs showed a certain level of prosperity, but that was it. She stabled her team in the Dalmyn yard, rubbed them down, checked her manifest with the office clerk, and found a spot to change her clothes.

She wasn't unhappy about the rain, because when she reappeared her cloak covered her finery. While she waited for the carriage she had ordered, she chatted with the clerk, leading him to reach the conclusion that she was here to check up on Dalmyn interests. She hoped this explanation would steer him away from barroom speculation about why she would drive in as a teamster and leave as a lady. Or have a bundle in her luggage that looked a whole lot like a sword.

The Waring family were expecting her, and she could tell from their welcome that Shen had put them in the picture as to her social status. They were unfailingly polite, but in all the time she stayed with them, she could never achieve an easy familiarity.

She found she did better with his father. Nathe Waring was a true merchant: good manners, smooth talk, all business. When they discussed the condition of the roads and he found her familiar with the reasons for the rising costs of freighting, he treated her like an equal.

With his wife, it was more difficult. Merte was a plain, hardworking woman with a good heart. Aleria could see where Shen got his friendly ways. His mother was a sweetheart, but she couldn't seem to relax in Aleria's company. Aleria struggled to find things that they could talk about, but every time she started on a new subject, the woman was so deferential that the conversation soon turned into a lecture, with Merte nodding and saying "Yes, of course," in all the right places.

Even in the kitchen. Aleria had no idea how much time a normal merchant's wife spent on the running of her household. Since her own mother took an active role in the kitchen, she didn't know what to expect.

It turned out that Merte had a hand in all the cooking, depending on her hired girls only for the simple, repetitive tasks. Seeking a chance for conversation, Aleria scouted out the kitchen as soon as she found an opportunity. The moment she set foot in the door, all action came to a halt.

"Lady Aleria! What are you doing here?"

She tried a casual smile. "Just looking around." She did so. "This looks like a very convenient kitchen."

"Thank you, my Lady. Thank you."

There was a brief silence. Uncertain at the absence of an invitation, Aleria stepped forward hesitantly. "Well, don't mind me. You just go about what you were doing."

There was immediate consternation. "But Lady Aleria. Your dress!"

"Oh. Good idea. I should really have an apron."

They bustled around frantically, finding and choosing for her what they considered an appropriate apron. From the look of it, the garment she was given was never intended for actual cooking, and she resolved to be very careful with it.

When she was suitably clad, there was another silence. "Go ahead. Don't worry about me. What are you making?"

It turned out they were making "...just a simple country-style beet soup."

"Oh. My mother makes beet soup sometimes."

They looked at her expectantly. She wracked her brains, trying to remember. "She chops the beets and boils them together with the leaves."

"Yes, yes, I have heard some people do that."

"She sometimes uses milk, sometimes yoghurt. Which do you use?"

"Whatever you say, my Lady."

She winced inwardly and ploughed on. "She chops cucumbers in, I think, and radishes when they're in season."

"What a marvellous idea!"

Out of inspiration, Aleria looked around at her little audience. "But I'm sure you make this often. You must know much more about it than I do. How do you prepare it?"

Merte shuffled her feet. "Just in the normal, country fashion."

"Oh. How do you do that?"

"Nothing as interesting as the way you do it, I'm sure."

Aleria thought furiously. There was some problem here, but she couldn't for the life of her figure out what it was. Either Merte didn't want to reveal her recipe, or Aleria was overstepping some unseen boundary. As usual. She forced the crooked grin off her face.

"Well, I'm sure you don't want me cooking. You go ahead and do what you usually do."

Merte's eyes went wide with horror. "Of course, of course, Lady Aleria. I never meant to suggest that you should..."

Aleria grinned. "And a good thing, too. The last time I tried my hand in the kitchen, I made such a mess that my mother ran me out with a broom!"

The maids tittered, Merte pretended to be scandalized by such behaviour, and the tension was broken. Aleria waited a while, then made a dignified retreat, deciding that she would have to find more neutral ground for her attempts to make the woman comfortable in her presence.

A separate problem was how to try Shen out on the spying business. She needed to get an idea of his interest, but allow herself an escape from the topic if she got the wrong responses.

One day she got the opening she needed. He was always interested in her stories of how decisions were made in the kingdom at large, and she had worked the conversation around to the road safety problem.

"But it's so hard to do anything about it. I mean someone like me. There's nothing I can do."

She pounced. "Don't you think that every person has the responsibility to do what he can to see to the safety of the kingdom?"

78

"Theoretically. I just don't see any way that a small family like mine, and a single person like me, can have any effect."

She nodded seriously. "I think many people feel like that. But if everyone just worried about his own profits, and didn't do anything for the common good, where would we be?"

He assumed that lecturing pose which was beginning to annoy her. "I know this might be hard for you to understand, Aleria, but for us merchants, the ability to make a profit must take precedence over everything else. If our business isn't successful we can't feed our families. We have no money, no power, no influence to do anything to help, and what good is that to anyone?"

"Nobody expects you to leave your business to fail while you go around doing valiant deeds for the good of the kingdom. But what about doing your share for the sake of everyone else?"

He smiled in a superior way. "I don't think, somehow, that out here in the real world people act like that."

She had to bite her tongue to stop from reminding him how small his world was. "I suppose you would know how the real world goes, because you live in it."

Some of the sharpness must have shown through in her voice, because he paused and looked at her, his head on one side.

"This is a very strange conversation, Aleria. Why are you asking me these questions?"

Time to toss it off as girlish curiosity. "Just trying to find out what kind of person you are. Don't you have conversations with your friends about serious things?"

"Of course I do!"

"Well, there you are, then." She supported this enigmatic response with a bright smile that successfully diverted his interest.

Aleria was disappointed, but satisfied as well. Shen was too concerned with his own interests to be useful to her in this matter. When trouble came, he would side with the party that offered him the best deal. The king needed someone with a larger view of the world, someone with more loyalty to the kingdom. She would have to look elsewhere or find a way to get the information herself.

10.   The Invitation Comes

It was the fourth day of her visit, and Shen and Aleria were just leaving the house, when a rider on a sturdy roan hunter reined in at the gate. Aleria noted the plumed hat, the length of his boots and the manicured dark beard and sized him up as someone important.

"Ah, it is Shen, the young merchant traveller. How is your business progressing?"

"We are moving a reasonable amount of stock, my Lord. Your recent order did not come amiss."

"Good, good." The noble swung down off his horse, revealing that he was about Shen's height, though heavier in the shoulders. He pinned Shen with his stare. "No problems with the bandits?"

"No, my Lord. We have been making larger caravans with our more expensive goods and that seems to have deterred them."

The lord nodded. "Good, good. I hope your luck continues. Is your father at home?"

"No, my Lord. He is down at the warehouse."

"As he should be. As he should be, at this time of day." The man turned slightly, as if just noticing her for the first time, and his smile broadened. "And this would be Lady Aleria."

Shen stepped forward. "Yes, Lord Fauvé. This is Aleria Dalmyn, who is visiting us from the Capital."

He bowed over her hand, and she curtsied in the proper response. This brought a twinkle to his eye. "A very graceful curtsey, my Lady. Do I detect a gentle upbringing?"

"I hate to be one to disappoint you, my Lord, but I am simply a carter's daughter, having a visit with fellow merchants and doing a small amount of business to make my trip worth the while."

He wagged a finger at her. "And that is not how a carter's daughter speaks, either. You are of the Dalmyn family, are you not?"

She regarded him a moment. "I am at a loss, my Lord, to understand how one of your rank would be aware of a lowly visitor such as myself."

"It is a poor liege who does not know what is happening in his demesne." He lowered his head, raised his eyebrows. "And you have neatly turned my question aside."

She pretended to hesitate, taking the moment to decide how he knew so much. Perhaps the turncoat pedlar. Was he playing cat-and-mouse with her? She shrugged. "I can claim a share of the Dalmyn blood. Not that it does me much good."

"Aha! So you are related to Kensel anDalmyn, and his Exalted wife, Lady Leniema. That means you are a bit more than a simple carter's daughter." He gave her a mock frown. "The question then arises; what is a lady of a Ranking family doing, driving a wagon so far from home?"

Aleria smiled, with a twist. "AnDalmyn may be a lord, and his lady may be of Exalted Rank, but the rest of us have to make our way as we can. I find we are treated with more respect if we make ourselves useful. Lord Dalmyn is that sort of man." She laid a hand on Shen's shoulder. "And I have friends to visit. So here I am."

He returned the smile, with what seemed genuine pleasure. "Ah, but here you should not be, Lady Aleria. Here you should not be. You are Ranked, and we must see that you are treated as such."

"Thank you, my Lord, but I am quite pleased to be visiting with the Waring family. They have been gracious and generous to me."

"It does credit to them, and credit to their class, that you should feel that way. No one has ever considered the Waring family inhospitable." He included Shen in his expansive gesture.

"However, I suggest you have done your duty in staying here this long, and now you may indulge yourself. May I send a carriage for you this afternoon?"

Aleria hoped the jolt of excitement did not show. *This is it!* "I thank you for your consideration, my Lord. I must take time to discuss this with my hosts. I do not know if they had any plans…" She glanced at Shen.

He shook his head. "We had talked about inviting some friends in, a few days from now…"

Fauvé clapped him on the shoulder. "…and so you must allow me to be the host. I will send a carriage for the Lady and a message for your father, inviting you all to the castle for an evening of dining, music, and dance. How does that suit you?"

There was no refusing the Lord, although Aleria suspected that Shen was as eager for this opportunity as she was. They both agreed, and Fauvé swung up on his horse. He saluted them with a sweep of his riding crop, then slapped his mount smartly with it and galloped away.

They stood a moment in silence, watching him depart. "So that's your Lord Fauvé.'

"It seems to be."

She glanced at him. "Will this be a problem for your parents? I don't like to just run out on them so suddenly."

He grinned. "Since his Lordship has decreed it, there's not much any of us can do, is there? I'm sure the blow will be softened by the invitation. They come, but rarely. Wait and see how many others he invites."

She nodded. "Well, I suppose I'd better get my things packed."

"That should take you a few minutes."

She grinned and strode into the house.

She was gratified that afternoon when the lord sent what must be his best carriage for her, complete with a footman in livery. She merely had to indicate her small trunk and it was swung aboard with due ceremony, the door held open with a flourish. She stepped up, settled herself and turned to wave to Shen and his mother. "I'll see you in a few days, then."

"Yes, my Lady. It has been a pleasure to have you visit with us."

She leaned on the windowsill. "And thank you so much for having me here, Madam Waring. You have been truly gracious."

Shen nodded to the driver, who snapped his whip over the backs of the matched team, and they were off. She sat upright, ignoring the comfort of the seat, emotions conflicting. *Now I'm getting somewhere!*

At the manor house, Lord Fauvé was there to hand her out of the carriage and see her to her suite of rooms. Well, it wasn't actually a suite, just a small bedroom/sitting room combination, and the functionary facilities were at the end of the hall, as they often were in older buildings where plumbing had arrived centuries after the original construction.

She smiled graciously at her host and said polite things about her room. After all, this was a long way from the Capital, and he had done a credible, if clumsy, job of furnishing it. The wallpaper was a rather overwhelming shade of red, and the draperies around the bed were of a striped material that was popular when she was twelve. Nonetheless...

"I'll leave you to get settled, my Lady. I'm afraid we dine and retire rather early out here in the country. Most of us are up with the sun."

"Oh, I'm used to that, my Lord. I'm at the yard at eight, workday mornings."

"Creditable, I'm sure, my Lady."

She smiled again. "Thank you, my Lord."

He turned to a plain older woman standing just outside the door. "This is Rumani, my housekeeper. If there is anything you need, just ask her."

"Hello, Rumani." she held out her hand. "I am Aleria, and I am pleased to be of your acquaintance."

The woman gave a quick glance to her lord then reached out in return, a large, roughened hand with firm strength. "Pleased myself, my Lady." She stepped back, her hand disappearing again in the folds of her apron.

Lord Fauvé smiled. "You'll be well taken care of, then." He took his leave, and the housekeeper, after an enquiring glance at her guest, followed him

Aleria looked around the room and began to unpack. She used the dark, old-fashioned carved armoire to stow her belongings, laid her toiletries on the equally dark and cumbersome dressing table, and that was it. When Fauvé had been gone for some time, she went to the door and looked out. She made sure of her exit route, only a couple of turns and a half-staircase to the courtyard. The hallway was empty and dim, lighted by a narrow window at the end. She strolled to the window and looked out on a rather pretty scene, over green countryside with whitewashed wooden cottages. She also noted that the casement was only latched in place, and thick, new-looking shutters with arrow slits in them were folded back against the wall. One thing about a pleasant panoramic scene; it also made a good field of fire. From the disturbed earth, it looked as if the area had been cleared of brush

Gordon A. Long

lately. Looking over, she could see fresh stone in some of the walls. She thought about that as she strolled back to her room.

* * *

The lord had prepared a small fete for her that night. It was sort of cute, she thought, with she and her host the only couple on the dance floor, the orchestra merely a country fiddle, a bass and an oboe. She had noted the number of instruments racked beside the oboist, and concluded that he must be the music master. Sure enough, for the next tune – which she was obliged to dance with one of the young men – he picked up a brass hunting horn for the start, switched to a flute for the bridge, then back to the horn for the coda. He was a reasonable player on both, and she clapped cheerfully at the end.

"You are versatile musician, sir."

"Thank you, my Lady. Do you play?"

"Not to your standard, sir. I can squeak a tune out of a violin, though the harpsichord is more my instrument."

"I regret we have no harpsichord here, my Lady."

"That's no difficulty. I prefer to listen to my betters any day."

"Oh, surely you are being modest, my Lady." Lord Fauvé smiled indulgently. "Here, Saleri, let's have your fiddle."

The music master handed her a violin, and she took a moment to look it over. It seemed a reasonable instrument. She tucked it under her chin and bowed a quick scale. It was not as clear in tone as her own, but it would do. She took it down again.

"What shall we play, gentlemen?"

"What do you know, my Lady?"

She frowned, then smiled. "Since there seem to be no other ladies available, I suppose a gentleman's reel would be appropriate. Fortunately, I happen to know one. The "Hornpipe in F?"

The other violinist looked hesitant, but the music master smiled. "Its the standard reel pattern, Ghant. You'll pick it up." He raised the horn again, nodded the beat to her, and off they went.

Aleria was a bit out of practice, but she soon started to get into the piece. The music master kept with her perfectly, and sure

84

enough the second violinist was soon chipping in with the harmony.

After two verses, she signalled them to stop. "No one is dancing!"

Fauvé shrugged. "Our music master has attempted to teach us some dances, but these men are more comfortable learning steps with a weapon in hand."

"Lord Fauvé, I only know this one good dance number. If you gentlemen don't make use of it, the party is going to end rather quickly."

He smiled. "Well spoken. As I recall, that dance requires two men, and it seems," his eyes scanned the small group sitting there stiffly, "I'm the only one who knows it."

"Well, then I guess they'll have to learn it, won't they? Come on, I think I can play and walk the movements. We'll show them."

She tucked the violin more firmly under her chin and stood. It was a bit of a laugh, trying to do the dance and keep the tune flowing, but the other musicians were more solidly behind her now, and Lord Fauvé, with high good humour, filled in when she lapsed on the dance steps. When they had finished, she was a bit out of breath and warm. They all laughed and their small audience clapped enthusiastically.

"Thank you, gentlemen. Now it's your turn."

They looked to each other doubtfully, waiting for someone to go first. She set her violin aside, reached for the hand of the nearest. "Come on. You've seen it, now. It's easy to learn."

He obeyed with relish, the others more slowly, and she took charge. "Three of you line up with Lord Fauvé, the other two with me. The extra man will just have to watch the paired figures. Now, the first step goes like this. One, two and cross over. Got that?"

She worked them through it and, buoyed by her enthusiasm, they soon had it to a reasonable level. These men had trained in physical skills all their lives, and this dance was much simpler than any of the advanced sword training patterns.

"I think you have it, gentlemen. I am going to step back to my musician's role, since this is not a dance for ladies. Follow Lord Fauvé. Ready, Maestro?" She waited for the music master to give the count, and off they went. By now the men were into the fun of the game, and she could see them using their moves to vie for superiority as the dance was intended: a series of patterns designed to show off physical strength and agility. Since they were new to the dance, all of them, with the exception of Lord Fauvé, were soon breathless and stumbling. The dance ended in a jumble of limbs and a roar of laughter.

She lowered her instrument and signalled them to be seated. "You have done very well, gentlemen, and now I will give you a chance to listen. And rest."

They gave an appreciative chuckle.

She turned to the music master. "I assume you know the *Lark's Lament?*" It was a rather simple piece that most intermediate violin students learned.

He nodded and picked up his flute. "May I improvise in the bridge?"

She nodded. "Unless I start losing the tune. Then come down to the lyric line and help me out."

He smiled happily, and they began. She could tell from the way he was playing that he enjoyed working with someone even of her low calibre, so she settled down to do her best. The other violinist knew the piece too, and the bassist ran a very simple line, but he was dead steady on the time. As a result, the piece went creditably, except for a small bit in the minuet where she had been admiring the flautist's improvisation and had to scramble to concentrate on her own tune, which was quite counter to his.

When they had finished, the audience applauded loudly, either from appreciation for the music, or understanding of the complexity of their accomplishment; it didn't matter. Applause was applause, and they took their bows with cheerful aplomb.

Buoyed by her success, she insisted on dancing a turn with each of the men, at least the ones she could persuade. One was too shy to even try, and one started taking liberties with the placement of his hands before they had even got started, so she cut his turn short, noting him as a future concern. Even in this protected place, she still carried her hideout, although in consideration of the filmy sleeves of her gown it was back on her leg at the moment. She had devised a loop that allowed her to hang it hilt-down, and she could get at it quickly if the need arose.

The evening lasted a bit longer than expected, and she noticed a few stifled yawns during her second stint on the violin. When she was done that piece she bowed graciously to her host. "I do not mean to keep your hard-working men from the sleep they need, my Lord."

He smiled cheerfully. "They're young, my Lady. If they can't dance all night and work all day, what kind of men can they call themselves?"

Nonetheless, he was not averse to calling it a night, and soon she was being escorted to her room by a yawning maid with a torch. She pulled her skirts in.

"Careful with that thing, please. Don't you use candles around here?"

"Oh! I'm so sorry. They called me to hurry, and I just grabbed what I could. There'll be candles in yer room...my Lady."

"That's fine, don't worry about it. We'll walk slower, and the sparks won't fly so badly."

The girl flashed a shy smile and moved ahead, stretching the torch out in front of her like regimental colours.

When they reached Aleria's rooms, the maid found and lit several candles. "There you go, my Lady. Is there anything more you need?"

"No, thank you, although I don't know your name."

"I'm Dallya, my Lady." She paused, then remembered she was supposed to curtsey.

"Well, thank you very much for the escort, Dallya. What is the usual schedule in the morning?"

"Well, the men's usually up just after sunrise, this time of the year. Lord Fauvé, he ain't a lie-abed type, and he snaps the whip pretty sharp. I'm sure you don't have to get up then, my Lady."

"Oh, I'm used to it. I'll be up when I hear others stirring."

"Would you like coffee in your room, my Lady?"

"That would be very nice, Dallya. Will that be a problem?"

"Oh, no, my Lady. I gotta be up with the cook to help with the breakfast anyways. If I bring you yer coffee, that gets me out of the kitchen for a while."

Aleria grinned. *Servants love a chance to change their routine. Can't blame them.* "Then you'll have to come and talk to me while

I drink my coffee. I'm sure a lady of my stature requires someone to help her dress."

"Oh." The girl seemed uncertain. "Do you?"

"As it happens, I don't, but who else needs to know that?"

The light dawned on her face. "Oh."

"Right. While I have my coffee and dress, you can tell me all about what I need to know to get around here smoothly. Can you do that?"

"I dunno, I guess so. If you got any questions, I c'n answer 'em, I guess."

"Perfect. You get yourself off to bed, now and I'll see you in the morning."

"Certainly...my Lady. Good night. Sleep well." She curtseyed and turned to go. As she left, she stopped and checked the inner bolt on the door, nodding to herself when it moved smoothly. She glanced back to see that Aleria was watching, then went out, her torch drifting sparks behind her, and closed the door firmly.

Aleria mused over that last gesture, then went over and slid the bolt home. She could take a hint, but she wondered why the girl had thought it necessary.

11. Life in the Manor

The next morning Dallya was conveniently walking down the hall when she went out to the functionary. The girl smiled, signalled 'one moment,' and turned back. Soon there was hot coffee and a small, fresh roll on a tray beside the bed. Aleria was already clothed when the servant arrived, so if she had been expecting to witness some arcane dressing ritual of the Ranking classes, she was disappointed. Instead, Aleria nodded to a bench. "So, tell me. When am I expected, and where?"

Dallya sat and thought a moment. "Well, if yer gonna have breakfast with Lord Fauvé, you'll have to go pretty quick. He's not down yet, but he will be soon, 'cause they sent his coffee up same time as I come here. The others'll follow soon after or feel the sharp side of his tongue." She smiled. "That might be interestin' this mornin', you keepin' them all up late last night."

"That was late?"

"Oh, yes. We ain't had anyone up that late, mid-week, for a long time." She paused, glanced shyly, "You play beautiful music."

"Well, thanks. Back home, I'm not considered very good. Your music master is a fine musician." A slight exaggeration to a servant would do no one any harm.

"Yes. He's a nice man, though so timid, don't you think?"

She frowned. "Not when he's playing."

"No, I just mean in general. Sort of slides around, you know, keeps out of people's way." She shrugged. "I guess if I was a musician in this bunch, I would, too."

Aleria nodded in sympathy.

"All right. So that's breakfast. What then?"

Dallya spent the next few minutes giving Aleria all the minute details of life in a country manor. Soon she lifted her head, listening. "There. That's the main door openin'. Lord Fauvé is down."

"Thank you, Dallya. We will wait a reasonable moment, then make our entrance."

They shared a smile, and Aleria moved to a stool. "Will you check my hair at the back?"

Dallya jumped up eagerly. "Certainly, my Lady. Oh, it looks perfect. So long and wavy."

Aleria glanced up at the girl's tangled mop. "Wavy isn't the fashion in the Capital, right now. At home I curl mine every day. You'd make quite a hit with all your ringlets."

Her hand flew to her head. "Really, my Lady?"

"Certainly. The girls with naturally curly hair are pulling it straight back from their brow to a band just behind their ears. Then they let the rest spill down their backs, intertwined with ribbons. Don't bother to try that, though. It takes the maid a half an hour to get the right look."

Dallya smoothed her hair back, "Like this, though?"

"That's right. You could use a bandanna, if you liked. Do you want me to try?"

The hand dropped as if it was burned. "Oh, no, my Lady. Not here."

She looked doubtfully at the girl. "All right." Then she smiled. "I think we have kept them waiting long enough. Let us depart."

Dallya smiled back and opened the door, curtseyed. "Right this way, my Lady."

Aleria strode out. "And when we get to the hall, you open the door, step inside, half-turn, and curtsey. Then I will make my entrance."

The girl scurried ahead, wiped away her grin and did as she was bid.

The gesture was wasted. Lord Fauvé was there speaking to Danton, the overseer. One other young man looked around with bleary eyes and sat up a bit straighter. The rest stared at their food with little enthusiasm.

Fauvé's eyes brightened. "Ah, our fair guest rises early. Serves her right, after keeping us up until the wee hours of the night."

"A slight exaggeration, if my Lord doesn't mind being corrected."

"Surely you wouldn't let the truth get in the way of a good story."

"If you wish, my Lord. What has the kitchen prepared to break our fast?"

His hand indicated the table, which was well furnished with covered dishes. She seated herself and glanced over at Dallya, hovering behind her. After a moment's thought, the girl reached over and began lifting lids.

Aleria made her choices, hinting to the servant to load her plate. She saw no need to be delicate. No telling what she might be doing today, and the country ham looked especially good, the egg yolks a bright yellow she was not used to seeing in the city.

"What do you have planned today, lord Fauvé?"

He smiled. "Nothing that would interest you, I'm afraid. Mostly riding my demesne, supervising, talking to the peasants about their problems, that sort of boring thing."

"Oh. I can ride."

"I'm sure you can."

"But I would like to see your demesne. That is, if I wouldn't be in the way."

"Not at all. I think you'll be bored, but if you really want to go, we will be leaving in..." he glanced up at Danton, "...an hour."

"That will give us plenty of time to finish the entries, my Lord."

He nodded, turned back to her. "An hour, then. Do you have riding clothes with you?"

She laughed. "My driving skirt will be sufficient. As long as we're not meeting with the other ladies of the local gentry. I'm sure they expect better of a girl from the big city."

"That reminds me. I promised young Waring I would invite his parents and some of the other merchants up for an evening. Would the day after tomorrow suit you?"

"My schedule is rather in your hands, my Lord."

He turned to his overseer. "Make that an hour and a half, Danton. It seems I have invitations to pen."

"I don't want to put you to extra trouble. Could I do that?"

His face brightened. "Now, that would be a wonderful idea. I'm sure your penmanship is far superior to mine. The local ladies will be much happier to receive an invitation from you."

After breakfast, he escorted her to a crowded office, shoved a ragged space clear on a table cluttered with papers, writing implements, a broken dagger, and what looked like a piece of partially-stitched harness. He grinned self-consciously. "I'm afraid we're rather rough around here. Will this do?"

She searched around for what she needed. "Do you have some prettier paper? And a list of who's to be invited?"

He pawed through a smaller desk and found some uneven sheets of linen-cloth, which he handed her. "Let me think." He picked up a pencil and a scrap of paper, scribbled down a few names, thought more, "...and a couple of young ladies..." he put down two more names, and handed her the paper.

"Oh, that's only six letters. I'll have those done in no time. What hour should I say?"

"I don't know. What's a good time?"

She considered. "Well, we should work backwards from when they will be going home." She raised her eyebrows at him.

"It's Feast day the next day, so they'll stay for a light midnight supper, leave around one."

"And what kind of entertainment do we have?"

He grinned. "I'm afraid you'll be the main attraction, as you were so gracious to be last night. I'll get in another violin, and some of the young ladies will want to sing." He made a face. "I'm sure you will appreciate the subject of their tunes much more than we rough men do."

"So let's say a half-hour for singing, an hour for dancing. How many courses for the dinner?"

He seemed about to shrug, stopped himself. "We should consult the cook."

"I'll tell you what. We'll set two hours for the meal, and I'll adjust it if the cook advises."

"Fine with me."

"Good. Let's see. Allowing half an hour for drinks before, two for dinner, another half hour for the men to have cigars and brandy while the ladies retire to gossip, one and a half for entertainment, that means close to five hours before the midnight supper, which all the good families serve at eleven-thirty, gives us six thirty for the start, so we say six, so they can all arrive fashionably late." She turned to him. "Will they?"

He grinned and shook his head. "The merchants pride themselves on their punctuality."

"All right. We'll say six-thirty. Is that normal for around here?"

"About right. I never knew why, though. You're pretty good at this."

She smiled up at him. "Why thank you, sir. Even someone of my status has all the proper training."

He became serious. "I don't think you should down-play your Ranking so much." He smiled again. "Here in the country, I suspect you outRank most of the local nobility, and don't think they won't know it. Later in the week, I'll invite some of them to drop around. You'll be surprised at how little different they are from our more recent guests." He nodded to the list in her hand.

"Thank you, Lord Fauvé. That sounds marvellous. I'll check with the kitchen, and then write these up." She made a mental note that she had overplayed her role a bit.

"Good. If you have them ready when we go, we can deliver some of them personally, and send the rest."

He turned it the doorway. "And I don't think we need to be quite so formal. Could we drop the 'Lord' and 'Lady,' at least in private?"

She dimpled prettily for him. "Certainly, Fauvé. I'd like that. It's so much more...normal sounding."

He smiled, nodded and left.

She waited, glancing over the list to make sure she could understand his scribble. No sense in offending someone by spelling a name wrong. She looked around the room, wondering if she could take advantage of the time to snoop a bit. Then she shook her head and scoffed at herself. *And there I find, conveniently on his desk, a list of all the bandits and how much each one has been paid, and when. On the first day. I don't think, somehow, it works like that.*

She considered offering to clean up, but once again, if he allowed her to, it would mean that there was nothing to find.

She shrugged and went to find the kitchen.

It wasn't difficult. The noise, bustle and cheerful female voices that were missing in the rest of the house overflowed all the way up the stairwell to the main hall. She stood in the doorway watching. The cook would be the tall, thin woman chopping herbs at a central table. The two girls scrubbing vegetables glanced at her frequently for approval. The housekeeper, what was her name? Yes, Rumani, was folding napkins in the linen room across the kitchen. A young boy was turning a spit with three chickens on it, and the cook was keeping a close eye on him, gesturing him to continue when he seemed to be losing concentration.

The cook called a quick, incomprehensible, question to Rumani, who paused to think before she answered.

"Seven, I think…" then she noticed Aleria. "Oh, my Lady…"

A gradual silence descended on the kitchen. Aleria stepped in. "Good morning, Rumani. I need to speak to the cook."

"Certainly, my Lady." the stout woman bustled forward. "This is Pareni. Pareni this is the young lady from the city. Aleria Dalmyn."

The cook curtseyed properly. "What can I help you with, my Lady?"

Aleria nodded her due and explained about the dinner.

The cook glanced to Rumani, then around the kitchen. "All right, you bunch, you've heard the gossip. We're doing a dinner in two days. So get back to work or we won't have one tonight."

The two girls grinned at each other and went back to their vegetables. The cook made certain that the boy, who had stopped completely, was running the spit at the right speed, then turned her attention to the subject. Between them, the three women set the menu for the evening, the type of service and the number of staff needed. They were done quickly, as it was a rather small dinner. The cook slapped her hands together.

"I must say, my Lady, that was smoothly done. I wish for certain we had someone like you above stairs. It would make my job easier, I'm sure."

Rumani smiled. "I don't think Lady Aleria is campaigning for the position, Pareni."

The cook had turned, clapping her hands loudly. "Berben!" The boy looked up and hurried to turn the spit again. Pareni turned back to them. "Sorry, my Lady. The boy's mostly deaf and has the concentration of…" she shrugged, "…well, of any boy his age I suppose. He'll learn."

Aleria smiled. "As long as he doesn't burn the fowl."

"Oh, don't you worry, my Lady. I'll be certain of that."

Aleria regarded the boy for a moment. "Boring job. We have a device in the kitchen: a weight on a chain. You only have to pull the weight up every time you baste the roast."

The cook's eye gleamed. "Really? I'll have to tell lord Fauvé. He likes to have the best."

Aleria shrugged. "I don't think it's very complicated. It's just a chain on a pulley in the ceiling, and a cog of the right size on the spit handle. Ours has three different-sized cogs, so you can set it to different speeds. If you want it to go fast, you add to the weight."

The cook looked at her. "What's a lady like yourself know about Mechanicals?"

She laughed. "She knows when she's been told off to watch a roast and let it burn. My mother takes a very serious hand in the kitchen."

"Well, it's to our advantage here, my Lady. Do you think the local smith could make one for me?"

"He should be able to, or order parts from any foundry in Domaland. Or one of the importers can get them. I'll draw up a diagram for him."

"Thank you, my Lady."

"But then Berben won't have a job."

The woman frowned in thought. "Oh, we'll find something else for him, never you worry."

"And now I have to get ready for a ride. What do you expect the weather to be like?"

Rumani shrugged. "Taine has wonderful weather in the fall, my Lady. Several times a day."

Aleria laughed. "In other words, take a parasol and an umbrella."

"I doubt if your horse would understand, my Lady."

"No, I'll have to make do with my slicker."

"Have a nice ride, my Lady."

"I'm sure I will. I love this countryside. It's still green, even so late in the year. Everything has gone brown, farther east."

"We pay for that, my Lady." The housekeeper gestured skyward. "Every day, this time of year."

She shrugged. "If it rains, it rains."

Both older women laughed. "That's very true, my Lady. How thoughtful you are."

Aleria grinned and turned away. The warm camaraderie of the kitchen contrasted so harshly with the barren cold of the rest of the house. Shaking her head, she returned to her rooms.

* * *

It was a pleasant but frustrating day. Pleasant because the weather cooperated, with white clouds scudding past rapidly, bringing no rain. Sunshine bathed them at intervals, but the heat of summer seemed to be gone.

It was frustrating because, watch as she might, she saw nothing more than a careful lord checking the welfare of his demesne and his people. Once again she scoffed at her naive hopes, but there were no secret notes, no bags of money slipped into waiting pockets, no suspicious strangers lurking.

They detoured into the village to deliver three invitations to ladies who were obviously expecting them and one who wasn't. She seemed disconcerted until she registered that Aleria was to be present. Then she looked much happier.

As they rode away Fauvé brushed his hand along his horse's mane in a gesture of satisfaction. "I've tried to get that lady up to visit a few times, her and her daughters, but somehow they have never made it. I wonder if they'll find a reason to beg off this time."

"Daughters?"

"Yes. She has two daughters getting to marriageable age, now. Don't see why she doesn't shop them around a bit more, as a good merchant should." He laughed at his own joke.

"Oh. I think I met them last week. They seem to me a bit young for marriage."

"Not out here in the country. We live hard lives, get our pleasures when we can, and die young." He glanced at her. "It's true. Check the Royal Census figures. Average age of death decreases as you move away from the Capital."

"I suppose. Fewer doctors, more dangerous work..."

"...bandits and uprisings."

"Those, too, I suppose."

"Oh, yes.' He looked over at her earnestly. "Always you must believe that."

"I heard you mention bandits to Shen. Some of the teamsters were talking about them, too. Is it a real problem?"

"Definitely, and they seem to be centred around here, somehow. Rather embarrassing from my point of view."

"I can see it might be worse than embarrassing."

"Yes. We don't seem to be able to catch them. Almost as if someone is tipping them off to our activities. Very frustrating."

"Is there danger here?"

"Oh, no. You don't need to worry on my land. The attacks have all been out in the countryside, along the roads. Merchants attacked and their goods stolen."

She nodded. "So they are well-organized and looking for more than simple loot. They'd need someone to sell the stolen goods to."

"You understand this better than I would expect."

"I'm a carter. We know all about bandits."

"I suppose you do."

They rode on, enjoying the fine, early fall day. They lunched at a prosperous farmhouse where the farm wife was proud to serve her best cooking, which was wonderful, on her best linen, self-spun and -woven, on her best crockery, which was plain by Capital standards. Aleria thoroughly enjoyed the food and the company. Here was a woman happy with her role in life, and standing back for no one, not even her liege lord.

"You gotta get yourself married, Lord Fauvé. This havin' a castle with no lady in it is no good: not for you nor for your people. A single man can't lead a demesne, and I hope you'll forgive me for talkin' plain."

Fauvé laughed. "Why wouldn't I forgive you this time, Tintalga? I just haven't been thinking along those lines yet. Other things to get organized first, before I start a family."

Aleria chuckled. "What was that you said about living a hard life and dying young? Maybe you'd better get to the fun part of it before it's over."

Tintalga joined in the laugh. "There you go, sir. Your own words turned back on you. What are you scared of? Don't see yourself bein' tied down to one woman?"

"I'm not concerned about that. It's the children part I'm not sure of. What do you say to a two-year-old?"

"Speakin' from thirty years experience, seven kids that lived, and two grand-ones on the way, I'd say, not much. A two-year-old mostly says it to you, and it's mostly 'No!'"

"See what I mean?" The lord threw up his hands. "Scares me to death."

Tintalga dropped a familiar hand on his shoulder. "Don't worry. When they're your own, it's altogether different."

As they rode away, their stomachs sore from overeating and laughter, Fauvé chuckled softly. "She's a character."

"She certainly is. Why do you let her talk to you that way?"

"Nobody else has the nerve. Sometimes she says things I need to hear."

Aleria nodded. "I can see how that would be useful. And nobody else is likely to try it, just because she does."

"Sure enough they wouldn't. She'd be the first to slap them down," he grinned over at Aleria. "She's jealous of her prerogatives, is Tintalga."

The rest of the day was more riding, more visits, more talk of fields and crops and fertilizer. She got the impression that Fauvé was a progressive lord, pushing his tenant farmers to try more productive modern methods and not always having success.

As they left one farm, he slapped his riding crop angrily against his leg, hard enough to startle his horse into a hop-and-jump, which he stopped with a quick wrench of the reins. "You can't prove them wrong, you know."

"What do you mean?"

"Take Pesers, there. He wants to sow his crops by hand in the old broadcast method. I'm well satisfied that you waste almost half the seed that way: uneven spread, falling on poor soil, taken by birds, plus the wasted ground where no seed falls. The yield is only about three bushels of grain for one bushel of seed.

"Now, if a man could afford to buy one of those new horse-drawn seeders that inserts the seed into the ground and covers it, I have been told the yield rises to almost ten for one. None of my farmers can afford one of those, nor can I. But if Pesers would only use a hand-held, Mechanical broadcast spreader, and rake the soil

Into Trouble

over the seed to protect it, he could get four or five bushels of harvest to one of seed.

"Now, I can't stand in the field and make him do it, but I can put on enough pressure that he'll try. But he won't work it right, and the machine will break down, and he won't do the raking right, and guess what? Come harvest time, he'll have no more grain than he would have by his old method. Why change?"

"I can see that would be a problem."

"I don't really want to turn him out, because he doesn't cause any other trouble. He pays his dues faithfully. They just aren't as much as they could be, and he's working just as hard as everyone else. But we're all suffering because of it."

"We don't have those problems in cartage."

"Then you're lucky. Why not?"

"Competition. You come up with a new way to save time or increase load capacity, the problem is to hide it from your competitors, because they'll all be stealing the idea as soon as they can."

"Which creates a different set of problems."

She nodded. "I guess every occupation has its own troubles. I don't think I'd want to change mine for yours, though."

"Well, there won't be any trouble between us, then, because I have no urge to go off cavorting all over the realm. I like to ride my land and see what I've accomplished, and try to do more."

She nodded. "I can see that."

They rode in companionable silence, while Aleria tried to reconcile this concerned landowner with the criminal mastermind they were searching out. Well, an ambitious man could be ambitious in many parts of his life.

Her next letter home took on a different tone.

My Dearest Love,

It is with trepidation I write to you, my dear, concerning our Love. When faced with the Reality of the situation, with me all the way out here and you still back there, I can't help but wonder if we were mistaken in our Feelings.

There is no question in my mind that there is some Feeling present, as I sense it everywhere. However, I must wonder if our passion was not truly Love, but some other Thing we dreamed up because it fulfilled our needs at the time.

It would be terribly unhappy if what we thought was Love turned to be some other Frame of Mind completely, and we spent our time chasing this Chimera, while the real emotion resided elsewhere.

I grieve to upset you with these thoughts, my Love, and I dearly hope that I find myself in error. Perhaps this is only a momentary lapse of my passion, due to the hardships and anxiety of travelling. I will strive to bring my thoughts into line with our former Hopes and Aspirations.

Ever Yours, even in doubt,

Aleria

She folded the letter, made certain it was properly sealed, and put it in her satchel. She would drop it off at the Royal Post when she was next in town, trusting no one at Fauvé's manor with the task. She hoped Raif wouldn't be too upset at this missive, at least not upset enough to go off on a tangent. Especially one that brought him to Taine. Still, she could not downplay her doubts.

Well, he would know soon enough. The Post moved rapidly. It had taken her three weeks to get here from the Capital; it would take three days for the letter to get back.

12.   The Bandits Strike

The following day, another robbery occurred.

News came with a messenger who had pushed his labouring horse into a dark lather. Aleria's first hint of trouble was the uneven pounding of hooves and shouting, silenced by Fauvé's stern voice. She rushed to the courtyard to see two men supporting the rider while he made his report. Then all was action again, and within a few minutes a troop of about fifteen soldiers was mounted and following Fauvé out the main gate.

Silence descended, broken only by the clopping of the hooves of the horse as one of the boys led it, head drooping, into the stable. Aleria turned to help Rumani bring the messenger into the main hall. He didn't seem to be wounded, just exhausted. As they plied him with cool drink and soft cushions, he recovered slowly. He was a young lad, and the experience had left him shaken.

"They was all dead, Rumani. I saw 'em. Five at least. Just layin' there by the road. I think two was bandits, three was traders. One broke wagon, sacks of flour spilled all over the place, a dead horse still in the traces. Everythin' else was gone."

"How long do you think you missed them by?"

The boy turned to Aleria, shuddering. "Not by much, let me tell you, lady. One of the guys was still alive when I got there, but he was...he was bleedin' real bad, and I couldn't help him." He turned back to Rumani, clutched her hand. "There was too much blood, Rumani. He just faded out while I was tryin' to stop it. I knew he was dead, so I checked the others, and then I figured Lord Fauve would want to know. Maybe he can catch them this time."

The housekeeper rubbed her hand through his hair. "You did exactly right, Genis. You got here as fast as you could."

The boy's head came up. "My horse! I rode her pretty hard..." he began to rise, but Aleria stopped him with a gentle hand on his shoulder. "You stay there and rest. I'll go check."

"Thank you, lady. She's my Dad's horse. He don't usually let me ride her. If anythin' went wrong..."

"You didn't do anything wrong, Genis. I'll go and see that she's being treated properly."

With a nod to Rumani, she strode out into the sunlight and over to the stables. Two of the hands were giving the horse a rubdown as she stood, munching happily at a bucket of oats.

"Did you water her?"

"Just a bit. We'll wait till she cools some more, then water her again."

She nodded. "I can see you know your business. Genis is worried about her. How is she?"

The elder of the hands chuckled. "Too certain he's worried. This horse is his father's pet. Came to a choice, don't know whether he'd save the kid or the horse."

The man spat on the floor. "Naw, to be fair, he'd save the lad. Sure loves this horse, though. She deserves it. Runs like the wind."

"Well, if anything will give Lord Fauvé a chance to catch those bandits, this will. The boy did a good job," she slapped the horse's rump, "and so did the horse."

They nodded in agreement and went back to their task. She returned to the house. The boy looked up anxiously when she entered, and she smiled down at him. "She's chomping oats and enjoying a rub-down. You can go out in a while and walk her around so she doesn't stiffen up. I'll help you look her over more carefully, then, if you like."

The boy nodded gratefully. "Thanks so much, my Lady. That horse is real important."

"Well, she's more important now, because if Lord Fauvé and his men catch those bandits, she'll be a hero, and so will you."

"Do ya think so?"

"No doubt about it. Your father will be proud of both of you."

Genis brightened at this. The horror of the scene would be fading. He started to discuss the merits of the horse with Rumani, leaving Aleria to muse over the possible course of events. If Fauvé was behind this, he would have been ready. What would he do, given this timely warning? He would know where the bandits were going, and would find a way to lead his men in the opposite direction. It would be the only thing he could do. If they caught up with any of the bandits, he would have to attack, make sure they got killed before they could talk.

She would be interested to see how the chase came out.

Several hours later, when the troop returned tired but elated, she got her answer and it answered nothing. The younger members of the party enthusiastically told everyone who would listen about their success, partial though it might have been.

"They were smart enough to split up, but we didn't. We took the trail that had the most horses on it, the heaviest loaded. They had taken one of the wagons, tried to get the whole load away." The youth paused to take a drink of his ale, and another took up the story.

"Thanks to young Genis, we were pretty close behind them. They must have realized we were coming, because after about an hour, we came upon the wagon, with the horses and part of the goods gone. The heavier stuff - flour, grain, and that - was still there. Also one of the bandits, wounded. We just left him there and pushed on. He was dead when we came back."

One of the servant girls had the temerity to speak. "What happened then?"

The first lad took the stage again. "We thought we might be close to catching them, so we really hoofed it. They were headed for that forest over beyond Felzer's farm. We caught up with two of them because their horses played out. They made it into the forest, though, so we had trouble catching them. Lord Fauvé ran one down, just when the man was nocking an arrow to shoot him."

The listeners gasped at the idea of a bandit with a bow. The boy nodded and continued. "Charged right into him, got him with one sweep of his sword."

"What happened to the other?"

"He got away. Headed up into the rocks where our horses couldn't go. We pushed on after the rest, but we couldn't catch them."

Fauvé slammed down his mug. "Our horses were too tired. They'd run too far, and it became obvious that we were getting farther and farther behind, so we came back. I sent Gates and a soldier to follow them on foot, at least get an idea where they went. They'll never catch up to them, though."

"So the wagons lost three men, and four bandits were killed."

"Yes, Danto, if you're keeping score, we did better this time. But the merchants have lost half their goods, either stolen or destroyed, and three of their horses. Too bad the wounded bandit died before we got a chance to question him." He tapped his mug on the table several times with increasing force. "Damn, but it's frustrating to be so close behind them, and have to let them go."

"Well, at least you got your chance, Lord Fauvé. You took that bowman down with as sweet a slice as I've ever seen." Nerval grinned. "And he was getting set to skewer you."

Fauvé winced. "I didn't have any choice, really. I came around that corner in the trail, and there he was. If I had turned to run, he'd have got me for sure. It was better to charge ahead and hope I got to him before he had a chance to get a full draw."

"You can't argue with success, my Lord."

"Thanks, Nerval. I'd rather not have that kind of glory. If I'd had more time to think, I might have taken him alive. We need information, not bodies."

Aleria watched this performance with interest. As far as she could see, the facts were pretty clear. Two bandits dead in the attack, one died on the trail, and one killed in the heat of battle. Only the killing of the bowman might have been avoided, but it sounded like it was a pretty tense situation at the time.

Of course, you don't have to kill a bowman. A slash to his bowstring and he becomes quite harmless. She looked at the assembled company, but no one seemed in a mood to ask that kind of question. Their lord was the hero of the hour, Genis the messenger was getting his share of the praise, and everyone was quite happy at the outcome.

"We'll have to wait and see what Gates comes back with." Fauvé shook his head.

She realized that Dallya was standing beside her. "Who is Gates?"

"He's the huntsman, my Lady. You might have seen him around. Long hair, greased leather coat, tall, old-fashioned riding boots, although he walks almost everywhere."

"Is he a good tracker?"

"Lord Fauvé thinks so." She shrugged. "The Lord doesn't have much use for slackers. He must be. Maybe he'll come up with something."

The two men came in several hours later, footsore and disgusted.

"They cut through those woods and picked up a track that runs around the shoulder of the mountain. Took it down to where it hits the road to Montila. They'll be long gone with their loot."

"Good work, Gates," Fauvé glanced around. "Somebody get them a drink." He looked at his retainers again, thinking. "Rost. Take a couple of men, fresh horses, and get out on the Montila road. Ask everyone you see, all the farmers along there, if they saw anyone like who we're looking for. About ten men, three dray horses in pulling harnesses but carrying packs. That might have drawn some attention. Some of them might have been wounded. Got that?"

"Yes, sir." The mercenary saluted smartly, pointed to two men, and left quickly.

"Now, about the other ones. Gates, do you think there's any hope of finding where they went?"

"Don't think so, my Lord. We're too long behind them, now. They'll pull the same stunt – cut back down to the road somewhere farther along. They're in smaller groups, even harder to trace."

Aleria leaned forward. "Is there a chance you could at least see which direction they went? If they headed towards Montila, that would tell us something."

The huntsman nodded, looked to his lord for confirmation.

"Yes, that's a good idea. Have something to eat and drink, Gates, and we'll go back out there and look around. We'll trail those other two groups, see if anything shows up." He looked grim. "I guess we might as well take some horses and a wagon, clean everything up."

"I sent a messenger to Chaden Luger, my Lord. They were his wagons and I thought he should know."

"Good work, Danto. If I don't see him out there, I'll drop in on him tomorrow, at least pay my respects. Who did he lose?"

"A driver and two hired guards, I think."

"It doesn't matter who it was." Fauvé's face clouded again. "It's three men murdered by those devils. We've got to do more about this."

If it was an act, it was a good one. Aleria didn't hear any false notes. He seemed exactly like a man whose demesne has been threatened, determined to do something about it. But nothing he had done had threatened the bandits seriously, and some of his actions could be questioned. Still, not having anyone with military experience to ask, there was little she could do. For once she wished she had a more comprehensive code, so she could give Raif more information.

Wait a minute. Why shouldn't I? If something so exciting happened, why wouldn't I write a detailed account to send to my lover?

That night, while it was all fresh in her mind, she wrote again.

My Dearest Love,

You will find it hard to believe the Exciting Events that have been happening here! There has been another bandit attack, and I was able to witness part of the Drama of it. The saga began when a young lad came galloping into the castle courtyard on a totally exhausted horse. The poor animal seemed to be gasping her last, and the rider was nearly as worn.

We all rushed down to see what was wrong. There was a whole lot of shouting and running about, and fifteen soldiers quickly mounted and rode in brave array out of the gate, Lord Fauvé in the lead.

I helped to bring the messenger into the castle. The poor boy was shaking with Fatigue and Fear and my heart went out to him…

She wrote on in this vein, gushing about how exciting it was but making sure all the pertinent details were in. When she was finished she sealed it with an extra pat of satisfaction. That was information Raif and his mysterious superior officer could chew on for a while. She doubted they would come up with anything she hadn't, but at least she was providing information.

For whatever good it would do. She couldn't mail it tomorrow, because of preparing for the merchants' visit, and the next day was a Feast day, but she would be sure to send it the day after that. Raif had to know, and it was the best she could do.

13.   A Disturbing Letter

Despite the raid, the planned social evening with the merchants went on. Fauvé took the time to explain it to Aleria. "We have to keep up the appearance of normalcy. If Chaden Luger wants to talk about his losses, it will give me the opportunity to make my points with enough of his fellow-merchants there to show that it is important."

She smiled. "Of course, you're on their side."

"I most certainly am, and I'm sure they are very aware of my efforts."

"But it doesn't hurt to let them know one more time."

"Exactly." He smiled knowingly at her. "I keep forgetting your background. It's good to share my problems with a sympathetic ear."

She surprised herself with a feeling of heat rising up her neck. To cover, she rose and paced across his office. "But you're not talking to the people who can help you."

"Oh, I suppose the merchants could, if it was that important to their profits to spend the money. But they would then want a voice in how the money was spent. If I solve the problem myself, I maintain control."

She nodded. "You always pay for help, no matter how freely it comes."

"I think you understand."

Once again, Aleria was torn. If he was putting on a show, it was a superb one. If he meant what he said, she agreed completely.

So the bright cloak of the evening's festivities had a darker lining, but the sense of shared concern pulled the group together, so all was relaxed and friendly from the start.

Since Aleria had met most of the guests and had planned the evening, it seemed natural for her to slip into the hostess role. The servants looked to her for their cues, and she found that she loved waving her hand and seeing something which took careful planning come off looking easy. From their responses, she thought that the merchant's wives – and they were the ones who knew best – were impressed.

Shen seemed quite content to be placed high in the rankings, but not close at all to Aleria, who presided from the foot of the table. She had winked at him as he entered and paid his respects, and that seemed to satisfy him.

She was especially gratified with the reception of the meal. Hearing the cook's laments about the lack of interesting spices available to her, Aleria had remembered the packs of her mother's special herbs that she had brought with her as presents. With the sudden move to the manor, she had forgotten to give them to Shen's mother, and now she thought they would go to good use, so she got them out. Pareni rose to the occasion and produced a meal that had the men eating thirds and the merchant women sharing glances of jealous wonder.

The entertainment went likewise. This was a much more cosmopolitan crowd than Fauvé's young backwoods lords, with ladies to fill out the dances, so a wider range of musical styles was possible. The music master was in heaven.

Aleria played either the hostess or the violin most of the time, but she managed to get a few dances in, one with Shen, two with Fauvé, and the others with the more important patriarchs. There were only two young men in the merchant party, so the young lords got a chance to show their abilities to the five girls, two of whom, Aleria privately agreed, were too young for such attention. When she saw their mother becoming anxious, she pulled the two over to sit with her for a while, and asked them questions about their lives, told them stories of the Capital, and kept their attention on other things than young men. When the youngest was yawning and refusing dances because of fatigue, she tossed their mother a grin and returned her daughters to her.

"I think they've had all they need of this, Ma'am."

The mother smiled. "Oh, probably. But now they won't be pestering me so much about having to live 'out in the forest', as they have been recently."

"I suppose you have told them that a truly interesting person is interesting, wherever she goes?"

The mother stared pointedly at the elder girl, who was taking in this conversation. "Yes, but I'm glad they'll hear it from you as well."

Aleria shook her head and returned to the rest of the party.

Soon it was all over: the last course of food was eaten, the guests were bid adieu, the hall was clear. She and lord Fauvé stood supervising the servants cleaning up the scraps and replacing the tables to their usual places.

"A very successful evening, don't you think?"

Aleria nodded. "It went smoothly. Did you get what you were after?'

He grinned down at her, fatigue smoothing the usual sharpness of his features. "And what makes you think I was after anything?"

She regarded him a moment. "Who has time to throw a party for no reason except pleasure?"

"Pleasure isn't a good enough reason?"

He had to be joking. "The ostensible reason for this party was to placate the merchants for lifting me out of their circle. If that was the only reason for it, I think it wouldn't be good for my sense of self-importance."

"I thought you came out looking quite important. Those women knew who was in charge tonight. They've never been treated to the like here before."

"And you still haven't answered my question."

It was his turn to regard her. "And you think I should?"

She gave a ladylike shrug. "In order to tell me how your plans went tonight, you would have to give me some idea what your plans were, and since they are none of my business, I suppose it is a bit forward of me to expect and answer."

He nodded slowly. "Quite true. However, you have worked hard and successfully on my behalf, so I should give you some recompense. Yes, the evening was successful from my point of view. I was able to discuss our most important topic in a more relaxed setting, and I could demonstrate solidarity with those of my supporters who needed that type of flattery. You were instrumental in creating an atmosphere which aided me to achieve those ends so I would like to thank you for your help."

He took her left hand and raised it gallantly to his right cheek.

She repressed the urge to pull it back. She could feel the bristly touch of his beard on the back of her hand, and she was forced to look straight into his eyes. She could read nothing.

Later, after she had bid him a gracious good night, she lay awake wondering. In retrospect, it had not been an overly familiar gesture. The left-to-right salute was the most formal. But there was more to it than that. First, why the urge to pull back? Given their relative ages and Ranks and her knowledge of him, that seemed a reasonable reaction. Much more interesting was the second question: why she had resisted the urge. Probably just her good manners. She tossed restlessly, but soon the day's toil sent her to sleep.

* * *

A few days later she was just sitting down to luncheon when Lord Fauvé strode into the hall, a satisfied look on his face. He was holding a letter, which he tapped against his hand.

"What do you know about somebody called," he looked at the letter, "Raif anCanah?"

She hid a jolt of dismay. "Um...he's the heir to the anCanah Dukedom. He's...I don't know...about twenty-two, maybe twenty-three years old, been in the Royal Army for a while, just resigned his commission, and is doing I-don't-know-what at the moment. Either helping with the family interests or working for the Crown, I suppose. Isn't that what those sorts usually do?"

"But you know him?"

"Well, sort of. I mean, I know who he is. He probably knows who I am, vaguely. Lord Dalmyn does business with the Duke's interests." She was beginning to calm down, now. It seemed to have been an honest question. "Why do you want to know about Raif anCanah?"

"He's coming here!"

"Is that good?" *Definitely not good. I have everything in hand here. What is he doing, coming out to spoil it all?*

"I think so. My bandit problem has finally received some notice. The king is sending this anCanah to investigate."

"Oh. I guess he is working for the Realm, then."

"It looks like it. What sort of person is he?"

She shrugged. "I don't know much more than his public persona. As you might expect, he's intelligent, well schooled, polite, handsome, all that sort of thing. Many of the girls in my class were quite gaga over him, but he's a bit too elevated for us, you know."

"And you? Were you gaga over him?"

"Not likely. Too much flash, dash, and everything he wants, any time he raises a finger. I wouldn't want to be married to someone like that. Better he stick to his own kind."

"So he's smooth, is he?"

"If you mean, can he do a turn on the dance floor, play a gavotte on the harpsichord, or toy with a lady's heart, then yes, he's smooth."

"A bit of a rake, is he?"

"I wouldn't say that. Not more than the rest of his class. He's just got a reputation for being smooth, that's all."

"But he's young for such an important duty." The handsome face clouded. "Or maybe they don't see it as an important duty."

"Oh, I don't think you need to be worried about that. His father is very influential, and this sort of thing is exactly what he'd want his son to take on. Canah isn't that far from here, is it?"

"No, we're practically neighbours. Drat it, the man should be sympathetic. They had more than their share of trouble over there, last year."

"There you go. Maybe the Duke wants his son out here to make an alliance, look for common interests. Maybe between the two of you, you can solve this problem."

She smiled cheerfully, but her mind was whirling. His reaction had been very interesting. The idea of developing a powerful ally seemed to have set him thinking deep, and not happy, thoughts.

Then Fauvé seemed to realize that she was there, and his brow cleared. "Yes...yes, that could be a very good thing." He slapped the letter on his palm again. "At least we're getting some action."

"When is this representative coming?"

"He's a bit vague. Says he'll be following the letter."

"Typical. Raises a finger and expects everyone to rotate around it."

The lord grinned. "Now, Aleria. Do I detect just the slightest hint of reverse snobbery there? Be honest. If the Duke anCanah made noises about arranging a marriage with his son, wouldn't you come running?"

"Oh, I'd be running all right. In the other direction."

He gave her a piercing glance, and she wondered if she'd overdone it. "That's a pretty strong reaction. Is there something about this man you haven't told me?"

"No, no, it's not him. It's the whole bunch of them. You don't deal with them on a daily basis, like we have to in Kingsport. You think it would be wonderful to be part of that group. Let me tell you, you would never get to be part of the group. No matter how much money or influence you had, if you weren't born to it, you'd always be on the outside."

The lord smiled indulgently at her. "I can see you have been on the wrong end of their snobbery, Aleria, and I'm sorry for that. Don't worry. We'll handle this young lord."

"Oh!" She put on her 'girlish mistake' face. "Don't think I'm warning you about him in particular. He might turn out to be completely nice, once you get to know him." She smiled ruefully. "I guess I'm letting my prejudices get in my way. I'm sorry I spoke like that."

"No, no, I asked you for your feelings, and you gave them, honestly. Don't be sorry." He smiled. "It will certainly liven up our little parties, anyway, having someone from the Capital - I mean someone new from the Capital – tell us the latest gossip,"

She nodded. "I'm sorry, I haven't been much use in that sense. What do I know about what's going on with the rich and powerful?"

"Aleria, you have done a marvellous job of raising our spirits, embattled as we are. It has been truly a pleasure to be your host."

He seemed so sincere that she couldn't help but smile. "Thank you, lord Fauvé. You are too kind."

"Not at all."

14.   A Successful Evening

The social evening with the nobility was far more interesting from Aleria's point of view. She had been even more correct with the invitations and had taken more pains to shape the manor up into a home worthy of entertaining. Mostly, she wanted to compare Fauvé to others of his station in the area.

Speaking honestly, he came off very well.

There were representatives of six families present. The senior Rank was Lord Eclade: an elderly man, upright to the point of stiffness. From what Aleria could see, he couldn't think any farther than a repetition of the tenets of the Ranking system. All stay in their proper places, follow their orders, do what they are told, and everything will be fine. There were three other couples, middle-aged and placid, who would be willing to follow any strong lead so long as it did not disturb the even tenor of their lives. Another manor was represented by a callow young fellow who gravitated to his like in Fauvé's retainers and spent the evening drinking too much with them. Aleria gathered that his father was still very much in charge of their demesne and gave him little chance to exercise his position or prerogatives.

And then there was the Bayern family. Lord Job Bayern was a pleasant enough fellow, about thirty. But his wife had her sister visiting, and between the two of them they took up about half the space in the room. They sang every song. They danced every dance with anyone who asked, and went out of their way to ask anyone who had not tried. This was much to the discomfiture of some of the young men, who were unceremoniously hauled onto the floor blushing and protesting, but invariably left smiling, if warm.

Aleria couldn't help but like them, especially Mimay, whose laugh was just a bit softer than her sister's, and who seemed to have a small amount of pity for her victims. Her elder sister, Lady Katry, took her own boisterous nature for granted and assumed everyone else would follow her lead.

It was fun for Aleria to slip behind her violin and let these two give new meaning to the expression 'social whirl.' More like spin, she thought privately, as she watched them form a reel, somehow

113

extracting eight dancers from the crowd. Each had paired up with one of the reluctant young men and proceeded to teach him his steps, keep up her own, and somehow encourage all the other dancers to out-perform their capacities. Aleria tossed an evil grin to the music master, and they put an extra bounce into their playing.

At the end, there were eight red-faced, gasping dancers stumbling to their seats. Receiving a nod from Rumani, hovering in the doorway, Aleria called a temporary halt.

"Gentles all. You have done more than your share to enliven the evening. The orchestra needs a break. Cool drinks are available on the terrace."

She swept her hand towards the open doorway and the crowd, with grateful applause, filed out into the cool evening air. Since there was no terrace, Aleria had organized torches to light one scoured-clean corner of the courtyard. Darkness hid the barns and stables all around, and a few strategically placed benches defined the area further.

Dallya and two other girls were stationed behind a cloth-covered trestle table dispensing the punch.

As she surveyed the scene with some satisfaction she was aware of someone to her right, breathing heavily. She turned to see Mimay, fluttering a bright handkerchief in front of her face.

"A nice idea, Lady Aleria. I'm sure glad to be outside, I'll tell you."

"That last reel was a good one."

The woman glanced at her suspiciously. "Did I detect a change in the tempo, near the end?"

"You may have," Aleria spoke blithely. "The orchestra perhaps got caught up in the enthusiasm of the dancers."

"Huh! You like to have killed me. And my sister only three months from her confinement."

Aleria frowned in amazement. "Your sister just had a baby, and she's out bouncing around like that?"

Mimay shrugged. "We're a tough lot. I came up to help her get over it, but she was out of bed and running the house again four days later."

Aleria looked at the other woman, now laughing loudly at something Lord Fauvé had said, with new respect. "She's certainly...energetic, isn't she?"

Mimay shrugged. "Runs in the family. Our father was an amazing fighter, till he got himself killed. Lord Rogan. You may have heard of him."

Aleria nodded. "You're the daughters of Lord Rogan of Kant?"

"That's us."

"We were all told about him. He was the hero of the Alghen wars, wasn't he?"

"A lot of good it did us when he didn't come back."

"Yes, but he saved an untold number of lives with his defence of Alghly."

"And died on the battlements, almost single-handedly turning back the enemy's last, desperate charge. The relief column showed up three hours later. Four hours late, as far as I'm concerned."

"He was a real hero. You must be terribly proud of him."

The woman turned to face her, sized her up a moment before speaking. "My Lady, we may be terribly proud of our men, but pride doesn't fill the larder. Why do you think my sister ended up married to a small-time lord this far from the centre of the realm?"

Aleria grinned. "I don't know. Because so many people were afraid of her?"

Mimay laughed, a great explosion of sound, and slapped Aleria on the shoulder. Then she laid her hand on the shoulder again, squeezed harder, frowned. "That isn't the shoulder of a delicate lady from the upper Ranks."

Aleria returned the stare calmly, flexed her arm out of the woman's grasp. "I'm not exactly delicate. I drive horses, remember."

"Right. And organize fetes like this," she gestured broadly, "without turning a hair, just in your spare time."

"I do have the proper schooling."

The woman looked at her, head cocked to one side. "That's all right. I'm not the curious sort. You tell your story your way."

"I always do."

There was nothing left to say on that subject, so they turned and watched the party for a moment.

Gordon A. Long

"It's a good bash, Lady Aleria. We haven't seen the like around here for years. Especially in this hall."

"So I gather."

"Oh, Fauvé is a good enough man, I suppose. A little rough around the edges. He just isn't too interested in the social side."

"Do I detect a glint of interest?"

"No," Mimay paused, as if to consider her reaction. "No, you don't. Not sure why. He's the leader in these parts and reaching for more, but somehow I'm not interested."

"Plenty of other harvests to reap, back home?"

Mimay shrugged. "Not really. I have a good name, but no money, and a certain reputation for...straightforwardness."

"Now isn't that strange. I've heard that said about me, as well."

They smiled at each other. Finally Mimay spoke. "Well, it doesn't make us especially marriageable, but it makes for an interesting life."

"Hmm. An interesting life. Some would call that a curse."

"I don't, and neither do you, I can tell. A boring life. Now that would be a curse."

"I'd have to agree."

Mimay glanced at her slyly. "It wouldn't be a boring life with Lord Fauvé."

"Whoa!" She held up her hands. "I think you're taking a big step, there."

"Am I?" The other woman gestured across the party, to where the subject of their conversation was holding forth to several other men. "He's not bad looking, he's got a decent living, he doesn't drink, swear, or laze around..."

"...and I'm not interested in getting married at the moment."

"You aren't? Really? I figure most women our age are interested in getting married."

"Not that interested. Besides, like you say. If he's that good a catch, how did he get to this age without getting nabbed?"

Mimay grinned. "Maybe because he feels like you do. Maybe he's not ready. Maybe the right lady hasn't thrown herself at his feet."

"Mimay, I am not about to throw myself at anyone's feet, thank you very much."

116

"We're in agreement there, Aleria." She stared a moment. "But if you were?"

She followed her new friend's eyes. "I don't think so. I don't know why, but the answer is still, 'No'."

"Hmm." The other woman looked around. "Enough serious talk. Everybody's had their drink, had their rest. I'm going to take that fiddle from you, and you're going to do your share of the dancing."

"You are?"

"You think a soldier's daughter can't make beautiful music? Just you listen."

She stormed over to the music master and towed him back inside. Aleria, smiling, signalled the servants to collect the cups as the guests, noticing the action, began to move towards the main hall.

The party rolled on much longer than Aleria had planned, but everyone seemed to be having such a good time it was hard to quit. This time it really was the wee hours of the morning when the guests began to trickle away. Predictably, Lord and Lady Bayern and her redoubtable sister were last. As they were saying their good-byes, Lady Katry buttonholed her. "My sister says I have to invite you to visit."

Aleria pretended to be miffed. "Well, don't make any extra effort."

The loud laugh rang out. "And I see what she means. You have to come and see us. I have my lovely children to show off, you know."

Aleria searched for an appropriate response. "I'm sure they are very beautiful."

"Oh, yes. And intelligent, and musical and artistic too."

"Especially the one who is only three months old."

"We are still guessing a bit with that one."

Aleria laughed. "We'll, I'd love to come and see them. Perhaps I could drop over some afternoon next week."

"Oh, we're too far away to come for the afternoon. We're staying with the Eclade family tonight. A straight ride to our manor is almost two hours. You must come overnight."

"That would be nice. Let's ask Lord Fauvé what he has planned for the coming week."

It turned out that Fauvé had no specific social events, and seemed rather relieved that she was finding her own amusements, so she arranged to visit them in three days.

Once they were gone, the silence that descended on the manor seemed more profound.

Fauvé glanced over at Aleria. "Rather a force of nature, aren't they?"

"I like them. They have so much life."

He pretended to wipe sweat from his brow. "More than I have, after a long day's work."

"Don't tell me you're tired! What happened to dancing all night, and working all day, and calling yourself a man?"

He smiled, then looked at her. "You remember things, don't you?"

"I've always had a good memory. For important things."

"And that was important?"

She shrugged. "A sweeping statement is always interesting. I like to see if the person lives up to his words."

"Hmm. So I have been judged, have I?"

"Depends on how tired you complain to be." She then realized how her words might be taken, and was glad the dim light hid the heat that suffused her face. "I don't have any boast to uphold. I'm worn out."

"Well, I release you from having to show your pretty face at breakfast, which I will have at the usual time. The rest of my people didn't get a party tonight, and they will be working tomorrow."

She laughed. "I believe I have piqued your pride, Fauvé."

"Perhaps a little. However, I am not feeling up to any other challenges. Once again, thank you for the work you did on my behalf today. I know you took great pains that this should go well, and you were very successful."

"Thank you, Fauvé. It was truly a pleasure. Now, as I said, I am a bit fatigued, and I will bid you good night."

She smiled pleasantly, and giving him no chance for any formal gesture, turned away and went straight to her rooms. Dallya, who must have been keeping an eye open, met her there and made sure, as she always did, that Aleria had everything she needed.

"That was some party, my Lady. You lot sure can dance."

Aleria grinned. "Some of us certainly can."

"Them ladies from Bayern are really somethin' aren't they? Hear tell their servants can't keep up. They get goin' on somethin', and they keep workin' and they don't stop till the girls start fallin' down, they're so tired."

"Well, be thankful you're working here, then, where there isn't anybody like that."

"Oh, I dunno, my Lady. Girls like workin' there, even so."

"That's a good recommendation. I hope the staff in my house will say that about me."

"Oh, I'm sure they will, my Lady."

"And you had to say that, didn't you?"

Dallya, by now used to Aleria's humour, grinned. "You did a good job of makin' me, my Lady."

"A skill honed by years of ladies' finishing school. Now get out of here, or I'm the one who's going to fall down."

The girl turned in the doorway. "You danced and played as hard as any of 'em, my Lady, and you worked through the whole day before. Good night, my Lady."

Aleria locked the door and slipped into bed, a glow warming her breast. She remembered her mother saying that an honest compliment from a servant was worth the formal flattery of a dozen nobles. Now she understood.

15. Reinforcements

A few days later Aleria was roused from a rather boring afternoon by the sound of hooves trotting up to the gate. There was a bustle in the dirt-floored courtyard that was too small to be called a bailey, and the sound of men's voices. She strolled into the main hall in time to see Fauvé and Raif enter, followed by several soldiers in Canah livery. Fauvé spied her first.

"My Lord, perhaps you know Lady Aleria Dalmyn?"

"Aleria Dalmyn." Raif sounded puzzled. "Yes, I know her..." He turned surprised eyes on her. "Lady Aleria! What are you doing here?"

"Hello, Lord anCanah." She dropped an appropriate curtsey. "I was visiting with some friends, and Lord Fauvé was kind enough to offer his hospitality."

"You're out here by yourself? Is that wise?" He turned to Fauvé as if uncertain.

"That's what I thought, my Lord. Everything is all right, now, though. I have taken her under my wing, and between the two of us, I'm sure we can arrange her safe return to the Capital."

Raif favoured her with a pleased smile. "I'm sure we can."

Inwardly fuming, she smiled sweetly. "You are so kind, gentlemen."

They both bowed, then turned and strolled inside, forgetting her. She stood there, watching everyone move past her, until she had control of her movements and could stroll after them. *So that's how it's going to be. I can play along. I just hope that Raif isn't going to get caught up in his role again. I'll straighten him around this time.*

The problem was to get him alone. Lord Fauvé, pleased with his important visitor and the interest and deference he was shown, monopolized Raif's time, and Aleria was starting to get frustrated. Then she remembered her conversation about Raif. What if she were to act like Fauvé had suggested?

It wasn't hard to demonstrate interest, and she could see Fauvé pick up on it immediately.

"Aleria, we have been ignoring you terribly. Why don't you show Lord Raif our new garden? I think the fall colours are magnificent."

"Oh! That's a good idea. Lord anCanah has a marvellous garden at his seat in the Capital. Maybe if I give him a good tour here, Lord Raif will return the favour when we get back." She gave him a smile that would have melted pine tar in January.

Raif nodded. "That sounds like a possibility. Lead on, fair maiden."

With a gay wave to the lord, she took Raif's arm and towed him away, conscious of Fauvé's smug private smile to her as she left.

Once they were in the garden she made sure they were away from any possible listening ears before she spoke. "I'm beginning to find that man a bore."

"That's good."

"It is?"

"Yes. You have to realize that we were getting pretty anxious, back in the Capital."

"Define 'we,' Raif."

"I mean me, your father, and my superior."

"You thought Lord Fauvé might have turned my head."

"It was a possibility. Now that I've met the man, I'm beginning to get the picture."

"What picture is that?" She allowed a mild edge to enter her voice.

"The picture of how he operates. He had my number before I'd been here five minutes."

"He had?"

"Oh, yes. He has me pegged as a young, ambitious type. Inexperienced, but slick."

"That's good, Raif. That's just about how I painted you."

"And how have you painted you?"

"Well, I did let him know I didn't have much use for your sort. He's very amused at my transparent play for your attention, now."

"Ah. And what about your love letters to someone else?"

"I'm sure it has confirmed his opinion of the fickle nature of the female gender."

"He may know more than that."

121

"What do you mean?"

"It's possible that your letters have been tampered with. Not for sure. A few of the more recent ones have been damaged in transit. Seals cracked, but not completely broken, that sort of thing."

"Ones that came from here?"

"Only since you got to Taine."

"Hmm. Now that I think about it, the seal on one of your letters didn't look quite right. I thought you were just being sloppy, or the mail was roughly handled. What other things worried you?"

"Well, it's just that we were so sure we had something, and you come out here, and you spend all this time, and we know you're staying with the man and then...nothing. Surely you would have picked up something by now."

She fought down a guilty pang. "That's just it, Raif. I don't have anything. Nothing! He hasn't stepped out of line. He hasn't laid a hand on me, made an untoward offer or offended my dignity. He hasn't met with anyone unsavoury, not in my presence. I can't go following him around in the night." She threw up her hands. "I'm not that stupid."

They stood in thoughtful silence a moment.

"He has been doing some upgrading to his manor."

"What sort?"

She shrugged. "You could suggest that it makes it more defensible. Or it could just be good stewardship. It wasn't enough to put in one of my letters, if I could have figured out a way to say it."

"I'll keep my eyes open."

"You say my letters may have been tampered with. 'May have been.' By whom? I agree he's the first suspect, but there is no evidence. None, Raif. He has behaved like a perfect gentleman of Ranked Class for two whole weeks. I'm sorry, but I guess I've failed. Or he's innocent. One or the other."

Raif nodded. "Let's see how things go, now that I'm here."

She fought down a sharp reaction. "How are we going to handle this?"

He glanced around. "First off, we're going to have to play the game a little closer. You're supposed to be a mere acquaintance showing me the garden in order to attract my attention, and we've been standing in one place talking seriously for too long. You haven't touched my hand, or turned demurely away or done any one of a hundred things a girl does when she's flirting."

She stared at him in amazement. "Tutoring from the expert."

He tilted his head, and offered his arm formally. "If you would walk this way, my Lady, I think we can talk without being overheard. You must remember where I took my training."

She sobered. "Yes. In a place where one small slip could mean death. I take your point." She waved her hand at some roughly sculptured flowerbeds. "This should give you a good idea of the type of man you're dealing with. He tries hard, but he doesn't have much idea."

"Not a paragon of the gardener's art, I wouldn't say."

She grinned up at him, hung on his arm. "This from a man who has never touched the handle of a shovel."

"That shows what you know about life in His Majesty's Army, my dear. Now, how are we going to handle this?"

"What do we want?"

"We want evidence that he's supporting the thieves."

"How do we get it?"

"I don't know. I have my plans for the negotiations. I was hoping for some ideas from you."

She shrugged. "I'm sorry, Raif, but short of following him when he goes out at night..."

"...which I absolutely forbid."

She glanced sideways. "I wasn't going to do it. I was thinking of you."

"Bad idea. Besides, he may not ever meet with them, himself."

"True. He has plenty of toadies around him."

"Such as?"

She thought. "Well, your pedlar seems to have gone along his way. I never saw him. There are several young men of questionable Ranking. Younger sons with no prospects, you know the sort. One called Nerval is particularly odious, but that's only a woman's opinion."

"What do you mean by that?"

"I mean that all the women in the manor give him a wide berth. I've seen servants scamper to leave a room rather than be left alone with him. I can draw my own conclusions, but that doesn't mean he's a criminal. Not the sort we're after, I mean."

"I'll note him. Who else?"

"There's an older man called Danto. He's the overseer. He seems all right, but he would be the obvious one to handle payoffs and the like."

"I'll keep watch on him, too."

"Then there's the mercenary Captain, Ussel."

"What's he like?"

She took Raif's arm and pulled him girlishly towards the gazebo near the pond. "I can't see him being the agent. Not that I like him. I haven't met any mercenaries, but he's about what I expected. Rough in his manners, foul-mouthed when he thinks I'm not around. However, he does have a reasonable amount of professional concern for his men and the job they are supposed to do. I heard him recently expressing frustration to Fauvé about his inability to track down the bandits. Said it was as if they knew he was coming. He had no idea anyone else was listening, so I assume it was an honest comment. There's another officer in the mercenaries, a sort of second-in-command named Rost. He's a bit older, seems very nice in a sardonic sort of way. He's got better manners: might even be Ranked. I hardly see him. But if he was the contact, he wouldn't be around much, would he?" She tossed her hands out in frustration. "I hate to say I don't think he is the guilty one, just from the fact that I sort of like him. That's not very useful."

She thought again. "No one else stands out. Lots of bravado and fancy weapons, but not enough talent, brains, or courage to organize this successful an operation."

"So we come back to Fauvé."

"Against whom I have found absolutely no evidence."

"Exactly."

"There is..."

"Yes? What?"

She shrugged, almost embarrassed. "There is a noticeable uncertainty among the staff. I mean the female staff. I don't think it means anything, other than that there is no lady here and some of the men are a pretty rough lot."

"How do you mean, unease?"

"Nothing specific. They are careful with locking their doors at night, and they tend to move in pairs a lot." She held her hands open. "I thought it might be because of Nerval, but he was away for a while and nothing changed. It might be just protective habits. I don't know."

She pretended to show him some flowerbeds he could see perfectly well for himself. In the process she turned him back to face the house, but she could see no one spying on them. "And are you going to tell me anything about your plans for the negotiations? Or is that information I don't need?"

"I'd prefer not to tell you everything."

"Because you don't trust me?" She held up a finger to stop his reaction.

He lowered his hands, bowed in a formal gesture for her to precede him into the gazebo. "No, it has nothing to do with not trusting you."

"All right. Tell me what you can."

"At the start I'm to seem uncooperative, to force his hand."

"So if you refuse him, and there's suddenly another bandit attack…"

"That will be a good indication."

"Do you think he's likely to be that stupid?"

"If he doesn't take the bait, he doesn't. Then we send him the soldiers."

"Send them?"

"That's right. He thinks the king is going to send him money to hire soldiers, so he can get more independent. Quite the opposite. The king will send his own men, take more control of the area. But Fauvé won't know that until they arrive. That's the fact you need to keep to yourself. I probably shouldn't have told you."

She shrugged. "I could have figured that out for myself, actually. Why hasn't Fauvé thought of it?"

"I'm sure he could, but his mind doesn't work that way. He's taking a calculated risk and all our responses have led him to understand that we're not thinking in that direction. People like to hear what they want to believe, especially clever ones who think they are fooling everyone."

She grinned. "If he's the culprit he's going to be very upset."

"And if he isn't, he's going to be very happy."

She nodded. "Well, I think we'd better go back to the 'castle.' Now that I have established my intentions it will amuse him to help me, because once again he has proven his intelligence at someone else's expense."

"Right. I'll leave first. We don't want to think you're making too much progress."

He strode out of the gazebo, and she waited a moment before tripping after him. She walked beside him for a moment, hesitated, then reached out and took his arm. He looked down at her, seemed to consider, then walked a bit closer.

"Did you ever think that we might be playing all this to a non-existent audience."

"We probably are. Consider it rehearsal. The more you practise, the less chance you'll make a slip when anyone is watching."

She nodded, serious this time. "Good advice from the expert."

"So we are agreed that we have no evidence to go on, and if we don't come up with something quite soon I should use my negotiating ploy?"

She nodded. They were nearing the house, so she said nothing.

"Two days then."

"Whatever you say, my Lord." She smiled sweetly, swung away on his arm so that he had to stiffen it to hold her up. He rolled his eyes at her, then put on a serious face.

"Thank you for the tour, my Lady. I am sure these gardens will be a wonder to the neighbourhood when they have had time to get settled in."

She grinned up at his subtle dig. Like their owner, the gardens would need a couple of generations to settle in.

16.   Changing Nappies

Aleria rode out to the Bayern demesne, escorted by two bored soldiers who made it plain from the beginning, while not saying a word to her, that they considered this a waste of time when they could be chasing bandits. She was tempted to make a shot at breaking through this prejudice, but then decided to act as her role would require; she ignored them.

The weather had settled into those beautiful fall days – clear and hot in the daytime, crisp and starlit at night– that lift the spirits and make you forget about the winter to come. She trotted her mare along the country road, enjoying the movement, the air cooling her face and the beauty of the changing leaves.

Then she remembered her role and slowed her horse to a walk, commenting to the soldier behind her how tiring it was, riding a horse instead of driving it. He mumbled something in response, and she rode on.

She had expected to be greeted with enthusiasm, but Bayern managed to surprise her, as she should have known it would. Entering the courtyard of the big, sprawling manor house, she was swarmed even before she dismounted by several children, small and smaller, who swirled around, calling out greetings, blithely ignoring the hooves of her horse. A laughing Mimay shooed them away, rescuing Aleria, who had gently reined her horse to stillness and sat, unsure what to do.

"You can get down. They won't bite."

"I thought my horse was going to step on one." She dismounted, watching where her feet went.

"Oh, they've been around stock all their lives. If they get stepped on, they learn faster. You notice none of them went anywhere near the heels."

Aleria shook her head and moved forward to receive a firm hug. "They don't seem to have suffered any because of it."

She was then introduced to a flurry of little faces, some shy, some bold. The only name she remembered was Chand, a four-year-old who stepped forward solemnly and offered his cheeks, one and then the other, for a formal kiss. Mimay winked at her over his head. "Watch out for that one."

"I can see why."

When she arose, her hostess was already unfastening her bags from the saddle. "Is this all you've brought?"

"Oh, I do apologize. I didn't know if I should bring my ball gown. The engraved invitation must have been lost in the Royal Mail."

"Don't worry, we had to cancel the formal garden party. We harvested the carrots yesterday, and it left a terrible mess."

Aleria laughed and took her bags, not without some force, from her hostess and slung them over her own shoulder. "So, in which hayloft am I billeted?"

Mimay frowned. "If some of this lot get in on you at six in the morning, you'll wish you did sleep somewhere else."

Aleria tousled a curled head that seemed to have attached itself to her. "I suppose I can handle it." She looked down. "If you took my hand instead of my leg, perhaps I could walk."

The response was a cheerful grin and a sticky hand entwined in hers. Thus encumbered, they stumped up the steps into the main hall, which seemed to contain a ball game going on between the tables.

She raised her voice above the ruckus. "Your sister mentioned several children. This seems to be rather a lot."

Mimay's laugh overwhelmed the din. "It's just harvest time. The parents are working in the fields, so we gather any children too young to help and keep them occupied. It was an idea of Katry's. The workers like it. They get more work done and the kids love it."

"I can see. Who looks after them?"

"Mostly me. As a genuine Ranked lady, I'm the only otherwise-useless person on the farm."

"So this is why I was invited? To be a substitute nanny?"

"Some of that. I could use a hand. And a break from runny noses and scraped knees. Maybe I'll even get some adult conversation between changing nappies."

"Well, I can provide the conversation until my voice wears out. However, my Lady, I should inform you that I do have certain standards."

"And what are those?"

"I feel I must draw the line at changing nappies. I've heard it's not so bad if it's your own child. I am looking forward to finding out the truth. I do not plan any testing ahead of time."

"Well enough. You take care of this one while I change that one."

Aleria took a sobbing child on her lap, wondering what to say. It turned out that no words were required, as the little girl squirmed into her arms and settled nicely.

The afternoon went like that. Between spates of childish calamity there was plenty of space to talk. By the time the workers returned to claim their broods at the end of the day, Aleria knew a great deal more about life in a country manor, and what being the daughter of an impoverished hero really meant. She also was developing an unabashed admiration for Mimay's ability to handle her charges. She remarked on it as they strolled inside.

"I have been watching you deal with the children. I always thought a person had to be careful how much attention you gave them: make them independent, make them stand up for themselves. You don't do that. Every child that comes to you gets your complete attention."

"I think they deserve it."

"Yes, but here's the interesting part. You give them complete attention, but they never stay. They are always gone again almost immediately."

"Yes, I find that's the way it works. They often don't need anything specific. They need to know I am here, and they need to know that I know they are here. Then they go on about their lives. If you know what I mean."

"Which means that they are truly independent."

Mimay shrugged. "That's not my doing. These are peasant children and their parents are working most of the day. They are cast on their own resources a lot of the time. They help each other out and live their own lives, almost from the beginning."

Aleria grinned. "I'm sure there's a message there for the pampered classes, but I'm not sure I want to be the one to send it."

"Me neither."

"Anyway, I have been watching you this afternoon and doing some thinking, and I have come to a conclusion."

"And what is that? To keep from having children until you are forty years old and your life is over anyway?"

"No. I think you need to get married and have a whole slew of children. You are so good with them."

Mimay smiled wryly. "That isn't one of the prime reasons a girl lists for getting married."

"Maybe it should be. We all should be doing things we're good at."

"What about you? What are you good at?"

Aleria shrugged ruefully. "So far, nothing much. I spent my girlhood perfecting the art of getting into trouble, and I haven't got much past that."

"I doubt that's true. Look at it the other way. I imagine you spent your girlhood perfecting the art of getting out of trouble, and as a result you have superior skills in that respect."

"I wish your theory had proved true in my recent life, but, sadly, that has not been the case."

"Could you give me an example?"

Aleria thought a moment. It could do no harm to her duty here. She told Mimay a heavily edited version of her escapade during Slathe's rebellion. She mentioned no names, and removed her relationship with Raif afterwards, but kept the rest pretty well factual. Katry and Job came in as she was starting, so she had to begin again. When she had finished, there was a long silence. Then Mimay raised both hands and slapped her thighs with satisfaction. "See? I told you. Excellent skills at getting out of trouble."

"I don't see what skills I had that got me anything. It seems to me I just endured what I had to, and did what I had to, and let luck take care of the rest."

Job shook his head. "I doubt if it went quite like that. I have been in battle myself, and I know that luck plays a part. I also know that the better you fight, the luckier you are. Of course, anyone can take that one unlucky arrow from a flight, but the man who has the best armour and gets his shield up quickest has the least chance of getting hit. It would have been the same with you. If you hadn't acted exactly right the outcome could have been much less successful."

"That's what the spy who rescued me said. He said I did it perfectly. If acting cowed and frightened was perfect, I did it perfectly."

"And were you cowed and frightened?"

"Frightened, always. Cowed, not often. Most of the time I was too angry."

Katry nodded. "Angry. My father always said it was the best way to keep yourself going. Pride and hope and love help, but a good, old-fashioned rage is what pulled him through."

Mimay shrugged. "Until he ran out of luck."

Her sister shook her head. "I think not. I think he just got a little more angry than usual. From what they told us, someone needed to. He saved them all."

The two sighed, together, as if it was some sort of ritual. There was a moment of silence, and they Mimay brightened. "But that was back then. This is today, and we have all sorts of things to talk about. You lose, by the way."

"I do?" Her sister didn't look too disappointed.

"Yes. She isn't the nappy-changing type."

"I didn't think so. But maybe if you put the pressure on..."

Mimay chuckled. "You don't put the pressure on this girl, Katry. You ask her nicely, and flatter her if you can get away with it, but you don't pressure."

It was Katry's turn to laugh loudly. "Good for you, Aleria." She paused, became more serious. "You see, there's a story here. The peasant children don't use nappies. They run around outside all summer with their bottoms bare and there isn't much need. However, when they come here, I insist that they wear them. We may be farmers, but I'm not having child manure in my hall. So someone has to do the changing, and since it's our idea, we have to do it. Only fair."

"Which means it's Mimay, because she does most of the child-minding. And she thought maybe she'd get me to take over that part?"

"You get the gist of it."

"Sorry to be such a poor guest."

"You really said that convincingly."

131

They all laughed comfortably, and Job rubbed his hands together. "Well, the rest of us have being doing easy and unimportant tasks related to harvesting, so pardon us if our tales of the day are not so interesting."

His sister-in-law slapped his arm as they turned into the house. "It must have gone well, or you wouldn't be so complacent about it, but we'll allow you the chance to tell it your way."

Dinner was ready, and they dug in with a will, especially those who had laboured in the fields all day. Even Katry, who was restricted by the need to nurse her baby frequently, seemed to have done her fair share and more, as her husband's grumbling attested.

"You shouldn't have her out in the heat of the day so much, dear."

Aleria privately grinned at the touch of pride in his voice.

"Nonsense. She is always well shaded. If I wasn't out there supervising those girls, they would make a complete mess of the winnowing."

"I know, I know. I just wish you weren't always stepping in to demonstrate for hours at a time."

"You know very well it wasn't for hours. I just had to stay with them for long enough that they could learn to copy me. There's a real technique required, and once they have it, they won't need the supervision."

"And if we had one of those new Mechanical threshers, we wouldn't need to winnow at all."

"When we can afford one, I'll be happy to stop."

He tossed up his hands in a silent plea to the gods for patience, and went back to his meal.

"When am I going to meet this paragon of babyhood? I was under the impression that I had been hauled all the way out here, the main reason being to ooh and aah over your progeny. Where are they?"

Mimay laughed. "You've had Ranya tagging after you most of the afternoon."

"Ranya? The one with the curls? She's yours?"

"Our eldest."

"Oh. Wait a minute. Let me guess. Chand?"

"How did you figure that out?"

"Only because he's a perfect gentleman."

They all laughed, the parents proudly. "I don't know where he gets it, around here."

"Maybe he's just trying to be different."

The supper and the conversation ran on, and Aleria had time to notice that her two escorts, seated at the lower tables, seemed not to join in any conversation, and one left as soon as he could get away. She wasted only one raised eyebrow. Whatever their problem, it was their loss.

Just before supper was finished, the man returned and sat down, but soon after, his companion left. Strange. Then it occurred to her. Were they taking turns watching her? It seemed hardly credible. She resolved to watch them, in her turn, and grinned at the idea.

After the meal was over, the children were presented, washed and tidied, for their pre-bedtime inspection. Gariella was, as expected, as cute as a three-month-old could be. Aleria made what she hoped sounded like the right noises of approval, although she could see Mimay's cynical grin in the background. After the baby was gone, Ranya gravitated to Aleria, and Chand once again carried through his formal ritual. Aleria, knowing that her reactions were the object of everyone's scrutiny, did the best she could, and soon the children were scampering away.

She turned to them shaking her head. "I am amazed."

"At what?"

She tossed a hand around in a huge arc. "This. The house, the children, the whole atmosphere." They were walking towards the private apartments, now, and Aleria checked to make sure they were out of earshot of her watchers in the main hall. "Do you know what it's like at Lord Fauvé's manor? Men. All men, and the female servants scurrying around and staying out of sight. The kitchen is the only happy place in the whole house. Unless you consider getting tipsy, singing off-colour songs and dancing around daggers stuck in the floor to be happy."

Job tossed his head. "I don't know. I can remember when I thought that sort of thing was all right."

"Perhaps, but not for a mature man."

133

"I thought I was quite mature at the time."

"Point proven."

The easy laughter flowed again, and Aleria felt bathed in it.

They sat in the lord's private sitting room for a while, and she got a chance to introduce her real interest into the conversation. "What do you people think of Lord Fauvé?"

Eyes turned to Job, and he answered with a shrug. "I suppose he's good for the region. He's progressive in his farming methods and his dealings with the merchants. That's good for all of us, because it attracts more business. He's also ambitious, that's plain. So far, none of his desires have been achieved at the expense of any of us, so, again, he's probably good for the area."

"But not necessarily."

Katry was squirming on her chair. "He hasn't said any of our real opinions, though."

"You mean your opinions, dear."

"And you agree, but you're too polite to say so. He's an ambitious man, and sooner or later, that sort always causes trouble. My father used to say that no one sleeps in the stall with his horse, no matter how hard it's raining. Sooner or later, you get stepped on." He glanced at her. "Been doing some work on his manor, I hear."

"I noticed some."

"Defensive improvements, would you say?"

"They might be seen as such."

He nodded. "So we could be in a stall with a horse."

Aleria thought it best to remain quiet.

Mimay raised a cautioning hand. "Not that we have anything against the man, personally. We don't want you to get that impression."

Her sister grinned. "In other words, if you have designs on marrying him, we wouldn't want to start off on the wrong foot with our new neighbour."

Aleria returned the smile. "I gather it's a country custom, this habit of marrying all the singles off to each other at the drop of a glove."

"Hah! And you're telling me it doesn't happen at Court?"

"Perhaps not so obviously. There are proprieties to be observed."

Job spread his hands. "The ladies are so bored out here in the country. Nothing to do but farm, nothing to gossip about but each other. They need the entertainment."

Aleria nodded. "Which is a reminder that you have farming to do tomorrow, and I suppose I have children to look after?" She looked to Mimay for confirmation.

"If you don't mind. We'll give you a scythe if you think it would be an easier day."

"But you must see the new wing in daylight."

"Wing? I saw some construction on the way in. I thought perhaps it was a new barn or something."

"Oh, no!" Katry was quick to respond. "I'm sure you have been hearing my sister complain about our genteel poverty, but I did not come here empty-handed. The new wing comes from my dowry. It's just the ground floor at the moment, but it will connect through here..." she pounded on the wall beside her, "...and double the size of this room, with an indoor functionary and a private ladies' room connecting to our bedroom on the other side. We will have a real suite of rooms to live in, then."

Job roused from his lethargy at this topic. "And later, when we can afford it, we will raise it to the next story, and have guest rooms up there."

"Well, I'll have to come back when the accommodation is worthy of my exalted status, then."

Mimay laughed. "When you've married someone rich enough to come here, and stupid enough to be persuaded?"

This banter continued as they rose, yawning, and strolled their separate ways to bed.

17. Another Way of Life

Morning light brought the pattering of feet in the hall. Aleria opened a bleary eye to see two small heads poking around the door. The moment they saw her awake, there were squeals of glee, and two little bodies burrowed under her blankets. For a brief moment, she hoped they would settle in for a while, but soon the twitching and giggling started and she gave up and allowed herself to be pulled into the tickling and wrestling.

"Are you winning or losing?"

All three stopped and looked up. It was Katry, Gariella on her hip, standing in the doorway.

"I think I've lost forever, Katry. Who turned these little animals loose? Shouldn't they be in cages?"

The two giggled and made animal noises, but their mother was all business. "All right. Fun's over. Lady Aleria has to get dressed, and we all have to eat breakfast."

They obeyed immediately, and Aleria was alone. The silence felt strange, though a relief. She dressed, straightened herself up, and headed down for breakfast.

Job was just finishing his coffee. "I'm sorry I was too busy to give you a tour of the demesne, yesterday. I have to do some rounds today, if you'd like to tag along."

Aleria grinned. "And neglect my child-minding duties? What a disappointment."

"You go ahead and get them started. I'll come and rescue you when I'm ready to leave, in about an hour."

"Fine. I'll go and tell my men what's going on. I think I'll ride back to Taine later on, towards evening. The afternoon was quite hot, yesterday."

"Good plan. You can help supervise lunch."

"That should be an experience."

Her guardians appeared, and she gave them the itinerary while they ate. Talden, the one who seemed to be the leader, nodded. "I'll ride along with you on this tour of the farm."

"I don't think there's any need for that. I'm hardly going to be attacked in the middle of the demesne."

He shook his head, perfectly serious. "Lord Fauvé said I was to watch over you, and if anythin' was to go wrong, it would be on my head. I'll tag along."

She stared at him a moment, coldly. It didn't seem as if he was giving her any choice in the matter. However, since she wasn't doing anything that needed privacy, and since there was nothing worth making a fuss over, she shrugged. "Lord Bayern is coming around for us in about an hour. Perhaps you could have our horses ready."

"Of course, my Lady."

It was the first time he had addressed her properly, and she once again favoured him with a stare before returning to the family at the other end of the hall. "That's fine. My horse will be ready in an hour. It seems I will have an escort."

Job frowned. "Him? That's hardly necessary."

"Talden takes his responsibilities seriously. Should one of your roosters go mad and attack me, he would defend my honour."

She turned in a business-like way, slapping her hands together and searching the corners of the room. "So, where are my charges for the day?"

Mimay laughed. "They'll be along in a while. We can take these two with us while we get started."

They were in the middle of some complicated game involving sticks and straws, and Aleria was just getting the rules straight, when Job appeared. "Ready for that rescue?"

Aleria stood up. "Since I seem about to be trounced by a five-year-old, I think now would be a very good time."

She looked apologetically at Mimay, who waved a dismissive hand. "I'll just step into your game and see if I can restore the honour of the adult world."

The boy she had been playing grinned. Perhaps he didn't understand what the adults were saying, but he could figure out what was going on. By the time Aleria and Job were across the room, there were two heads leaning in over the sticks in mutual concentration.

Her unwanted attendant was at least punctual, and her horse was saddled and waiting in the courtyard. Job nodded to the soldier and mounted, and they trotted out to the east.

137

"I have a farmer out here who is quite resistant to the new methods, and I want to check on his harvest."

"Still using hand-broadcast seeding, is he?"

He turned in the saddle. "You know about that?"

She smiled. "Lord Fauvé has the same problem."

"What's he doing about it?"

"There's nothing much he can think of. Keeping the pressure on, getting the farmers who will change to lead by example. The man's otherwise a good tenant, so he is loath to turn him out."

"Turn him out? Did he say that?"

"He only mentioned it as not being an option."

Job nodded. "That's what I meant last night. I doubt if any of the other lords in the area would have even discussed it, option or not. Some of these families have been on their land longer than we have. They don't own it outright, but..."

She nodded. "The old feudal habits die hard. That's bad in some ways but good in others. I have heard my father comment that if the lords would forget the new laws of land ownership and remember their own responsibilities under the terms of their fiefs, then they would find their demesnes running much better."

"Interesting to hear that from city gentry."

She remembered her role. "If my father had any influence, it would be more useful."

He glanced at her. "Your family seems very progressive, at least to us, out in the country."

"I don't think we're that different from many. When you live in a city and make your living in a trade you tend to lose the connection with the old ways."

"I suppose. And is Lord anDalmyn as progressive?"

"I would think so. After all, he lives in the city and makes his living in a trade."

"He does?"

"Oh, yes. The family estate is very small. Nowhere near big enough to support all of us. I'm sure he owns other land, but the cartage is our livelihood, no question about that."

"I see. Interesting."

"Yes, I'm hearing from various people that the power is moving into the hands of the merchants. Any Ranked folk who wish to keep their prerogatives had better keep that in mind. Kensel anDalmyn certainly does."

"You seem to know a lot about him."

"Certainly. A good merchant keeps his managers in touch with what's going on. My father follows that advice, and in turn tells me what he knows." *There. Not one actual lie in the whole story.*

It seemed to satisfy the other, and their talk turned to the farm.

Once again, Aleria was treated to a tour of a country estate, and to a view of the lord dealing with his tenants. She could see that Job had a much more friendly, easy, way with them, but could not see that it made their work any better. Both estates seemed to be well run and tidy, and both sets of commoners treated their lord with respect. It was hard to tell which one was wrong, if either was. She recalled the manner her father maintained with his workers, and thought he must be somewhere in between the two.

Job dropped her off in the courtyard just in time to meet Katry, coming out of the house with the ever-present Gariella, this time in a sort of sling over her shoulder.

"Are you coming to see the new wing?"

"If I can get past Mimay without being seen and put to work."

"Let's do that." Job glanced around. "I don't like all those children running about where the men are working, and if she comes there's no keeping them out."

Aleria acted impressed by the new building, which was a rather small project, as far as she could see, but the workmanship looked good and she could envision the difference it would make to their living space. She glanced around for something to say. "The new end wall comes very close to that barn."

Job glanced at his wife before answering. "Well, I did notice that, yes. It has...purposes that way."

"You mean for defence?" Aleria looked down. "I see. You have put extra footings here, for a gate. A heavy one."

"Yes. It seemed prudent, since we were doing the rest of the work at the time."

She nodded. "Yes, that will be a good addition." She swung and surveyed the rest of the courtyard. "All you would need is a short wall to fill that gap between the silo and that shed, there, and you could button this place up tight as anything."

Job ducked his head, mumbling something about it being possible. His wife rounded on him. "So that's it!"

He made an unsuccessful attempt to look puzzled. "What, my dear?"

"That's why you bought that extra stone. That you said we didn't really need, but the price was good and we could save it for the upper story, later."

"Well, the price was good, and we could save it..."

"Or we could build a short wall and complete our defences?" She shook her head, turned to Aleria. "He is so stupid sometimes. Here he is, married to a general's daughter, and he thinks I'll be upset with a plan to make our home safer."

She slipped over to her husband, held his arm with both of hers. "I think it's a marvellous idea. Mind you, I would have liked to have some furniture for the new rooms..." she glared up at him in mock anger.

"I know, I know, dear. We'll keep looking around. Now let's not air our family problems in public."

Aleria grinned. "Yes, I wouldn't want you to ruin the picture of filial bliss I have created."

"There you go." He nodded wisely. "You are spoiling a young lady's dreams, and she has yet to experience lunch."

A patter of feet on gravel alerted them. "And we have been discovered. Let's get out of here before the little ones start eating the cement."

They returned to the courtyard, to be surrounded by a gaggle of voices informing them that lunch was waiting.

When it came right down to it, lunch wasn't bad at all. The children fed themselves and each other and all the adults had to do was keep the plates moving. The older children sometimes made an attempt to clean up the spills, although that often made the mess worse. In all, Aleria found it hilarious.

"You do this every day?"

"Just in harvest time."

"No days off?"

"If the weather is good, Feastday is just another day to get the crops in."

Aleria nodded. "I know. If you're on the road with an important cargo, it's hard to rationalize sitting still and paying inn fees. I sometimes think that if we didn't have to rest the horses, we'd work every day of year."

"Yet you like the job."

Basic honesty pulled Aleria back closer to truth. "I'm not on the road all the time, so I can't say. I work in the office and the yard most days."

"In the yard?"

"I've been known to load a wagon or two of lumber," she flexed her arm, "as long as the planks aren't too heavy."

"The gentry from the city surprises us again."

Aleria looked at her new friend, aware that she might be leaving soon. "Are you staying in Bayern long?"

Mimay thought a moment. "I started out wanting to go home quite quickly. Katry didn't need help with the baby. Then this," she indicated the children, "got in the way. So now I'll stay till the harvest is over. After that, I'll see. I like it here."

Aleria nodded. "I can see how you would. Never have to sit still, always something needs doing."

"That's right, and it's the need part that appeals to me the most. Don't worry. I can sit still if I have to. But I like a useful life."

Aleria shook her head. "The problem is to find one. I'm not doing too well, so far."

"Manor life does that for me. I'm always doing something important, here, even in some small way."

"Like stopping that little boy from eating whatever is in his hand?"

Mimay glanced over, looked again and frowned, then jumped up and strode over to the lad, who was messing about on the floor in the corner. "What do you have there, child?"

The boy grinned, held up something.

She took it gently. "Hmm. I'm not sure what that is. I doubt that it tastes very good though." She pretended to nibble it, wrinkled her nose. "No, definitely icky." She tossed it in her hand a few times, and then seemed to notice something the other children were doing. The boy's eyes followed. When Aleria looked a moment later, the object had disappeared.

"Nice work. I once met a thief who was good at distracting people's attention from his hands."

Miman shrugged. "Some day he may have to eat a dead beetle to find out whether he likes the taste. But not while I'm in charge." She shuddered delicately, placed the bug on a dirty plate, and began scraping the other plates on top. "It's the slop bucket for this. The pigs won't mind."

Aleria helped clean up and then they took the children outside. She remembered a game she had played when she was young – she couldn't remember how young – and decided to teach it to the older ones. Soon she had all of them merrily hopping over and ducking under sticks. It hadn't occurred to her to tell them not to use the sticks for swords, but that was a minor hitch in the proceedings, and they had a lot of fun.

She was having so much fun that the afternoon was gone before she knew it, and Talden was leading her saddled horse from the stable, probably anxious to have this duty over with.

She bid farewell to all of them: a reverse of her introduction, with mobs of children at their feet. In the middle of it, Ranya pulled at her mother's arm, spoke into her ear.

"Oh, I don't know," Katry raised her eyebrows, "She's a very busy lady."

This time the little girl's voice rose over the babble. "Invite her to visit again, please, mama."

"It's your idea, go ahead."

Aleria watched in amusement and some other emotion she couldn't define as the little girl walked up to her with a determined look and curtseyed. "Lady Aleria, would you like to come back and visit us again, soon?"

She nodded formally. "I certainly would, although I may have to go back to Kingsport soon. I will send you a message if I can come."

"That will be very nice."

"Thank you for the invitation."

Ranya turned away, then broke and ran to push her face in her mother's skirt, whether in embarrassment or tears, Aleria never knew.

That small formality was an effective closure for their good-byes, and she swung up on her horse, turned carefully, and led her small detachment out the main gate, the older children running along at a safe distance from the horses.

Once the noise of the manor faded behind them, Aleria resisted the urge to make some comment to the soldiers following her. They would respond woodenly and spoil it all.

As she rode, she thought of her visit to the Bayern manor. It had been a complete change from the rest of her visit, and she felt a small twinge of guilt about ignoring her duties. Then she shrugged it off. She had been gaining valuable information about the neighbourhood. As far as she could tell, all the local gentry were quite happy to have Lord Fauvé play whatever ambitious games he wished, as long as his desires did not extend to their demesnes. The merchants would follow along with anyone who flattered them socially and actively supported their enterprises.

Yes, Fauvé had a good, solid basis for a small empire of his own out here at the edge of the realm. But did that mean rebellion?

She was brought out of her thoughts by Talden riding up beside her. "I was just thinking, my Lady, that the next stretch is a good place for an ambush. I'll ride ahead and check it out."

"Aren't we quite close to home?"

"Yes. Once we're through this stretch of trees, you'll be quite safe. Besk will be following the whole way."

"I see." In other words, he was going to head home first and leave her to her own devices. She was glad to have his gloomy presence gone. She wasn't worried about bandits here in the centre of Fauvé's demesne and her sword hilt rose unobtrusively in front of her left leg.

He nodded, not waiting for any response, and rode off at a brisk trot.

She wondered how Fauvé would feel about this abandonment of duties and speculated if it would be worth it to say something to test his reaction. Such pettiness was beneath her unless it served a useful purpose, so she decided to let it go unless someone asked her.

The other soldier jogged on a reasonable distance behind her, lost in whatever thought he was capable of, so she ignored him and went on her solitary way.

She arrived in time to get cleaned up for supper. Fauvé asked little about her visit, only the usual polite and meaningless enquiries about the comfort of her travel and the health of those in Bayern. She took advantage of the opportunity to emphasise her preference for driving over riding, and left it at that.

Fauvé was interested in his peer's problems with backward farming techniques, and seemed disappointed but not surprised that Bayern was having no more success than he was himself. He listened to her gossip about the other manor, showed a slight interest in the new building and their consequent need for furniture, but otherwise seemed to be occupied with his own thoughts. She soon ran out of ideas and that was the extent of their supper exchange.

Later on Raif and Fauvé were deep in conversation, and since there seemed nothing entertaining going on in the manor that night, she retired to her rooms early.

She found herself pacing the room and decided she was bored. It was understandable in view of the starkness of this manor, compared to where she had just been.

Shrugging, she took refuge in her usual activities. Dallya was surprised, and even a bit frightened, to find Aleria sweaty and panting, running through her sword exercises.

"What are you doing, my Lady?" She set the tray down and stood back, regarding Aleria with amazement.

"I'm sitting on a stool doing embroidery, Dallya. What do you think?"

For a moment, she thought the wit had been wasted, but then the girl's face cleared. "Oh. I see. Yes, my Lady." She thought a moment. "That's a pretty big needle you got there."

Aleria looked at her sword as if for the first time. "Yes, but it does the job it's made for."

"I suppose it does, my Lady."

Aleria wiped the sword with an oiled cloth, sheathed it and sat on the bench, reaching for the drink. "Thanks, Dallya. A workout makes you thirsty, warm day like this." She took a deep draught.

"So sit down a moment and tell me what's been going on since I left a whole day ago."

Dallya sat down quickly, as if afraid the opportunity would go away. "Not much, my Lady. Boring evening last night, with you away."

Aleria shook her head. "I was here tonight, and I didn't hear much applause. Is Lord Fauvé worried about something?"

"We're not sure, my Lady. He did get a message yesterday that he didn't seem happy about. Not too upset, you know, just thoughtful. It wasn't a real letter from the King's Messengers. Just a note on folded paper."

It was so easy to get information that Aleria felt almost guilty. The women in the castle watched their lord carefully, noting even the smallest change in mood and passing it quickly through their grapevine . Aleria had been accepted into that information system, and she felt sometimes as if she was abusing a trust.

"Anything else?"

"He'n' Lord Canah spent a lotta time talkin'. Guess that's to be expected."

"I suppose so. That's what Lord Raif came to do."

"He's handsome, ain't he? Dresses so beautiful."

"Yes, he is good looking, and educated and polite. And I don't have a chance in a million, since you didn't ask. But a girl's got to try, doesn't she?" *I must be a poor spy, when I feel bad about planting even a simple misdirection like that. Word might get around, though. Maybe she's been set to spy on me. Maybe I'm a bad spy because I don't like this sort of thing at all.*

"Talden came back early. I thought he was protectin' you?"

"Yes, he said he was checking ambush points ahead, but he never got back to us. Does lord Fauvé know?"

"Oh, yes. He reported straight to the lord the moment he got in. He wasn't far in front of you."

"Hmm." She filed that away. Fauvé knew and wasn't upset. That didn't match with his concern about bandits.

"Any word on the bandit problem?"

"The men he sent out came back and reported, but you'll have to ask him what they said, because I don't know."

"I didn't expect you would, so I will ask him. Thanks again for the drink, Dallya. I think I'll go to bed now."

"Could I ask you one question, my Lady?"

"Of course."

"Well, it's like this, my Lady. I notice that with you, it's always 'please' and 'thank you' and using my name. I ain't heard that before. I'm used to 'girl, get me this,' and 'hey, you, where's the ale?' What's the point? I have to do what you say, whether it pleases me or not. Why bother?"

Aleria grinned. "I guess I say 'please' because you don't really have to do anything for me. You can always refuse."

"Sure. And walk out the door to...what? No, a servant like me ain't got too many choices, my Lady, and everyone knows it, and I think you do too. So why do you still ask, polite like that?"

"It's a good question, Dallya, and I shouldn't joke about it. My parents told me the answer long ago. It has to do with treating people like people." She looked at the puzzled frown on the servant's face.

"When you use courtesy to someone, you are recognizing that she is a person with feelings. The fact of whether she has to obey is completely aside from that. My mother put it this way; yes, you have to obey me, but how you feel about obeying is up to you. If I ignore that, you can feel any way you like, and it probably won't be good. If I am polite, I show concern for how you feel and I hope that will make you feel better, rather than worse."

"But why should you care about how I feel?"

"As I said before. Because you are a person, just like I am. What kind of person would I be if I didn't care about other people's feelings?"

"Oh."

"The problem you're having, Dallya, is that a lot of people don't think of servants as people with feelings. My parents also said a lot of things about how it showed what kind of person I was, and that showing respect to others showed respect for myself. I'm still working on that bit."

Dallya grinned. "Yeah, my Mum said stuff like that, too." She frowned. "But I think it works."

"It does? I'm so glad."

146

"No, I mean it. Look at you. You show respect to me and that shows me that you're worth respecting."

"I don't think our mothers were talking about making impressions on other people."

"No, I guess not. It still seems right to me, though, now that I've met somebody who does it."

"Well, I guess that's good, then. Is that why you've been calling me 'my Lady' so much, lately?"

"Oh that's easier, if you think about it. If I'm serving someone important, that makes me more important, too."

"So you're getting above yourself, are you?"

"That's right, my Lady. Keepin' her Ladyship talkin' when she said she wanted to go to bed. I'm right uppity, I am."

"Well, I think I had better put you in your place, then."

Dallya scooped up the empty cup, slapped it on the tray. "Which is in the kitchen, helpin' with the final cleanup." She gazed around the room. "Will you be needin' anythin' else," she paused and emphasised the words, "my Lady?"

Aleria put on emphasis of her own. "No, thank you, Dallya."

The girl nodded deeply, partly in acceptance, partly in obeisance, then spoiled it with a grin. "Good night, my Lady."

Aleria resisted the desire to throw a pillow. "Good night, Dallya." The door closed softly, and she threw herself on the bed, chuckling. *Deep thoughts from a serving girl. Hmm.*

18.   New Tactics

Fauvé had a smug look on his face the next morning at breakfast, but he said nothing, and Aleria had no reason to ask, so she ignored him and made small talk with Raif while they ate. However, the older lord could not maintain his secret, and stood in a formal manner when he saw that they had finished eating.

"Lord anCanah, Lady Aleria, I have a small announcement."

They glanced at each other, then gave him their attention.

"It has not escaped my notice, nor that of anyone in this demesne, how much Lady Aleria's visit has meant to us. She has been a cheerful and uncomplaining guest, despite our rough ways out here on the frontier of the realm. She has been instrumental in creating a flowering of culture in our little castle, the like of which no one has seen for many a year. She has sung, played, danced, and acted as hostess several times. Our lives have basked in her warmth." He looked down at her fondly.

Aleria caught herself beginning to frown, and pasted a pleasant smile on her face. *What was this all about?* She was careful not to glance at Raif.

"We are aware that she may be leaving us soon, and we do not want her toil to go unacknowledged. So tonight we have planned a little surprise for her. Tonight, Aleria, you will not sing, you will not play, and you will only dance if you choose. We will be entertained by a well-known entertainer who is passing through Taine at the moment. The ladies of the staff have promised to go all out in their preparation of the meal." He raised a finger. "With no help from you. Partly in order to demonstrate that we do have the ability to create a soirée without your assistance, although we would much rather not. Your instructions are to relax and play the lady of leisure for the day, and spend your time anticipating our poor efforts to entertain you tonight."

He stepped over and held out his hand, beaming down at her, and she felt her face grow hot as she took it and rose to make an appropriate curtsey.

"My Lord, I don't know what to say. I have tried to be a good guest and contribute to the community. It will be a great pleasure to enjoy the evening that I'm sure you will organize with great success." She turned to Raif with another formal curtsey. "My Lord anCanah, you will be pleased to join us?"

He laughed. "I can scarcely be expected to dine at the local inn, can I?"

She took his cue and slapped his hand coyly. "My Lord, you mock my poor attempt at good manners." She turned her back to him and nodded to Fauvé. "My Lord, I am in your debt."

He nodded in response, clicked his heels together and made a military turn. Then she could see his shoulders lose their formal pose as he glanced at Danton, the overseer, and motioned the man to follow him. Business as usual.

She turned to Raif, but made no comment. They were going to have to let this one play out, and too much discussion could cause suspicion.

* * *

Predictably, the day dragged. After all, part of her reason for making herself useful was to escape the crushing boredom of country life. So when dinnertime dragged itself into view, she was quite looking forward to the evening.

In general, it didn't go too badly. She was seated at the head of the table, with Raif and Fauvé on either side vying for her attention. The food was good, as she knew it would be. The entertainment was passable. The minstrel, while perhaps not well known in the Capital, was an experienced professional with a good range of pieces, from comic through historical to romantic. He and Saleri provided the high point of the evening for her, because they were both far beyond her own ability, and their guitar and violin duet was excellent.

Throughout it all, she played her role, she thought, to perfection. She toyed with each man's attention as she was expected to, and tried not to enjoy it too much. *This is all a charade. I think.*

And through the evening, she was watching her host, trying to see what was going on in his head. *Why is he doing this? What does he really want?* The evening ended and she still had no answer. Unable to talk privately with Rafe, she strolled off to bed, trying not to feel exhilarated by the attention. Dallya glanced at her a few times, then took her cue and said little, slipping out and closing the door before Aleria noticed she was leaving.

After a long time lying with the same thoughts spinning through her head, Aleria decided that whatever was going on, she could see nothing that could reveal her position or do her harm, and there was an end to it. She rolled over one more time and composed herself to sleep.

* * *

The following morning she took her time getting up, and she and Raif contrived to stay late at breakfast. Fauvé went out about his business at his usual time, leaving them alone.

Aleria looked around to be sure that they were unobserved, then leaned closer. "So what do you make of all that?"

He shrugged. "You've been here longer than I have. What do you think?"

"I don't know. It's not like him. Usually he's much more reserved. He doesn't gush. In fact, he rarely shows any strong emotions at all. The idea of him being tender, or in love, or jealous is just beyond imagining."

Raif burst out laughing. "You've got it. He's jealous!"

"What?...oh. Yes, that had occurred to me."

"With all the attention I've been giving you, he's making sure you realize that he's here and appreciates you."

"I suppose." She shook her head. "But you see how it goes? It doesn't help. That's the problem I've been dealing with the whole time. We have no idea whether anything he does is a clever ploy, a natural reaction or something else we haven't thought of."

"I'm beginning to see the problem." He stared at her a moment. "If he is working something up, he seems to have it focused on you. You watch yourself."

She shuddered. "After the last time, I'm forced to agree." There was a short silence as they both thought about the last time. "So what do we do now?"

"Well, I have to agree that your approach hasn't had any success. Either he's innocent or he's too smart to let anything slip. That leaves it up to me."

"What are you going to do? If you should be telling me."

"I've been playing it coy so far. Now I'm going to start pushing it a bit, as we discussed. Then we'll see how he reacts."

She nodded. "Fair enough. I can't think of any way I can help, but I'm here if you need me."

"You've done your share and more. I appreciate your effort."

She grinned at him. "Not you, too!"

He smiled. "I never could resist a challenge."

"Spare me the embarrassment."

"I will do what I can to keep you out of it...servant coming."

She nodded and searched her mind for another topic.

"Have you seen Mito lately?"

"Ah...yes, I have."

Aleria came alert. "Why the hesitation? Is something wrong?"

"Oh, no, nothing's wrong. Everything is going very well, actually."

"Then why the trouble telling me?"

He grinned at her. "Well, I never know how you're going to react, so I have to think how to put certain matters. Then there's the security aspect. I have to decide whether you should know. Very complicated."

"Now you have my interest really piqued. What have you done?"

"No, no, don't round on me with your eyes blazing. I haven't touched a hair of her pretty head. Quite the contrary."

Aleria held her stare a moment, just to let him know he wasn't getting off easy. "All right. That was enough preparation. Now just tell me what's going on."

He shrugged. "It's rather simple, when I come to tell it. I've had to...um...take Mito more into my confidence than I had first expected."

"That's all?"

His face became serious. "Yes, and that isn't the 'all' as you seem to imply. That's why I thought long and hard about it, and why I was worried about your reaction. Up to this point, she has had nothing to do with this spying business except to pass letters to me. You have made it clear that her reputation for openness and honesty is paramount to her. So bringing her in further could have been a mistake, but only from her point of view.

"You realize, Aleria, that once you have given someone a piece of information, for good or ill, there's no taking it back. They know, and they are vulnerable to the hazards of that knowledge. And you have to accept the consequences too."

She thought about that, then looked over at him with a grin. "Why Raif. Do I detect a hint of forethought in your actions? I don't recall being on the receiving end of such sensitivity, myself."

He scoffed. "Right. And I'm supposed to ask my fencing partner before I make a touch, in case I might hurt him."

He turned to her. "Look, Aleria, I give people the consideration I think they need. In your case, I think sometimes I overestimate your strength, and for that I apologize. With someone like Mito, it's a whole different situation."

"I think you'll find that she's a lot stronger than she seems."

"It's her reputation, not her personal strength that I'm concerned about."

She nodded. "Well, that's as it should be. I agree completely." She turned and walked on. "So what prompted this monumental change in procedure?"

"It was your letters. I told you we needed a better code."

"I thought my message was quite clear, even if my results may not have been as we wished."

"That wasn't it. I just couldn't figure out what was going on."

"Ah. Whether my head had been turned."

"I have to admit it, yes. I was trying to get all the information I could out of your letters, and I just wasn't getting anywhere. I don't know you well enough."

"Aha. So you went to the expert."

"I did. As I said, I thought long and hard about it, but I considered the importance of the situation, and I finally decided that Mito was my best choice. Nobody knows you better, and she was already involved."

"I see."

"When it came down to it, I had to balance your certain exposure to physical danger against a hypothetical threat to her reputation. When I laid it out like that, there was little question. She agreed, by the way."

"She would. And did you get anything out of her?"

"Quite a bit. It's amazing how much information you put in those letters, once they were explained to me."

"Good. I'm glad Mito knows. Not telling her bothered me just about as much as telling her would have."

"The problem was, she couldn't make up her mind, either. She leaned towards believing your instincts, but then, she admitted that she's your friend, so she's biased."

She chuckled. "So despite your agonizing choice and the risk you ran, you ended up no further ahead."

"Exactly. Very frustrating."

"I see. So here you are."

"I didn't have any other choice. And Mito agreed."

She nodded. "Well, I have to say that makes me feel a bit better. I'll be honest, I was concerned at first that you were meddling again, but I see that you took whatever action you could. I also understand your frustration. I've been feeling the same way. What do we do now?"

He shrugged. "Keep on living your life here as you have been. You'll be coming back to the Capital with me when I leave, success or not. I assume that's a given."

"We'll agree for once. I had my chance, and if I wasn't successful, I know when to quit."

He glanced over at her, grinning. "Why, Aleria. Do I detect a touch of maturity and sensibility?"

"Don't press your luck."

"I won't, and I see our host returning. Time for me to beat a subtle retreat." He rose, bowed over her hand and turned away to pass Fauvé as he departed. Aleria detected a tilt of his head as he passed, and pictured a conspiratorial wink, which she knew would have infuriated her, had this recent conversation not taken place.

Fauvé was smugly jovial as he approached, but she had no trouble in squashing her irritation. She had a task to accomplish.

"So our young friends in Bayern are in need of furniture?"

Aleria touched his sleeve lightly. "Don't you tell them I said that."

He grinned down at her. "You have hit the problem exactly. I have a whole granary full of old furniture I never use. Some of it is of good quality. However, I could never offer an old piece of furniture, no matter how useful it might be." He opened his hands helplessly.

"You couldn't."

His brow wrinkled.

"But I could."

"Aha!" He smiled. "You do have a grasp of the subtleties."

"Right. If I were to stumble over a nice piece of furniture or two that just need some refinishing, and were to ask you for them, as a favour..."

"...and if I were to give them to you, no one would feel upset."

"So why are we sitting here talking about it?"

He allowed her to pull him to his feet. "I suspect a visit to the west granary is imminent."

She glanced back at him. "Oh. Unless you're busy..."

"No, no, Bayerin is a valuable ally. If I can aid them without stepping on their pride I'm all in favour. Lead on."

He signalled to a couple of servants as they left the hall, and soon she was happily directing a dusty, uncomplaining crew, who lugged, overturned and restacked the mass of old chairs, beds, benches, chests, armoires and other detritus of years of changing style and inherited interests.

Finally she had it down to five items: two armoires, a chest, a chair, and a bench upholstered with tattered embroidery. She regarded her choices with satisfaction, then looked uncertainly at her host.

He nodded. "You have a good eye for quality, my Lady."

"Oh, I wasn't suggesting that you give them all..."

His chin gestured towards one of the armoires. "That one has been in my family for untold generations. I won't be getting rid of it. The others are fine. Why don't you pick, say, three?"

"Are you sure?"

"Yes, I don't want to give too much. It might upset others, despite your intervention."

"Exactly. You think three would be all right?"

He grinned at her, reached out to push a wisp of hair out of her eyes. "As long as they're small enough to go in a wagon."

She patted her hair back and turned to the servants. "All right, boys. Put the two armoires back. One's too nice; the other's too big. We'll take the remaining three."

They didn't even glance at their lord for confirmation. While they reorganized the goods again, she turned to Fauvé. "They'll appreciate the chest for putting the baby's things in and I know Mimay will be able to fix up that bench. You should see her embroidery."

He nodded, satisfied. "Good enough. I suppose I should arrange a wagon."

"I could run them out! I'll just pick up a wagon at the Dalmyn yard. Maybe my old team is still there."

He shook his head. "I keep forgetting your abilities. I suppose you could, if you wished. I'll send an escort with you."

"That will be fine. I'll go tomorrow."

"We should check that with Lord Canah."

"I don't see any reason for that. Unless he has some new information about the bandits, he has nothing to do with me."

Fauvé grinned. "If you say so, my Lady."

"I do say so." She strode in front of him her head high, aware of the picture she presented.

She could hear him chuckle as he followed her.

It never occurred to her why he should be so pleased.

* * *

It was a beautiful fall day, and she was glad to be on the road again. Her horses were also ready for exercise, and she took pride in her driving skills. This trip had held all sorts of unexpected bonuses.

She glanced back over her shoulder. Nobody. So much for her vaunted escort. She snorted. *No wonder Lord Fauvé is having trouble with bandits. Completely useless. My two protectors forgetting their duty and haring off after some rabbit or other.* She reached down and patted the hilt of her sword, tucked close to hand under the wagon seat. *I can take care of myself.*

Then the two men stepped onto the road in front of her. Both hands busy with the reins, she had no time to reach for her sword before the smothering folds of blanket engulfed her from above.

19.   Abomination

This was not how it was supposed to happen. In all her nights of lying awake and preparing herself, she had always thought that she would fight. She would exact a toll on her attackers, even if she must surrender in the end. She had been given no such chance. This was painful, and all mixed up, and she couldn't think straight. At least her smock, thrown over her head, kept her from having to smell their breath. They were all ragged and dirty and they reeked. They struck her and pawed at her, but the outside damage was nothing compared to the feel of them entering her, befouling her innermost being. The injustice of it enraged her.

The only thing clear was the anger. In all her terrible dreams, she had never imagined how angry she would be. And as she lay under each one of them, in her pain and her shame, another feeling came over her. She felt a new being arising from her, out of her pain, and she stood over herself, and watched and was angry. She rose into this new state, and revelled in her fury, in her towering rage, her desire to revenge herself, to cut and flay. These men, these animals, these dregs of humanity. She imagined her sword cutting their flesh, and her pain receded. She focused on her anger, drawing it out further, gritting her teeth in rage, letting the moans turn to growls.

An involuntary scream burst from her. A biter. It wasn't enough that he got to rape her; he had to bite her breast as well. She gritted her teeth again and willed him to get on with it. She clawed the dress off her face to get a look at him. This one would pay. She watched the animal lust on his twisted face, and the horror of her situation bloated up inside her. She crammed it back down under her anger, which swelled in its place.

They would all pay, but she would save the biter till the last and make him pay dearly. The others, she would just kill. She let her mind drift into ways of killing these creatures.

Then the weight was off her, and there were no more. She moaned and drew her legs up, carefully, expecting a slap or a kick. None came.

She curled up, cuddling the pain in her centre, cushioned by her anger, and listened. They were congratulating themselves, the bastards, and joshing the fourth one for being so quick.

Fine. They were in a good mood. Now she had to keep them from killing her. Cradling her stomach, she felt along her left forearm. Yes, the dagger was still there, strapped hilt-down under her sleeve. At least one would pay, even if they decided to kill her. She curled up and waited, nursing her revenge.

Pain exploded in her back as a kick lifted her, screaming, to her feet. "Up off your ass, bitch! We ain't done yet."

Her anger at the indignity was overcome by the memory of Slathe's camp, and she forced herself to let her hair fall over her face, assuming the cringing pose she had practised so long. It seemed to satisfy him.

"Come on, bitch. We got some walkin' to do." It was the biter, she was sure of it. What had the others called him? Brade? She peered up through her hair to be sure of him. He pushed her, and she exaggerated her stumble towards the back of the leader as he set off up the trail. As she walked, she retied the waistband of her smock. It was torn, but it kept the folds of cloth snugly around her. Somehow that helped, despite the heat.

As she blundered through the rocks, she made her plans. She checked her body. Pain, yes, but nothing to hinder her. Bruises, but nothing she hadn't experienced before. She could feel liquid seeping down her leg, but not much, and she turned her mind away from that, searing it dry with the heat of her anger. For that indignity, for invading her body with their sperm, wanting to make their child in her; for that, they would pay the most. As they walked, she wiped her legs with her smock until they were dry. No more wetness came. Good. If she had been bleeding, it had stopped.

She glanced around through her lowered hair, assessing the enemy, her condition, her situation.

This hike was a good sign. If they were going to do some walking, that meant they had decided to keep her for a while. A while was all she needed. They had no idea what they had taken on. The blanket, thrown over her head from the trees above, had prevented her from fighting properly and revealing her skills. She wondered where her sword was. With any luck, one of them would have found it under the wagon seat and brought it along. If she could get her hand on her sword, on any sword...

As she paced along, careful to keep her head down and stumble often, she thought back to the attack. She had been driving along, nobody in sight, when two of them had stepped out of the bush on either side of the road. Somebody in those overhanging trees must have dropped the blanket on her. They had wrapped her up, thrown her into the wagon bed, and whipped up the horses over a rough road. Not too far, as she could remember, although she had been too busy struggling to notice.

They had left the horses and wagon behind, because the trail they were following was too narrow. They were ascending a series of switchbacks and her captors were sweating in the unseasonable heat. She slowed and stumbled again, was rewarded with a shove to her back, which she allowed to carry her to the ground. Then she scrambled up before he could kick her. This Brade character was definitely going to pay.

She grinned to herself as he gasped and wheezed behind her, his knee-length greatcoat flapping around his legs. With his long, curly hair and his wide-brimmed hat, he looked like a refugee from fifty years ago, but the heat must be killing him. This lot was a bunch of lazy layabouts. In fact, she wondered if any one of the four could catch her if she simply ran away. That was an idea to keep for later. *Right now, I have them all together, tired and sore, and that was the way I want them.*

They broke into the open at the crest of a hill. A cool breeze lifted her hair for a pleasant moment, but her captors hurried her down the other side, only slowing when they reached the obscurity of the trees again. Then the leader cut left onto a little-used animal trail that threaded through some boulders and stunted trees, ending in a small clearing, with willows suggesting a creek on the far side. There was a rough camp here, with a lean-to, a fire pit, a scattering of packs and not much else.

No horses. That was good, because they wouldn't be so ready to get rid of her as long as she could walk with them. They would kill her the moment she became any kind of problem.

Gordon A. Long

Come to think of it, what was their plan? Out of the scramble of memories of the attack, a voice called out, "That's the one."

They had been after her. They had been waiting specifically for her. This was planned!

There was only one possibility. She remembered Raif's words. *An atrocity with an important person involved might give Fauvé the leverage he needs.*

That had to be it. Fauvé had set her up. Raif was right. He had been playing her for a fool the whole time. *Still no proof. All this pain, and still no proof. How can I fix that?* She pushed the pain and shame aside, controlled her anger and concentrated on solving the problem.

Now she wondered if they planned to kill her at all. Or maybe this bunch had been hired to kill her and had decided on some freelance entertainment before they completed the job. She would have to listen very carefully. A plan began to grow in her mind.

Predictably, when they hit camp she was ordered to clean up, cook food, and carry water, supervised by the youngest bandit, an acned scarecrow with a limp. He carried a rusted flintlock pistol cradled in his arms as if it was a treasure. It looked like an antique, and she wondered if it even worked.

Once the bucket was full, she looked at the running water, felt the crusted skin on her thighs.

"Turn around."

"Whadaya mean?"

"I mean turn your back."

"Why?"

She stared at him. "I've just been raped. I want to wash myself off."

His face went red to his hairline, and he turned away.

"Don't worry, I'm not going to run off." Squatting, she pulled up her dress and splashed the wonderfully cool water over her legs and crotch. She felt a strange reluctance to touch herself, afraid of what she might discover, so she was content to dry off gingerly with the hem of her skirt. There didn't seem to be too much pain, anyway. She stood.

"All done."

He turned, his glance dropping to her legs, then hastily back up to her face, and the blush flared again.

"Thanks." She smiled at him and swished her hips as she turned back to camp with the bucket. No sense wasting an opportunity. She had this one pretty well off balance.

She wasn't hungry, but she ate anyway; her body needed fuel. Once they had eaten and rested, she wondered if there would be more "entertainment." She hoped not. She was feeling bruised and sore enough and didn't want to go through that all again. Not that it would matter in the long run, but it would be a bit of a triumph if she could get them before they did her any more damage.

She figured a couple of them wouldn't be interested. The kid especially. The biter would. Sex wasn't sex for him, it was power, and he could never get enough.

Fortunately, they seemed worn out by the afternoon's exertions. One lay down on his bedroll and was soon snoring. The biter was fixing something on his pack. She cleaned up as quietly as possible, trying to draw no attention to herself, as she had in Slathe's camp. It seemed she was successful, for they paid her no mind. She managed to get a smear or two of ash and dirt on her face and in her hair as she worked. Her idea began to take shape.

When the biter got up and left the clearing, presumably for hygienic reasons, she slipped over to the leader, a taller man wearing a bandana instead of a hat, with a wide baldric supporting his sword. He probably thought he looked swashbuckling.

"What's your name, big fella? I gotta know what to call you."

He looked down at her. "You can call me Tallis."

"All right Tallis. I can't say I'm pleased to meet you, but I did, so here we are. I'm Maricopa."

"What?"

"Maricopa. Is there somethin' wrong with my name?"

"It ain't your name. You're Aleria Dalmyn."

"Who? Aleria anDalmyn? That's the boss's daughter. I bet she's in the capital right now, dancin' with royalty, not out here in the boondocks, screwin' bandits."

"Whataya mean? We was told to look for a woman drivin' a two-horse Dalmyn wagon. That's you. Aleria."

161

She shook her head. "Nope. Aleria Dalmyn is about five years younger'n me, an' a whole lot prettier. I just drive the Dalmyn wagons. I bin doin' it for three years now, light loads, empty returns, that sorta thing. First run-in I've had with bandits. Can't say as I'm impressed. Hell, that was the worst sex I ever had."

"What?"

"Tallis. Whaddaya think? I'm some kind of virgin or somethin'? You think I got this drivin' job without easin' my way with a coupla the foremen?"

Tallis glanced over at his sleeping companion. "I don't know what we're gonna do with you."

She shrugged. "I sort of figured you'd do what bandits usually do. When you've had enough fun, you turn me loose, I walk to the nearest farm, and you skedaddle the other way."

She glanced at him from under lowered eyebrows. "Now, if you was to kill me, there'd be king's soldiers and Dalmyn mercenaries bustin' the bushes from here to breakfast time. You're much better lettin' me go. I c'n understand you boys wantin' some fun. Must be lonely, on the run all the time."

She slipped her hand up her sleeve to feel the comforting steel of her hideaway dagger. "But next time, let's do it proper. None of this skirt over my head and everybody standin' round."

She tried to smile at him. "I do much better with a soft bedroll under me."

He reached out and squeezed her breast, not too hard. She steeled herself and leaned into his hand. "That's right, Tallis. I can see you know how to please the girls."

At that moment, there was a crackling in the bushes. Tallis snatched his hand back, and Aleria took a chance.

"But one thing, Tallis. I'm special nice to you, you gotta protect me."

"Protect you?"

"Yeah. That Brade guy. He can have his turn with the rest, but he's mean. You gotta keep him from hurtin' me. I ain't no use to anybody, all busted up. You can handle him. You're the leader. I can tell."

"Yeah, he is mean. But I can handle him. I'll think about it."

Brade stomped into camp, snarling. "What're you two gettin' chummy about?"

Tallis leaned back against the ridge pole of the lean-to. "Well, I was just gettin' some information from our little captive, here. I think we got a problem. Better wake Vel up. He'll want to hear this."

Brade nudged his partner with his foot, not quite hard enough to call it a kick. "Hey, Vel. Wake up. Tallis says we got a problem."

They gathered around, the younger lad sidling up, not quite part of the circle.

Tallis tossed a thumb towards Aleria. "She says she ain't Aleria Dalmyn. She says her name's Maricopa, and she's just a driver."

"Bullshit! She's lyin'. Come here, slut." He grabbed Aleria by the hair and tilted up her head.

Tallis waved a hand. "Take it easy, Brade. Don't damage the goods."

"I thought we was supposed to damage the goods a bit. Wasn't that the whole idea?"

Aleria gripped this fact. *'Damage the goods a bit' doesn't sound like killing me.* As Brade released his hold, she slumped into her habitual posture. She sneered up at him through her hair. "Take a look at the wagon seat, mister. You figure any lady's gonna sit on that plank for long?"

Tallis ignored her. "Yeah, but if you ain't the right person, then we ain't gonna get paid. I don't mind a bit of entertainment, but we didn't get enough out of that wagon to make up for the money we was promised. Maybe this Aleria is drivin' by, right now, and here we are, entertainin' a teamster."

"Hell, you're right about that." Brade turned to the youngster. "Kid, you get back to the road and keep watch."

"Aw, Brade, that's a long way and it's still hot."

"Are you arguin' with me, kid?"

"No, Brade, I'm not arguin'. You just send somebody out to take over in a while, hey?" He started away, then tossed a final comment over his shoulder. "It gets real borin' out there."

Then he turned back. "What do I do if I see her?"

Tallis must have decided it was time to exert his leadership. "You high-tail it back to camp and we'll figure it out from there.

She's only goin' out to Bayern. We'll just catch her on the way back."

Aleria's mind whirled. A very few people had known where she was going. Fauvé being the main one. She gritted her teeth and stood silent, making her plans.

The leader turned to the fourth bandit. "Vel, I think you better skip into town and make contact. Maybe our client can give us some way of figurin' out who we have here."

"And leave you to have all the fun?"

Tallis laughed. "Don't worry. There's plenty to go round. You can have a turn, all your own, when you get back. That right, Maricopa?"

She shrugged. "Sure. Fair's fair. You'll get your share, same as the rest."

The bandit rose and pulled his boots back on, unaware of the true meaning of her promise. She couldn't believe her luck. She was going to be left with just the two of them. Now, where was her sword?

Sure enough she spotted it, the hilt jutting from the leader's pack. *How convenient. Now what?* As the one called Vel strode grumbling up the trail, she considered her options. Better not push it. She had some time, now.

She busied herself about the camp: tidying up, banking the fire, scrubbing the pans. She waited long enough for the men to settle and a little longer to screw up her courage. Finally she forced herself to risk it. She touched the dagger on her arm once for luck. "Hey, Tallis, I need some water."

"So, go get some."

"All right." She wondered if he was going to let her go by herself, but she hadn't walked more than a few steps before he rose, shrugged off his baldric and followed her. *He's leaving his sword! My luck seems to be improving.* When she reached the stream, she took her time in a crouch, filling the bucket.

Sure enough, he reached down and caressed her bottom. She smiled up at him.

"Primed to go again, already, big fella?"

He looked over his shoulder at the camp. "Yeah. I do better without an audience, too. Especially that audience."

"Wanta find a nice mossy bank?"

He grinned, his rotten teeth spoiling the effect. "Sounds good to me."

He turned and raised his voice. "Hey, Brade. The lady and me's takin' a little walk."

"Yeah. Don't get lost."

"Don't worry, we'll be back. And we'll both be smilin'!"

Brade waved his hand in disgust and flopped down beside the fire.

Aleria started off up the creek. "Oughta be some nice, soft, moss under those willows, there."

"Whatever you say, sweetheart. You just get yourself ready for some fine entertainment."

"Now ain't I just pantin' and not from the heat." She tossed this over her shoulder as she scrambled up the streambed.

Sure enough, it was cool in the shade of the willows, and soon they found a reasonable amount of moss. Tallis threw himself down. "Feels soft enough to me. Come on, sweetie. Come to papa."

She knelt at his side, rubbing one hand along his chest. "Now you just lie back for a moment and take it easy. We ain't in a hurry here, are we?"

He relaxed as she rubbed his chest, circling lower and lower. When he closed his eyes, she retrieved her dagger from her sleeve.

"Now I'm gonna show you a trick you ain't likely to forget. You just lay back and get ready. It's a lesson I learned from a girl I know. Too bad you won't have a chance to learn it properly."

"Huh?"

She jabbed the point of the dagger under his chin, not gently. "It's called the 'Hideaway Dagger Trick.' Goodbye, scum." She rammed the point as hard as she could into his brain. He stiffened. His eyes widened. Then he sagged. She held firmly, waiting, but he didn't move. She tugged the dagger, but it was stuck. She had to jerk it back and forth, blood pouring over her hands, to get it out.

Suddenly aware of her surroundings she crouched, the dagger held in front of her. *Brade. He's the violent one. How can I get him without his sword?* Ideas flashed through her head as she started forward. *There's always that way.* She shuddered at the thought of

Gordon A. Long

his touch, but tucked it away under the burden of necessity. *Hell, my shoulder hurt worse than this when Rilke threw me in barehand practice last fall.*

All was silent. She washed her hands and the dagger in the stream and moved slowly back towards the camp, all senses alert.

20.   A Long Walk

She chose a route that allowed her to approach the lean-to from the back, and peered through the thinning screen of willows. She could see no one moving around. *Good. I get to deal with Brade alone.*

A sudden thought jabbed her. *What if he's already coming for me? I wouldn't have much chance against that heavy cutlass he carries.* Glancing down at her frail dagger, she then peered through the trees around her, listening. Reassured by silence, she crept back towards the creek until she could see Brade, half-lying on one elbow, staring into the fire. His sword lay out of reach against his pack. She looked for her own hilt. It was still in plain sight, but there was no way to get to it without passing the bandit.

Forcing herself to calmness, she re-sheathed the dagger and stepped out of the bush. His eyes jerked up to her, but he didn't move.

She pointed a thumb over her shoulder. "Tallis wants you to join him."

"He wants me, let him come get me himself." He leered at her. "Obviously he couldn't keep you busy for long."

She smiled sweetly. "Oh, it was short, but it was a one-of-a-kind experience."

"Well, then, I guess it's my turn. Get over here, slut, and show me what you're good for."

She approached him slowly, circling towards her weapon. Just as he reached out to grab her dress, she darted aside, her hand clasping the reassuring grit of the hilt. The sword came out with a clean whistle, and she swept it around to threaten the astounded bandit. He half-rose, but her point pushed him back, weaving slow circles in front of his eyes as she talked.

"You know, Brade, you are the meanest bastard I've ever run across. I bet you've caused a lot of pain to a lot of women. I'm going to make sure you never do it again. No, you don't!"

He turned and lunged for his sword, but her edge slashed down across the back of his ankle, severing the tendon. A scream of agony tore from his throat. She resumed the sword movements in

167

front of his face. Her anger grew as she thought of her own torment.

"You know what it feels like to be helpless and in pain? To have somebody standing over you who is going to hurt you and you can't do anything about it? Well, this is how it feels, Brade. And don't bother looking to the woods for Tallis to save you, because I killed him first."

She slipped forward in a quick lunge and nicked his neck. He brought one bloody hand up from cradling his ankle to press against the wound. The sight reminded her of the blood on her legs, and her anger flared, threatening to overpower her. With an effort, she held her hand.

"This is your lucky day, Brade. If I was anybody else, I might take a long time killing you. But you know, there's a danger there. I might just enjoy myself too much, and then where would I be? So I think it would be better if I just killed you quick, before I start thinking about how much you hurt me. What do you say?"

She lanced forward again, this time scoring his cheek. He sat, staring at her, the blood running down.

"You're right. This isn't a time for conversation, Brade. It's a time for action. This is from me and all the other women you've hurt, Brade. Good bye."

She swung the sword in a larger arc, and the tip sliced through his throat. He fell backwards, making horrible choking sounds, the blood spewing. In a moment, he lay still.

She picked up the dishrag, cleaned the sword thoroughly, and looked around the camp. She rummaged through the leader's pack, but there seemed to be no papers or evidence of any kind. She did find twenty Crowns in a pouch in the bottom and she tucked them into her waistband. Then, with a final backwards glance, she left.

The sunlight was slanting through the trees when she reached the clearing where they had raped her. Her horses and wagon were gone, so she moved along. The spot held no special fear for her, as her head had been wrapped in blanket and skirt for most of the time.

Now she moved more carefully. She edged along the wagon track to the north, moving as silently as she could towards the highroad. Soon she could see the grove of trees overhanging the route. Peering out, she was able to reconstruct the attack. Tallis and Brade had been there, behind those bushes, because they jumped out and grabbed the horses. That left Vel in the tree with the blanket, and the kid behind that tree over there, to jump up on the wagon box behind her.

She circled cautiously, and sure enough, there he was, sitting in the same spot, slapping mosquitoes and muttering to himself.

Suddenly he stood up, and she faded behind a bush. He stared at the wagon track a moment, then dropped back down. As he sat, she moved forward. Soon he started up again, looking down the road for his relief. Again, she took advantage of his movement to close in.

It didn't take much of this game for her to reach the last tree behind him. Abandoning stealth, she stepped forward. He jumped up, swinging his pistol around, but it was too late. Her sword point took him in the chest, and he fell backwards to the ground. As she had promised herself, he got the quickest death. Again she cleaned her sword, and it shone silver in the setting sun.

Now the last one. He should be coming back from town by now, and she didn't know which route he would take. The only sure place to find him was at the camp.

It occurred to her that she should start back to the castle. She had only come an hour's drive, so she could make the return journey on foot before full dark. Then she thought of the anger. It still burned in her stomach, and she knew it wouldn't stop until she was done. Once the fourth man had paid, then the important work began. Fauvé was the one who had set this all in motion. Fauvé was the one who had used her as a pawn, played her for a fool. Fauvé would pay even more. She turned and headed back up the wagon track.

When she reached the camp the sun was down, but the light was good. Good enough to see that Vel had, indeed, returned. He was rummaging through the packs, cleaning out his dead friends before anyone else could. He was so intent that he never even heard her.

"You should have run when you could, Vel. Your greed killed you."

He spun around, dragging his sword from its scabbard. "What the hell happened here?"

"What happened here is still happening. Your friends have already paid for their entertainment, and it's your turn, now."

He grinned and stepped forward. "So you think you can wave that little sword around and I'm just going to fall in a faint?"

"No, I think first you're going to tell me all about the man who hired you, and then we'll see if I let you live."

He slid forward in a reasonable glisé. She beat his sword a couple of times, testing his wrist, which was strong enough, but much too slow. On the third move she started a beat, and when he moved to counter it she circled her tip under, came up on the outside and pushed his blade the other way, far out of line.

Her point entered his forearm, and he yelped and dropped his sword.

"Now you start talking. Who hired you?"

His eyes shifted right, then left.

"Take a look at Brade, there. He tried to run. Maybe I ought to just hamstring you and leave you here for the wolves and vultures. Who hired you? Talk!"

His shoulders drooped, his hands wavering. "I don't know."

Her sword point rose.

"No, no, I really don't know. This guy came up to us in a tavern. He hired us, gave us the orders and the first half of the money. We was supposed to get the rest when the job was done."

"And what was the job?"

"We were supposed to..." he glanced up at her fearfully.

"Supposed to what? Kill me? Beat me up? Rape me?"

"Just beat you up and take your stuff. That's all. We weren't gonna kill you."

"So the rape was just your own idea."

"It was Brade's. I swear it. I only went along because the others did."

"We'll see whether I believe you." She ran the sword along his ear in a quick lunge. "Now talk. Who was this guy? Describe him."

He felt his ear, looked at the blood on his hand, covered the ear tighter. She feinted with the tip, and he hastened to talk. "I dunno. Short, dark hair, well dressed. Had a red stone in his ring."

170

"Old? Young?"

"Sort of middle, I guess."

"That's all?"

"Yeah. The tavern was dark."

"You met him in broad daylight, today."

"No, he didn't show. He wasn't expecting a report until tomorrow night, and I couldn't find him."

"Which inn?"

"The Dragon."

"So this stranger hired you to beat me up and steal my rig and leave me there. You decided to have some fun, so you raped me. You were going to meet him tomorrow night at the Dragon for the rest of your pay. Is that it?"

"Yeah, sorta."

"Well, I can't think of any more questions to ask you. Your turn to pay."

"What?"

"You're going to die, Vel. You raped the daughter of an Exalted Family. I'm just saving you all the hassle of the trial."

Before he could speak again, she ran him through the heart, and he dropped without a sound.

As she walked down the trail in the deepening gloom she thought about the day. It had started very badly, but the ending had been satisfactory. She hadn't expected all that blood, though.

Then she was leaning against a tree, her stomach heaving. The greasy food from the bandit camp came up, leaving her shaking. Sobs wrenched at her body for a long time.

When her breathing evened she stumbled on through the dusk, her movement firming and her back straightening as she got into her stride. Again she thought of the day. The anger started again. The job wasn't finished. There was one more to go.

21. Retribution Falls

It was full dark and she was staggering with fatigue when she finally made it back to Fauvé's manor house. There could have been trouble at the gate, but she had little patience with the guard's uncertainty. She slipped to her rooms, found water and bathed herself as best she could.

She had hardly finished when footsteps pounded down the hallway, and Raif burst into the room.

"Aleria, you're a mess! They just told me. What happened?" He grabbed her arm to pull her closer to the light, but she twisted free.

"I've had a little too much of that already today, thank you. Keep your hands to yourself!"

He released her like a hot iron and peered at her face in deep concern. "What do you mean?"

She stepped to the door, closed it. The anger was starting again, and she used it to overcome her fatigue. She pushed Raif down on a bench and leaned over him. "I was waylaid out on the road. Four bandits. They grabbed me, beat me up, raped me, and intended to keep me for a plaything." She straightened up, her hand on her sword hilt. "They paid."

"They raped you?"

"Yes. It wasn't fun, but I got through it. It's amazing what you can survive when you don't have any choice. I guess you'd know about that."

"But...who...how...?

"That's the good part, Raif. You'll like this. They didn't do it on their own. They were paid. A small, dark man with fine clothes and a ruby ring. He'll be at the Dragon tomorrow night to pay them the rest of their money. I was set up, Raif, just like you said."

"Set up?"

"Don't keep flapping your lips, Raif. My two so-called escorts pulled the same stunt they used before, one fading out behind, the other rushing ahead. When I was alone the bandits attacked me. Almost nobody knew I'd be on that road today. That means I was set up, and we both know by whom, and why." She pointed towards the ceiling. "The question is, what are we going to do about it?"

Comprehension dawned on his face. Then he was on his feet, hand on his sword hilt. "I have a pretty good idea what we can do about it!"

She reached out and jammed his sword back into its scabbard. "No, Raif, this isn't the time to indulge in histrionics. This has to be done carefully. I've had several hours of walking to think about this. He set me up, and we have to return the compliment," she stared intently into his face.

"And then you can kill him."

He nodded, his arm relaxed. "You're right. We know for sure what's going on, but we don't have any proof. We need to manipulate him somehow."

She paced away from him, then turned back. "We have to use his weaknesses against him."

"Any ideas?"

She smiled grimly. "Oh, yes. His vanity. He's been sitting out here in the countryside thinking how grand and sophisticated he is, and what he deserves because of it. He has his fencing master, and his music master, and his little orchestra. He has no idea how pitiful he looks, but he has himself all puffed up. That's his weakness."

"What kind of fighter is he?"

"Reasonable. I saw them practising. He would overwhelm me with his superior strength."

"How about against a real swordsman?"

Her smile widened, but she narrowed her eyes. "I don't want to make you over-confident, but against you, he wouldn't make it through the third pass. And that's if you were being careful."

"So all we have to do is get him to draw on me."

"Are you willing to take the consequences? If you kill him in his own castle, with no support, and all those mercenaries around..."

He laughed. "Simple. Once he's dead, I tell everybody who I am, and why I'm here. I have papers from the king to prove it. They won't dare mess with me once he's gone. Besides, I do have support. I have you."

"Thanks, but I'm not up to a prolonged battle just now."

His face registered concern. "Are you all right?"

173

"Let me see. Raped, kicked, punched, killed four men, walked for two hours in the dark. I seem to be functioning. Let's get going. I want to see this finished."

"Killed them?" His eyes were wide.

"Oh, didn't I tell you? I got them separated and killed them, one at a time. Now it's your turn. Don't let me down. He dies tonight!"

"He has to draw on me in the presence of his supporters."

"And his mercenary Captain. There can't be anyone rushing to his defence. There can't be any doubt once he's dead."

"How can we do that?"

Her fatigue was gone, her mind whirling with ideas. "We use his own plot against him. It's supper time, isn't it?"

"Yes. We were just sitting around after the meal when they called me."

"So everybody's there in the banquet hall?"

"Every one of them."

"Perfect. What if you go in there, raging that he has allowed the daughter of an Exalted family to be waylaid, beaten, and raped within an hour's drive of his manor, and there he sits, with all his friends and his soldiers, doing nothing about it."

"Right. Then I get into the personal insults. His puny orchestra and their bad music, his fake culture, his poor cuisine."

She nodded happily. "Those are the things that will get him. He'll challenge you for sure."

"And then I kill him!"

"No! Not yet."

"What?"

"When he challenges you, you have second thoughts..."

"So it looks like I don't want any trouble, but got carried away..."

"But he'll take it for cowardice, and he'll push harder for a duel..."

"...and afterwards, I can say I tried to back down but he wouldn't let me."

"Remember...he killed a man at school."

"Hah! That sort always choose weak victims. We're making the choices now. Wait a minute. Who's the heir?"

"A mousey little cousin of some sort, about sixteen years old. Name's Farge"

"I'll make sure I promise him lots of support, keep the succession clean."

She nodded. "Sounds perfect. Let's go."

He stopped her. "Everybody will know you were raped."

Her chin came up. "What's my other choice? Try to hide it, and have that secret follow me around all my life?"

"Good girl!" He put an arm around her shoulders. "Let's go get him!"

"Raif, he has to pay."

"That's right. He has to pay."

Buoyed by their enthusiasm they made a fine entrance into the banquet, Raif striding ahead, dragging Aleria by one wrist behind him. She fell into her slouch. The stir they caused as they stormed up between the tables was enough to assure that all eyes were on them when they halted, panting, in front of the high table. Raif waited a moment more, then raised his voice.

"Fauvé, you have allowed this to go on long enough. Now behold the results of your inability to govern!"

"What are you talking about, young man?"

Looking up through her hair, Aleria noted a satisfied look on the lord's face.

"I am talking about this tragedy that you have allowed to occur in your demesne. This young woman has been robbed, beaten, and raped by your subjects and here you sit, with your lackeys and your soldiers, doing nothing!"

"What? Beaten and raped, you say?"

"Do not look so surprised! You must have known that sooner or later something like this would be the outcome of your ineptitude."

"My what?"

"Your inability to take care of these third-rate bandits, who have now become so bold that they attack at will. What kind of a lord are you? You sit here in your cute little manor house with your dancing master and your fencing master, I'm not sure which is which, listening to this country band you call an orchestra, eating swill that some charlatan has persuaded you is high cuisine, while your whole demesne falls to pieces around you. How could you have let this happen?"

Fauvé's face had paled as Raif spoke, and now he rose slowly, his hands quivering as he planted them on the table top in front of him. "Young man, I can understand you getting a bit carried away because of your anger, but you have overstepped several boundaries."

Raif laughed, spoke in a mincing voice, "Overstepped several boundaries, have I?"

His pitch dropped to a growl. "When I get back to the Capital, and the king finds out what has happened here, there will be some serious stepping. On you!"

"You dare to threaten me in my own castle?"

"Castle? You call this overgrown farmhouse a castle? My father's gardener lives in a better hut than this."

The lord's sword cleared its scabbard.

Raif took a step back, his hands empty before him. "Wait, I...I didn't come here for a fight. I want you to do something about these bandits!"

"If you didn't come here for a fight, then you should have curbed your tongue. It's too late, boy. You have said what you should not. I call insult, and you will pay."

"You insist on a duel?"

"Don't try to back out, coward!"

Raif waited, staring into his opponent's eyes, then slowly drew also, stepping sideways into the clear space before the head table. The witnesses would get an unobstructed view. Aleria slid sideways in the opposite direction, dropping her feigned cringe, regarding the others in the room to see their reactions.

The two lords touched swords, and Aleria's attention was drawn to the fight. In truth, she was worried. Raif had, as usual, been carried away with his own acting, and seemed in a complete rage. She hoped he would retain enough control to win the duel.

To her surprise, Fauvé seemed to be doing well. Raif was soon on the defensive, stepping backward while the lord attacked with a series of vicious overhand cuts. Her worry increased for a moment, and then she saw the form of the fight. Raif was defending, but his sword was weaving a shield around him that

Fauvé thrashed against with great vigour but little success. To the inexperienced eye it might look as if the older man had the advantage, but in fact he had none.

She noted Raif's face, usually dead calm as he fought, develop a slight smile. At the same moment, a bead of sweat burst on the older lord's brow, and his breath quickened. This was the point when Fauvé understood that he was completely outclassed.

In the heartbeat it took her to realize all this, the fight was over. Raif took the offensive, breaking the other lord's attack with two wicked beats that pushed the man's weakening wrist far out of line, followed by a quick thrust to the heart, withdrawn so rapidly that many watchers probably missed the hit.

Fauvé stood upright, staring at Raif, then folded to the floor.

There was a sudden silence in the hall, and then a general rush forward. Raif's voice cracked out, freezing them. "Stay where you are. You," he indicated the mercenary Captain, "and you," his sword pointed to the nearest diner, "check him over. I'm sure you'll find him dead. Where is Lord Farge?"

There was a pause, then a weak voice cracked out, "Uh, here, Sir?"

His eyes dragged the lad to his feet. "You are the designated heir, are you not?"

"I am? I mean, yes, I am." His back straightened.

"I hope you do a better job than your late cousin did." His voice rose. "As you are now aware, the king is taking more notice of what is happening in this district than some of you may have wished. If you haven't figured it out, I am Raif, Heir of anCanah, sent by his Majesty to investigate the situation, and I find it completely out of control."

He swung to face the rest of the hall. "Dinner is over, gentlefolk all. Go to your rooms or your homes and stay there until morning." His gaze swept the head table. "You will all meet with me in the council chamber to make sure of a smooth succession. Aleria?"

She had straightened her posture during the fight, and now she flung back her cloak, revealing a hand on her sword.

"Stick by Lord Farge, will you? We don't want any accidents."

"Right." She strode over to the youngster, bowed slightly. "Would you lead the way, my Lord?"

He nodded vigorously, stumbled over his chair as he rose, and started towards the door. She dropped her voice. "Slowly, lad. Show dignity. You have to take control of this lot, and quick."

He shot her a grateful glance and straightened his back, lengthened his stride. By the time they reached the chamber, he had found some poise. At her gesture, he stood by his chair until they were all seated except Raif. The boy nodded to transfer control of the meeting and collapsed into his seat, Aleria attending at his elbow.

Raif looked around. "First thing is the succession. Does anyone have any argument with Lord Farge's appointment?"

Danto, who had placed himself at the new lord's left, spoke immediately. "There shouldn't be, my Lord. He's the next living relative, and Lord Fauvé designated him last year officially."

"There is documentation for all this?"

The older man nodded. "Most of us here witnessed the ceremony."

Raif interlaced his fingers. "Now. Any comment on the way in which the former lord met his death?" His eye sought out the Captain, who looked around, got no support, and stood, almost to attention.

"It seemed quite clear, Sir. While there was insult given, it was perhaps understandable in the circumstances, if the lady is a friend of yours."

"She is."

"After that, Lord Fauvé insisted on the duel. He drew first, you tried to calm him, but he refused to withdraw. You killed him fairly, Sir."

Raif looked around the room, received no other comments. He nodded. "I'm sure the king will want unbiased reports. If you will all leave your names with this gentleman?" He raised his eyebrows at the older man.

"Danto, my Lord."

"Danto, will you take care of making a list, and keeping it until the king's emissary arrives?"

"Certainly."

"Thank you. Does anyone have any more business?

178

"Actually, I do." Nerval was leaning back in his chair, his eyes burning into Aleria's.

"Who are you and what is your business?"

"As everybody here knows, I am Nerval of Trescott. I am…I suppose I was, a friend of Lord Fauvé. And my business is that this whole thing looks a little too convenient to me."

Raif's brow clouded. "Convenient? Please explain."

The blonde man leaned back in his chair. "With pleasure. These events might seem very sudden, but you all appear quite prepared. It leads one to wonder how much of this was planned, and how much just happened. The girl, for example," the flick of his hand dismissed her, "doesn't seem to be acting much like a woman who has been raped."

Raif stepped forward, but Aleria was there first. She paced towards her enemy, eyes fixed on his. He rose as she approached, slid back a step. "What experience do you have with raped women, Nerval?"

"How does that matter?"

"And what does a raped woman act like? Weeping, afraid, hiding her head in shame?"

He shrugged. "Something like that."

She reached out and grabbed the front of his shirt. "And you like that, don't you?"

His smirk was more than she could abide. "You son of a bitch! You have, haven't you? Oh, I bet you don't call it 'rape'. You just call it 'manly assertiveness'. The woman isn't unwilling, only coy, or shy, or playing hard to get."

He swallowed, did not respond. She shook him a couple of times. "Did it ever occur to you that she might be angry?" She backhanded him across the face, cracking his head around. "That she might want to get revenge on the men that did it?" A forehand snapped his head the other way. "That she might be likely to take that anger out on anybody who got in her way afterwards?"

He recovered his balance and grabbed for her throat, but she blocked and followed with a solid reverse punch to the wind that doubled him over. As his head came down, she smashed her elbow up into his face, and he slammed erect against the wall.

He stood there, dazed, for a moment. Then the consciousness returned to his eyes, and his hand groped for his sword hilt.

"Oh, do it. Yes, please! Haul out your manhood so that I can lop it off!" She stared at him, her hand hovering over her own sword, and his arm fell, nerveless, to his side. She held him like that for a moment, then turned her back on him and returned to her place at the new lord's side.

Raif crossed his arms. "I take it that concern has been answered? Then may I suggest that those of you who are staying go to your rooms. Anyone leaving, please do so without pause. Nerval, that would include you, I think. Captain Ussel and I will meet with Lord Farge to ensure the proper safety of all."

Aleria calmed her breathing and watched them all as they left, but there seemed to be no conspiracies obvious. If they were smart enough they wouldn't start talking until they were out of sight, but she was keeping her eyes open. She approved of Raif's action. The mercenary Captain had control of more soldiers than everyone else put together. The sooner it came home to him that Farge was his best chance of getting the wages he was owed, the stronger would be his support.

Raif was talking, but she was having trouble paying attention to what he was saying. It was becoming difficult to stand, but she held her position with all her might. Raif needed her support. She stared at the far wall, willing her shaking knees to hold...

...then, somehow, she was on the floor, and Raif was holding her head up. "Aleria! Aleria! Wake up, girl. Talk to me!"

"Sorry. Did I fall asleep?...tired...walked a long way today...they...they...Raif, those men..."

"It's all right. Don't worry. Don't talk about it. You're safe now."

"Talk, don't talk...come on, Raif, what do you want?"

He grinned, looked up at the other two, who were leaning over anxiously. "She's started to argue again. She'll be fine."

She struggled to sit, and Dallya appeared with a goblet. Taking a sip, she found it warm and spicy. She drank a bit more, rested a moment, then passed the cup back and crawled to her feet.

"I think I'd better take a rest, Raif. You seem to have everything under control."

"That's a good idea. I think you overdid it, at the last, there."

She nodded. "Had to. I couldn't let him get away with that."

"I'm not arguing. It was a whole lot better than me killing another one." He looked around the room. "We need someone to see you to your rooms."

Rumani appeared from behind her, and Aleria could see several more women grouped by the door. "We'll take care of Lady Aleria, my Lord. Don't worry about her."

Raif stared at the woman. "We have to keep her safe."

The mercenary Captain stood. "I agree. I think I need to put my men out in the courtyard and the hallways, and send some patrols into the town," he turned to Farge, "if that suits you, my Lord."

The young man nodded. "I think the town patrols should be larger."

"Good idea, my Lord. I'll get on that right away and return immediately."

Raif and Aleria exchanged satisfied glances. All was going as it should. Aleria felt her knees weaken, but Dallya was there with a strong shoulder to lean on, and then she was surrounded by women, moving gently down the hallway.

Later, she was unsure of the sequence of events, but she remembered a hot, cleansing bath, more of the spiced drink and a warm, soft, bed that engulfed her. She peered out of the covers to see Rumani, sitting there in the dim candlelight. The woman noted her attention.

"There will be few of us sorry to see that one go, my Lady."

"Um." She wasn't sure which one the woman was talking about but couldn't find the energy to ask. Rumani seemed happy, though, so it probably didn't matter. Satisfied, she slept.

Gordon A. Long

22. Recovery

Aleria surfaced slowly from a long, deep, sleep. She had a vague feeling that something was wrong, so she resisted the pull of the conscious world as long as she could, nestled in the soft, safe, bed.

Suddenly, against her will, it all came rushing back to her. The attack, the rape, killing those men, her actions in the banquet room last night.

Her cheeks burned when she realized that she had passed out when Raif needed her most. This thought brought her to her feet, wincing with the pain of bruises and stretched muscles.

There was an exclamation, and she realized that she was not alone. A woman had been sitting in the chair beside her bed, one of the kitchen staff, perhaps? She remembered the evening vigil, but this seemed not to be the same person, who might have been Rumani.

"Are you all right, my Lady?"

She grimaced. "Much better that last night, but still hurting. What time is it?"

"Just gone nine, my Lady."

"How long have you been here?"

"Not long, my Lady."

She regarded the woman, older than most of the other servants. "Why are you here?"

"To see to you, my Lady."

"I needed seeing to?" She clambered back into the warmth of the eiderdown.

"We thought so."

"Who are 'we'?"

"The manor staff, my Lady."

She mused a moment. "So the servants took it on themselves to take care of me."

The woman's demeanour was unruffled. "We knew that Lord Farge would have a lot on his mind, my Lady."

"I'm not going to complain. What was in that drink you gave me?"

"I don't know, my Lady. One of the women makes it."

Ah. Might have known. "You have a woman who does this sort of thing?"

"Yes."

"Perhaps I should talk to her."

"We thought you might."

"You seem to think of everything."

"My Lady, when there is a manor without a lady, the women must take care of themselves."

She grimaced. "An understatement."

"Do you wish to see the Wise Woman now?"

She thought a moment. "Where's Raif... Lord anCanah?"

"He won't bother you until you are ready, my Lady."

She grinned. "He is a bit squashable, isn't he?"

The woman smiled. "He's a good lad. He was very concerned, and Rumani told him that you needed rest and that everything was under control. I think he was relieved."

"Yes, he's not very good at this sort of thing."

"Not many of them are."

"I'm not exactly an expert myself."

A sly grin quirked the woman's mouth. "Nor do you wish to become one, I'm sure."

"I'll support that idea."

The woman laid a hand on her arm gently. "You are very strong, my Lady. I will find the Wise Woman."

Aleria lay back in the pillows, savouring the cup of hot coffee that had appeared the moment the bedroom door was opened. She was interested to see what this Wise Woman would be like.

She was half expecting a wrinkled crone, but she was disappointed. The woman who entered was of plump middle age, with a business-like air.

"So you're the one slapped young Nerval silly last night?"

She shrugged. "I was a bit...out of sorts at the time."

"And how are you feeling now?"

"Very stiff and sore."

"Any specific damage?"

"Oh. You mean from..."

"From the rape, yes."

"I never looked."

183

"Would you like me to?"

Aleria had long suspected that the male doctors who usually examined her were rougher than required in order to maintain a distance from the patient. This woman's soft ministrations did nothing to dispel this notion.

After a brief inspection, she nodded. "No lasting damage. You're going to be sore for a while, but nothing serious."

Aleria straightened her clothing, waited for the inevitable.

"Now you're expecting the lecture."

"What lecture is that?"

The woman's mouth quirked. "The one that tells you how to feel, how to react, so that you can put this all behind you."

"Is that what I should expect?"

The woman shrugged. "I believe that's the usual formula."

"Which you don't think much of?"

"I believe that most people deal with tribulation in their own way. What works for another person might not work for you."

"I see. So what can you do for me?"

"Help you find out what works for you."

Aleria considered. "Fine. What works for me?"

The woman laughed at that. "I said help you, not do it for you."

Aleria shook her head. "The story of my life."

"It sounds like you have good parents."

"The very best." A sudden thought hit her. "Will they know?"

The woman shook her head. "It's hard to say."

"I need to do it. I have to tell them. Father will be very upset. I'll have to have this all solved before I tell him."

"All solved?"

"You know. I have to be able to reassure him that I'm all right, that it's all over, that he doesn't need to worry."

"You worry about your father. What about your mother?"

"She'll understand. She always does."

The woman seemed satisfied at this. "So how will you have this all solved?"

"I don't know. I did what I could yesterday. Now, I guess I'll just have to wait and see."

"What did you do yesterday?"

She paused a moment to see how it felt to say it out loud. "I killed them. I killed them all."

"So I heard."

"So why did you ask me?"

"To see if that was why you did it."

"I don't know why I did it. It just was what I had to do. I was very angry."

"Understandable."

"It was to me."

"Did you enjoy it?"

"Not especially. I mean, I was satisfied. But then I was sick."

The woman only nodded.

"And then I helped Raif deal with Fauvé, who set me up."

"And you cuffed young Nerval, put him to challenge, and he didn't dare draw his sword. He won't be able to show his face in this demesne again."

She felt a satisfied grin forming. "Oh, yes. Was that a good idea?"

The woman smiled, too. "As you may have gathered, the women in the region are well pleased."

"I wondered."

"Don't get me wrong. We would have rallied around you in any case. But to them," a wave of her hand indicated the whole area, "you are now a hero too."

Aleria felt a warm glow inside her. "That helps."

"Good."

There was a pleasant silence. Aleria cuddled in the blankets, watching the dust motes drift in a ray of sunlight pushing through a crack in the shutters. A reminder of the outside world.

"What's going on today?"

The woman smiled as if Aleria had done something right. "That is for you to find out, I suppose. Would you like to talk to Lord Raif?"

"Is he available?"

The woman smiled more broadly. "He has been showing up outside the door off and on for several hours. He was there when I came in."

"What?" She sat upright.

"Do not worry. I was speaking to him before you woke. He feels very guilty."

"Guilty? Raif? He's the one that warned me. He came out here to protect me."

"Yes, but he feels guilty because he was not able to protect you."

"Oh, great."

"Why is this a problem?"

"Because we get along strangely enough as it is, and him with a load of guilt is going to make it even more messy."

"I suspect you are right. Be easy on him."

She snorted. "I'm the one got raped. Why do I need to be easy on him?"

"Because I think you are handling it better than he is."

She realized that she was staring. The woman chuckled. "That's right. It's difficult for a man, you know. He has no idea how you feel, and no idea how to deal with you. You have to help him."

Aleria crossed her arms and looked full in the woman's face. "You're very good at what you do."

The older woman nodded, smiled softly. "There are many who believe so."

"Well, there's one more believer today. I thank you, Ma'am. You have helped me a lot."

"I think you have helped yourself a lot."

Aleria sobered. "When it comes down to it, what else can you do?"

"That seems to be true. In my experience, you are the only one who can cure yourself. The rest of us can only be there if you reach out to us."

Aleria smiled. "And, having listened to that, I suppose I can face Raif."

The woman stood. "I'm sure you'll do fine." She strode to the door, opened it, and motioned. Then she slipped out as Raif stormed in.

"Aleria..." he stopped in mid-stride, unsure what to do.

She grinned up at him. "Good morning Raif. I think what you want to do is rush over and give me a hug."

"Would that be all right?"

She held out her arms. "I need my friends, Raif."

186

He sat on the bed and held her gently, even delicately. She laughed and threw her arms around him, squeezed tightly. "I'm not porcelain, you know."

He returned the force of her embrace for a moment, then released her and sat up. "I can't believe how cheerful you are."

She shrugged. "I have people who care about me. We have achieved a minor political success, at some cost to me, I admit, but perhaps it was worth it."

"Do you think so?"

She grimaced. "Raif, if I didn't think so, then all my pain would be wasted, wouldn't it? How are things in general this morning?"

"Very quiet. The mercenaries are on patrol, everyone seems to be going about their business as usual, though quietly."

She nodded. "Sounds good. And Farge?"

He grinned. "I doubt if he slept last night. I do believe he intends to try his best. All he needs is support and advice."

"I seem to remember Danto being useful last night."

"Danto? Oh, yes, the overseer. His loyalty seems more to the manor that to whoever happens to be in charge."

"Admirable."

"I think he'll be a great help to the lad."

"What now?"

Raif pretended to consider, but she knew he had already figured it out.

"I think perhaps you need to go back to Kingsport. I'm sure you want to see a doctor."

"I suppose I should. I have been well cared for here."

His thumb indicated the door, his eyebrows raised.

"That's right. The local Wise Woman. She is very knowledgeable."

"Yes. She seemed to be. She put me in my place."

"What are you going to do now?"

"I need to stay here. I know everything is going well at the moment, but until we can get somebody else here to keep an eye on developments, anything could go wrong. A man like that collects a certain type around him. One of them might be capable of trying something. So I can't come with you."

"I understand, Raif. You don't need to come."

"Captain Ussel has promised ten of his best men to escort you."

She smiled. "Ten? I'm worth that much?"

He reached out and hugged her again. "Much more!"

She laughed, and after a moment pushed him away. "I know. Much more, but that's all you can afford."

She grabbed his arm. "But I'm in charge."

"What do you mean?"

"I am not going to ride back to the capital in a carriage, surrounded and protected by a bunch of men, telling me what to do and how to do it. I'm going back to the capital at the head of my escort. In charge."

He nodded. "I understand."

"Will they understand?"

He grinned. "If they don't. I'm sure you'll straighten them out."

"You have the truth, there. Now, you have to get out. I have to get dressed and see about breakfast." She shot a glance at him. "Have you eaten?"

"Not much. I'll have something hot sent up, and I'll join you."

"Great. We can talk some more."

He reached out, tousled her hair. "You're really something. You know that?"

"Huh! I've always known I was something. I'm still trying to find out what."

He rose, grinning, and strode out.

As it turned out, they had breakfast with the new lord, because he hadn't taken time to eat, either.

Aleria took him to task. "You have to take care of yourself, Lord Farge. You're no use to your people or your demesne if you're sick."

He ducked his head. "I'm sick, all right. I'm worried sick. This is going to be a rough duty for me. It would have been bad enough, but with all these bandits..." He threw his hand up.

"I wouldn't be too worried about the bandits. I think several of them left last night." Raif explained his theory about where the bandits were coming from.

Aleria stared at the table. "And I finished off a few. Not that they were much, as bandits go." At a sudden thought, her head rose. "Actually, I'd be worried for the next week or so. Some of that lot who just left might hang around, do some real banditry before they leave."

Raif nodded. "Good thinking, Aleria. You'll have to put out some more patrols, Lord Farge, and messengers to your neighbors. You've still got quite a few men, good ones, I mean, and I've got my five you can count on to help keep the castle safe. I'll ride out tomorrow and warn the other landowners. I think if we all push hard now we can solve this bandit problem for a while.

"Not that it ever goes away completely, but I think most of it will evaporate once there isn't any support from here."

Farge frowned. "You really think that Lord Fauvé was funding the bandits?"

Raif shrugged. "It's the best explanation I can come up with. Time will show us."

They all nodded wisely and left it at that.

It took two days for Aleria to get organized for the trip home. Between settling down the demesne and choosing her escort and a thousand other details, everything just moved slowly. Not that it bothered her; she felt in no rush. It was good to relax, let others make the moves. She was cosseted by the castle staff, and Raif was concerned, which was a pleasant change.

Of Shen and his friends, there was no sign. When she mentioned this to Raif, his answer was off-hand.

"The merchants always keep their heads down when there's a change of power. At least you hope they will. If they start blundering into politics, it means they think they have some control over what happens and then things can get very messy. Look at Domaland. They've pretty well taken over, there."

"You mean sometimes the merchants can affect the transfer of power? Even here in Galesia?"

"Certainly. Money speaks louder these days. A hundred years ago it couldn't have happened, but now the reason for a change of power is often that the previous lord couldn't manage his finances. In that situation, somebody with solid mercantile backing could make a good case for himself to take over."

"So why haven't I heard about this development? Why don't we have it happening everywhere?"

He grinned. "What does your father do with his time?"

"Ah. The merchants have already taken over."

He nodded. "They just happen to have the right names."

She pondered this for long enough that he looked at her curiously. "Whatever are you thinking?"

"I was just wondering what I could do with my life, you know?" She smiled up at him. "Those serious thoughts a young person has. I was just thinking that if I wanted to make my mark, have some control over my life, I couldn't go wrong by learning more about father's business."

"You ought to talk to my father!"

"Why is that?"

"Because that's what he keeps telling me." He gave a rueful grin.

"He's a smart man. Do you listen?"

"Mostly. After all, I'd like to make my mark too."

There was a short silence.

"So we don't expect to see any of the merchants showing up around here for the next couple of days."

He shook his head. "I doubt it. It's up to Farge. When things are settled enough, he'll send out an invitation."

"So be it. What about the Ranked class?"

He grinned. "That was different. You seem to have some support there."

"Mimay?"

"Her especially, although both Lord Bayern and his wife were appalled that you had been waylaid on your way to their demesne."

"I hope you told them..."

"I did. I also told them what you were doing here. I hope you don't mind. They were very upset, and it seemed to help to know that you had been injured in the line of duty."

She nodded. "They're soldier's daughters. That would mean a lot to them."

"Yes. Mimay asked a strange question, though. 'Was she angry?' What did she mean by that?"

Aleria found a chuckle at that. "Just a conversation we had about getting through a battle."

"Ah. She seemed quite satisfied when I told her how angry you were."

"It got me through."

"And now...?"

She laid a hand on his arm. "I need my friends, now, Raif."

He smiled, covered her hand with his own. "I feel rather helpless, but I'm here for whatever I can do."

"That kind of support is all you can give, Raif, and it's all I need. I have to do the rest myself."

She had enough support here in the manor, and more. The servants, especially the women, treated her like she was porcelain. The Wise Woman, whose name she never learned, appeared several times to talk and listen. The last afternoon, before Aleria left, she made sure that they had one more visit.

"I had a nightmare."

"The one you told me about?"

Aleria stopped in surprise. "Actually, I haven't had one of those lately. No, this one was about killing people."

"You, killing people? And that was bad? You call it a nightmare?"

She frowned. "I should hope so!"

"That seems a good response."

Aleria realized what the woman meant. "I see what you mean. Does everyone who kills people dream about it?"

"Many do. It's your brain's way of dealing with the horror. The only problem is if you don't see it as horrible."

Aleria shuddered. "I think I must be normal in that respect. Will they go away?"

The woman shrugged. "Depends."

"I've been through this all before with the other dreams." Aleria threw up her hands. "I learned to live with them."

The woman looked at her a moment. "Which would you prefer? These or the old ones?"

Aleria laughed. "These, I'm sure. What I don't want is both kinds."

"Your mind is trying to make sense of some terrible, senseless, events. Painful as well. It may take a while."

"I could handle it if I thought it had an end."

The woman smiled. "In my experience, these things all eventually pass. They may recur years from now, when something else is bothering you. But they will stop being an important influence on your life."

Aleria reached out impulsively and hugged the older woman. "You really are good at what you do."

After returning the hug for a moment, the woman stood. "I think my work has been done here. You will be seeing a doctor in the capital?"

"I suppose. I don't know what he can do for me that you haven't done already."

"That you and I haven't done already."

Aleria laughed. "I stand corrected."

"I was thinking about possible...effects."

"You mean in case I'm pregnant."

"You don't mince words, do you?"

"That's how I deal with things. So what if I'm pregnant? If I am, the doctor will know how to deal with that."

"Abortion?"

"Yes. I've thought about it. I can't see bringing a child like that into the world. Can you imagine the conversation?"

'Mummy, who was my daddy?'

'He was one of the scum who raped your mummy, dear.'

'Oh.'

"No, I want children some day, but not that badly."

The woman nodded. "Your choice, of course."

"It is my choice, but what's your opinion?"

"As usual, I think that what is best for you is what you think is best for you. In most cases, though, I have noted that the victim recovers quickest when there are the least lasting effects. A child is a very lasting effect.

"I'm not suggesting you should try to forget that you have been raped. That can cause problems too. I think you should let the incident recede naturally in your memory as more important, newer, events take over."

Aleria considered this. "Sounds good. I hope it works."

23. Not Exactly a Holiday

She left the manor on a fine fall morning, riding a spirited black gelding, the ten men of her escort lined up in pairs at her back, a supply wagon rattling merrily somewhere behind.

Raif didn't even look too worried as he saw her off. She had spent the last few days reassuring him that she was fine. She realized that she had also persuaded herself, and she did feel fine. A well-dressed dark man with a ruby ring had been arrested at the Dragon with twenty crowns in his pocket, and had turned out to be Raif's former pedlar. Not knowing that everyone else was dead, he had broken down under questioning and admitted his guilt, as well as his connection between Fauvé and the bandits. Raif had taken a troop of soldiers to the bandits' main camp and found it deserted. He estimated at least thirty men had stayed there. The mercenaries at the redoubt in the mountain pass had been happy to continue their contract with the new lord. Her wagonload of furniture had been found and delivered to the Beyern home. All the loose ends were tied up. It was time to move on.

As she rode, she wondered what to do about her escort. It was a five-day trip, and she didn't look forward to spending that time alone with strangers. The problem was how to break the reserve of these professional soldiers. She could tell by their demeanour that the captain had impressed them with the gravity of their duties. She would have to find a way to get through to them.

She called a halt when they passed through the grove of trees where she had been ambushed. She pulled her horse aside and there, behind the tree where the boy had died, was an unmarked grave.

She turned to Rost, the Guard officer. "That was one of them."

"Yes, my Lady."

"He was just a youngster. Thin, ugly, not too smart. Fell in with the wrong friends, I guess. It killed him."

"Yes, my Lady. Although I gather you had something to do with it."

She glanced at his face, but he seemed serious.

"I did, that." She turned her horse back to the road.

At lunchtime, they stopped at a pleasant spot near a stream. The teamster swung the supply wagon into its assigned place, and a familiar figure climbed down.

"Rumani!"

The servant grinned. "Yes, my Lady. You don't think we'd let you go all this way unattended?"

"I might have known you wouldn't. Thank you, Rumani. It's good to have you along."

"Right. Now let's see if any of these louts can cook." She strode to the back of the wagon and began snapping out orders.

The weather was fine and there were no manors nearby big enough to handle her escort, so they camped the first night. Her men functioned smoothly, pitching her tent at a careful distance from theirs: private, but protected. Once Aleria had arranged her belongings to her satisfaction she surveyed the camp. It didn't take her long to notice that there always seemed to be two soldiers somewhere nearby. She sought out the officer.

"Rost, am I going to be followed every step of this trip?"

"I'm not sure, my Lady. We have been ordered to protect you. Lord anCanah was very specific."

"I'm sure he was. I'll make you a deal. I'll promise not to leave camp without telling you, and your men can concentrate on guarding the whole camp and leave me the illusion that I'm free. How does that sound?"

"If I can count on you to hold your end of the bargain, it sounds fine."

"You suggest I might cheat on my own safety?"

"My Lady, I have done my share of escort duty. I find that many members of the Ranked classes have a different idea of what a promise is, especially when made to someone like me. Especially," an apologetic grin, "the young ladies."

She nodded. "I can understand that. Well, I can only assure you that I have had reason lately to learn the value of a good escort, and I will do my best to stay within whatever boundaries you deem appropriate."

"That suits me, my Lady."

"And me. Oh, one more thing."

"Yes, my Lady?"

She had spent the day figuring this out. "Do any of your men know quarterstaff?"

He took this strange request in stride. "Of course, my Lady."

"Do you think one of them would give me some pointers? I would like to continue my training, but I doubt if any of your men want to cross real swords with me in case of an accident. So I thought quarterstaff would be a better choice."

"Have you worked quarterstaff before, my Lady?"

"The basics plus the first four practice patterns."

"There shouldn't be a problem." He turned and signalled to a soldier nearby. "Would you cut a couple of quarterstaffs? One for you, one for Lady Aleria."

The man nodded and strode into the grove of trees nearby. He soon returned with two shafts of dead spruce, clean and light, and proceeded to trim them with his dagger.

He handed one to Aleria. "Does this suit, my Lady?"

She stepped clear and swung the staff experimentally. It was light and almost balanced. She started the first warm-up routine. After watching her a moment, the solder picked up his own weapon and sought his own space to warm up. She took that as a good sign.

Once they were ready, she looked at the soldier expectantly. He seemed to have no idea how to proceed, either.

"How would you like to work this, my Lady?"

"Well, first I should know your name. If I have bruises, I'd like to know who gave them to me."

He grinned. "In that case, perhaps it would be better for me if you didn't know."

"His name's Jano, and if he lays a bruise on you, he'll be on latrine duty for the rest of the trip!"

She turned to the officer. "No, no, it won't work that way. If he's afraid of bruising me he won't train me properly. I'm not experienced with staves, but I have been practicing other Arts of Battle for several years, now. I have given and taken bruises worse than I'll get from Jano."

The officer nodded. "All right, then, Jano. But I'll be watching."

She shook her head. Talking would do no good. She would have to show them. She walked to the centre of the open space and waited for the soldier to join her. "First doubles pattern?"

He nodded. "First pattern, my Lady."

They walked through the pattern the first time, then tried it again, half time. By the time they had finished, she had a pleasant warmth under her arms and she felt loose and ready. "Full speed?"

"If you wish, my Lady."

They ran through it at good speed, and she noted that he was pushing a bit harder than he had at first. When they were finished, they grounded their staves and grinned at each other.

"Any comments, Jano? I know that wasn't full speed."

He nodded. "Good enough for starters. Hold up your staff, please, in the overhand left position."

She complied.

He brought his staff around from the side. "You see, in this position, you are not pushing quite far enough away from your head. If I come even slightly from the side," he demonstrated, and the wood clunked her head gently.

She laughed. "First bruise, Jano."

"If you wish to call that a bruise, my Lady. Second pattern?"

She nodded, and they squared off.

By the time supper was ready, she was well sweated up and she could see that her opponent was working, too. As the training had progressed his moves had become faster, his blows firmer, and she had held up pretty well, she thought. They grounded their staves for the last time, gave the formal salute, and walked off the practice field together.

"Thank you, Jano. I enjoyed that."

"I did too, my Lady. You do credit to your trainers."

"I'm working with Master Ogima."

"Ah, yes. He trains the students at the Academy, doesn't he?"

She detected a patronizing air. "I'm not with the students. I work in his Masters Classes."

He glanced at her. "That explains it, then. He only takes the best." He saluted and turned to his tent.

There was warm water waiting in her tent, and she sponged off and changed into a clean robe before she appeared at the supper table. She passed a wink to Rumani as the woman gave her a glass of watered wine. "I need this. Just as much as that hot water."

"Gotta keep you in top condition, my Lady."

"Don't talk about me like I'm a prize racer."

"No my Lady."

"But keep the hot water coming."

"Yes, my Lady."

Aleria shot a glance at the older woman. "Do I detect a hint of sarcasm?"

"Of course not, my Lady. Far be it from me…"

"…I know, I know. Silly of me to mention it." She turned to her meal. "Nice stew."

The woman's head came up. "I brought my own spices, my Lady. Family secret."

Aleria paused to sense the lingering flavours before digging in again. "You can keep them secret as long as you keep feeding me the results."

The woman smiled and offered another ladlefull.

The trip went smoothly after that. The following evening she was able to inveigle her trainer into some free sparring: not full-speed, but undoubtedly free, as her bruised ribs attested. Jano got some razzing from his comrades at supper.

"Heard you hit the little lady today, Jano."

"Yeah. Heard she clipped you a couple of times too."

Jano grinned. "It was only part-speed. No damage done either way."

"You better hope there isn't."

"For certain. Lord anCanah hears you laid a staff on his lady, he'll do more than tap your ribs."

Aleria felt this needed a response. She raised her voice to carry to where they were seated. "I'm nobody's lady, but Lord anCanah hears Jano has been helping his friend train, he'll be more likely to reward him. Maybe with a promotion over you lot."

They scoffed at this, but through the laughter she could hear a note of respect. She resolved to make a thorough report to Raif. He would be expecting it, and Jano deserved it.

She was surprised that a man like Fauvé could attract what seemed to be a decent bunch of mercenaries. Their manners towards her were rough, but always respectful. To be sure, she had wondered whether their extreme reserve at first had a bit of fear in it, but the object of that fear seemed to be Raif. Fair enough.

Except for Rost, the officer. The sense of humour she had noted from the first had peeked through with increasing frequency, and she had begun to note his interactions with the others. He seemed to have the easy camaraderie that a good junior officer can develop with his men, yet still maintain discipline. She noted that his manners to her were smoother than those of the other soldiers, and he seemed to handle this small command without really trying. He rarely gave orders, seldom raised his voice, and never, except for the latrine comment, threatened any man with discipline.

In fact discipline, or the need for it, seemed to be missing. The soldiers went cheerfully about their duties, got along with each other in their rugged, joshing way, and treated both Aleria and Rumani with a careful pleasantry that made them feel accepted in a limited fashion. Curious, she commented to Rost one day as they sat their horses waiting for their troop to form up. His explanation was simple.

"I've known most of them for quite a while. I put this bunch together during the Bussot uprising three years ago. I think we were near you during Slathe's rebellion. We helped mop up a smaller army that was marching to reinforce him. Since then we've had no contract, and we signed on with Lord Fauvé this spring. It seemed like a good situation at first, but I was getting suspicious. We spent too much time chasing bandits that didn't seem to exist."

"What do you think was going on?"

"That was the problem. I couldn't figure out what was going on. I only know that we were wasting a lot of time."

She explained Raif's theory about how Fauvé might have been extorting money from the king to pay for chasing his own bandits, and the officer nodded.

"That would explain it, all right. We were never in the inner group, the ones with Fauvé from the start. The ones that disappeared the night he got killed. We never knew what they were doing."

"You were sort of a separate group, right to the last."

"Which is why Lord Canah chose us to look after you, I guess."

"Which is not why he chose you."

They both turned to see Rumani's wagon behind them. She was driving her own team today.

"What do you mean?"

"I mean that Lord Canah chose you lot because he asked me."

"He asked you?"

She grinned and clucked to her horses, moving them alongside the riders. "That's right. He knew if he asked me he'd get an honest answer. I knew there was none of Fauvé's lot in your troop, and that you was a good officer, so I recommended you."

The soldier doffed his campaign hat. "Then I have you to thank for this pleasant excursion, when I could have been sitting back in the barracks, playing on my lute."

She laughed. "You also could have been laid off. Think about it."

His eyebrows went up. "It's possible."

Aleria broke into this pleasant repartee. "You may also want to have a chat with the king's agent."

"Oh? About what?"

"Well, Raif...Lord Canah said there would be an investigation. They will want to know what you've just been telling me. It will help them figure out what was going on, and help clear you and your men at the same time."

"I'd be thankful for a chance to do that."

They jogged on. The weather stayed good, often cloudy but with only light showers, and the roads stayed firm. She practised quarterstaff with Jano every evening, and he taught her some new solo sword drills as well.

She was having such a good time that the nightmare caught her by surprise.

She awoke one night in smothering darkness. There was noise and shouting in the camp, and a horrible fear clutched at her. She started and almost screamed when the tent flap opened, silhouetting Rumani.

"What's wrong, my Lady?"

"I don't know. What's wrong?" She clung to the woman's forearms in the dark.

"You woke everyone up with your screaming, my Lady. That's what's wrong."

"Did I? Oh. Yes, I guess I might have. I was having a nightmare, I guess."

"That's all right, then."

Another figure appeared in the tent door. "What's happening?"

"Just a nightmare, Rost. You can tell the men to go back to sleep."

"Some nightmare. That scream brought me out of a sound sleep so fast I was on my feet with my sword in my hand before I woke up."

The servant's grin was wolfish in the light of his lamp. "Then it was a good drill for you, wasn't it? Proved that you're on your toes."

"Huh. Well, hope you get over the nightmare, my Lady. I'll go settle the camp down."

"Ask someone to stir up the fire and put some water in the kettle. I'll make her a pot of tea."

He nodded and departed, leaving the lamp with them, and soon the camp was quiet again.

"Wanta talk about it?"

"I don't know."

"Your choice. They say it helps."

"I suppose. I don't remember much. I had my sword, and there were men coming at me, and I was killing them. I wanted to stop killing, but they just kept coming. I wanted to tell them to stop, but I couldn't speak. It just got worse and worse, all the blood, and there were more and more of them, and finally..." She looked at the woman's concerned face, controlled the hysteria that was building at the back of her throat. "...I guess I found a way to wake myself up."

"Hmm. And the whole camp, unfortunately. How are you feeling, now?"

Aleria shook her head. "I'm more upset that I had another dream than anything else. I thought I was doing so well, and I was having such a good time..."

Rumani smiled sadly and shook her head. "You didn't think you were going to get over it that easily, did you?"

"Now that you mention it, no. But it was sure nice for a while, there."

"Why do you think the dream came tonight? Is something bothering you?"

"Something's bothering me, all right. We'll be in the Capital tomorrow and I'll have to tell my parents. That's not going to be easy."

"That explains it. How are you going to tell them?"

"I've been thinking about that all day. I suppose the best thing to do is sit them down and tell them together. They'll need each other's support. And I'll need my mother's support to calm Father down." She smiled. "He's a bit of trouble when he gets upset."

Which turned out to be an understatement.

24. Once More, Her Parents

She sat the two of them down and started her tale. It went badly from the first, as she could see her father's face getting red. When she got to the part about the rape, he leapt to his feet, shouting and pacing up and down the room, threatening everyone he could think of.

Aleria watched him in dismay. *My father, who never loses control. And this is all my fault.* She could feel the tears starting to build. Her mother slipped over and sat beside her, encircling her with a comforting arm.

"You don't have to go on, dear. I know how hard it must be."

"I have to, Mother. But I knew he would react like this."

Her mother looked at her a moment, then raised her voice. "Kensel AnDalmyn! Calm yourself! It's you that's causing her all this pain. She's not worried about being raped, she's worried about you ranting and raving."

Her father stopped in mid-stride. "What?"

"Sit down here and let Aleria tell this, as she has to. You're making it very difficult for her. Would you rather not know at all? Do you think that would be healthy for her, for us all?"

He shook his head. "But Leniema, we have to do something about this. Our daughter has been attacked. They must pay. They must be punished!"

Aleria found a bubble of laughter forcing its way up her throat. She held it back, and it came out a sob instead.

"I'm sorry, father. If I had been thinking I would have left one for you. It would have helped, I know."

"What do you mean, dear?"

She sat a moment, then looked straight up at him. "I killed them all, father. I got them separated from each other, and I killed them. One with my dagger, the others with my sword. Raif killed Fauvé. So they're all dead, father. I'm sorry, but there's nothing left for you to do."

"You killed them? Oh, my poor dear." He knelt beside her, took her in his arms, held her head against his breast. "What a horrible thing to have to do."

She relaxed against him, then squirmed gently away. "I had to, Father. I was angry, so angry, and I kept myself angry, because then I didn't have to be anything else. And because I was angry, I had to kill them. It got me through."

She watched him. He didn't seem to hear. He was sitting, his head bowed, his hands twisting in his lap.

"What's wrong, Father?"

He looked up at her. "I...I can't say, Aleria. I feel terrible, and I don't know which it is." His eyes were brimming with tears, ready to fall. "I don't know which is worse, that my daughter has been violated by those horrible men, or that you killed them."

"Do you think it was wrong to kill them?"

"No, no, it was what you had to do. But it will change you. Once you have killed someone, you will never be the same person you were."

"I understand that, Father. I can already tell."

"You can? How?"

She smiled wanly. "Well, my nightmares have changed."

Her mother's arm tightened around her.

"I just realized it last night. You know those nightmares I used to have? Brought on by the rebellion? I haven't had one of those since...well, since I was raped. I have new ones. Ones that involve killing people. You were right about that, Father."

He nodded, sadly. "It was the same with me."

"With you? I never knew you killed anyone."

He straightened. "It's not the kind of thing you brag to your daughter about. But I remember the nightmares."

"Who did you kill?"

He sat there looking at her. "I suppose this is an appropriate time. I have been in battle, Aleria. I have killed quite a few people, I suppose. In a large battle it's so mixed up, you never can be sure. No, it was the first killing that affected me."

He sat beside her, took her hands. "You have to realize that it was necessary. It was a duel. Not one of those silly duels that the young blades involve themselves in. This was a serious one. He was a bully. He would pick on someone and push him and push him until finally he couldn't be pushed any more. Then there would be a duel and this man would win. He had killed two young men and injured several more.

"Then he decided to pick on me. I made all the usual excuses for him. He was drunk, he just lost his temper, he didn't mean to insult me. All those reasonable reasons. Then I realized he was never going to stop. Finally, like all the others, I said, 'No more.'

"I called insult on him. We fought, but it was different. I had already decided to kill him, and I think he knew it. He may have been as good a swordsman as I.

"But in the end he didn't have the nerve. When he realized that I intended to kill him, he lost his composure and with it, his skill. I finished him on the next pass.

"So what was wrong with that?"

Her father shook his head, slowly. "There was nothing wrong. If anyone deserved to die, he did. It wasn't him. It was me. It changed me. I grew up in a great hurry. And then there were the nightmares."

"Ah. You too?"

"Yes. I won't inflict you with the details. But I had nightmares."

"But they went away."

"Yes, they did. With time."

"Good. I hope mine do. Soon." She grinned, one side of her mouth only. "They're beginning to cost me friends."

"What do you mean?"

"I woke up the whole camp last night, screaming."

"Oh. Your escort?"

"Yes. The mercenaries."

Her father grinned. "I've got news for you, there. Those men are used to that."

"They are?"

"They live by killing. You think they don't have dreams?"

"Oh."

"So don't worry about the dreams. If you're anything like the rest of us, you'll get over them."

She relaxed back into her mother's shoulder. "Best news I've heard for a while. With the other dreams, nobody said that."

She reached out and squeezed her father's hand. "Are you ready to hear some more?"

He nodded. "And this time I will try not to over-react. I didn't realize how much it bothered you."

"Thank you, Father."

She proceeded to tell the tale, right to the end. At times, she could see his lips tightening, but each time he would control himself and let her continue.

When she had finished, there was a long pause. She looked at her father, then twisted to see her mother's face. It hurt her to realize that she was the cause of so much pain.

"I have been a headstrong, wilful, brat, and I got what was coming to me."

To her surprise, it was her mother who reacted. "No, Aleria. Never say that. Headstrong you may be, wilful sometimes, but never say that you deserved what happened."

She shrugged. "You're right. Nobody deserves that. But look at the facts. Two times I run off and do something stupid. Two times it gets me into deep trouble. Do you think I'll ever learn?"

Her father took her hand. "Yes, but look at the results. You have done good service for the realm both times. Yes, I admit that the two of you look like a couple of kids going off on a lark, but once you got into the situation, you got results."

"Us two."

"Yes, you and Raif."

"Yes, I don't know what I would have done without Raif."

"Probably nothing. Fauvé would have got what he wanted – an incident involving someone important. You would have come home and left it to someone else to take care of that problem. I think the way you and Raif handled it was brilliant, and he couldn't have done it without you."

She managed a small grin. "I'll take the 'brilliant' part as an opinion, but the rest is fact. We managed to use my situation to good advantage, and it was my plan that succeeded. It helps, you know. It's sort of like I got injured in a war or something."

Her father nodded. "I'm glad it helps. I'm worried about this killing business, though." He laid a hand over hers. "You will never again be the daughter that went away from us."

She couldn't stand the look on his face, so she slapped his hand in irritation, twisted against her mother's arm. "Oh, father, don't be melodramatic. I'm still the same. Well, maybe not quite the same, but not enough to make any real difference."

Her mother smiled. "Well, you haven't changed in that respect, anyway."

"Right. So let's not have any more of this goopy-goopy stuff. I've told you the story. It all turned out right in the end. There we have it. That's the end."

"But it isn't ended."

She turned to her mother in surprise. "No?"

Liniema shook her head slowly. "Until you get to be a parent, I don't think you really understand. We have been watching you grow and change all your life, watching and worrying. It's not just us. All parents do. Most of the changes are good, some are more troublesome." She smiled wryly. "Whatever you decide to do next, we will find something to worry about there too."

"Oh. That sort of thing. I know what you mean. You're right. Until I have my own children to worry about, I won't really know. And then I'll be smugly superior to them about it as well."

She could see her mother's eyes narrow, just for a moment. "You are joking, aren't you?"

She pressed her lips together, could not keep them straight. "That's right, Mother. I'm trying to demonstrate that the old Aleria is still here, ready to pounce out at the slightest provocation."

"And this is supposed to reassure us."

"I do my best."

They all laughed, but there was a sad tinge to it, which she knew would be a long time disappearing.

* * *

Aleria finished her story and looked at her three friends, upright in their usual lounge chairs in her sitting room, their faces pale.

"I refuse to let myself become a victim. Not in my own head. I tried that for two weeks during Slathe's rebellion, and I didn't like it at all. It gave me all sorts of problems, especially the dreams. You know, I haven't had one of those dreams since."

Mito sniffed. "Right. Now you dream about killing people. Some improvement."

"But that's the point. Everybody tells me these dreams are a natural reaction and they will go away. The other dreams weren't going away."

She turned to the Twins. "You know that old saying about how a brave man dies only once, but a coward dies every day?"

They both nodded, puzzled.

"Well, I think it was like that with being raped. When I was caught up in that rebellion, I spent the whole time being afraid. Then when it was over, there was no end to it. I was afraid of the fear, afraid of my imagination of what it would be like. Then when the real thing happened, it wasn't as bad as my imagination, because I could do something about it."

Hana shuddered. "Yes. You killed them."

Aleria grinned. "Don't you think they deserved it?"

"Well, yes, but..."

She sobered. "I know. Father was worried about that, too. He said he wasn't sure which he was more worried about. Killing people changes you. I hope not too much."

Mito stared at her a moment. "Don't you think about it all the time? I would."

"Yes, I think about it. I'm already not sure I did the right thing. Oh, I had to kill the first man in order to escape, and he was the leader, so you could say he deserved it. The second one, the one that bit me, I have no qualms about killing. It was like destroying vermin. It's the third one I'm not so sure about. He was just a stupid, ugly kid, and I could have left him sitting there in the bush swatting mosquitoes, and gone home. So, yes, Mito, I'm still thinking about it. I should be. It helps get it straight. It's not like I'm happy about killing people."

She went over and sat by Mito, an arm around her shoulders. "So don't worry. I'm still the same old me. The dreams are even getting better. I haven't woken the whole house with my screaming, have I?"

"Did you really do that?"

"On the road home. The last night before we got here, I was so concerned about how I was going to tell my parents that I worried myself into another nightmare. Woke the whole camp up, screaming. Those poor soldiers!

207

Gordon A. Long

"Father says it happens quite often in the army, so they'd be used to it. I don't know. They seemed to be...well...kinder to me the next day. I hated that. I liked the officer better. He joked about it."

"He joked about your nightmares?" Gita's frown looked angry.

"Yes, I know it sounds cruel, but he was that sort of person. He joked with the men all the time, but some of his jokes had a real point, you know? Don't worry; the men picked up on it. I never saw him discipline anyone, rarely heard him give an order."

"Sounds like a strange kind of officer."

"Yes, but you should have seen those soldiers work. They just got everything done, quickly, efficiently, with no hassles. If I had to go off to war, that's the kind of troop I'd choose to go with."

"Now you're talking about going off to war. And you don't think you've changed?"

She laughed, "No, Gita. I'm not planning to go off to war, even if there was one to go to. I just used it as an example. I would have said something like that before this happened, when we were still in school together."

Mito frowned. "Yes, but then we'd have known you were just being silly. Now, I'm not sure any more."

"You see my problem. I haven't changed; it's the way everybody is treating me that has changed. The sooner you get back to normal, the sooner I will."

She paused a moment, then grinned. "Maybe I should do one of my old, crazy stunts, so you could all be aghast at my stupidity, just like normal."

"It's all right, Aleria."

"You don't have to."

"Honest!"

She laughed freely, now. "There! I feel better already!"

Mito threw a pillow at her.

Gita's eyes gleamed and she leaned forward. "But tell us again. Did you really grab that man and punch him, then elbow him in the face?"

"Oh, yes. He was one of *those*, you could tell. He had the nerve to say I wasn't acting like I'd been raped. I found out later that he'd been forcing himself on any of the women in the manor that he could."

She made a fist, looked at it thoughtfully. "You know, I've practised thousands of reverse punches in the past four years. Master Ogima says it's the strongest punch, because the power comes all the way from your back foot, planted on the floor. I never realized until now how strong it is. Believe me, it felt good, giving one to that bully."

"But you said he almost drew his sword?" Hana's eyes were wide.

"Oh, he thought about it. I was pleading with him to draw it. I'd have killed him, too. I think he knew that.

"He sure learned something about how raped women act! One of the serving girls said his nose was all swollen up. She said she hoped I had broken it."

Mito shuddered. "I'd just as soon not think about it. I know it's important to talk about bad things, Aleria, but now I'm worried you'll give me nightmares!"

"Well, what are friends for? Share the joy, share the sorrow, share the nightmares." She looked around. "Anything interesting happen here while I was gone?"

Soon after that the Twins had departed, and in the silence they left behind, Mito sat looking at Aleria.

"Where was Shen in all of this?"

"After the rape? I never saw him."

"He never even showed up?"

"Yes, I know. It hurt, but I can understand. He's a merchant. Until they know which way the wind is going to settle, they just hunker down and wait. Once the new lord is firmly in control, they'll swarm around him, offering support."

"But not for you, when you needed it."

She smiled ruefully. "No, I guess not."

25. Setting Them All Straight

Aleria looked around her sitting room with satisfaction. The warm colours, the soft furniture, and all her familiar objects gave her a sense of peace. Then she looked at Mito, slouched on the settee. Definitely slouched. *Mito never slouches.*

"Mito, what is the matter with you? "

The girl raised her head, looked straight into Aleria's eyes. "What do you mean?"

Aleria grinned. "Nice try, Mito, but you can't work the 'fawn-eyed innocence' trick on me. You've been preoccupied for two days. You're no fun at all."

"And if I'm not fun, what then?"

"Then, my dear, we find out what's bothering you, and we fix it, and then you're fun again."

"Not this time, Aleria. You can't fix this one. Not you."

"Oh, it's a guessing game, with clues. Our little Mito has a problem that she can't solve, and I, specifically, can't solve either. What a challenge! Let's see..."

She clapped her hands and spun back, an accusing finger pointing at her friend. "You're in love. That has to be it. Aha! Go ahead. Deny it. See? You can't. You're a terrible liar, so don't even bother.

"But love isn't a problem. So there's a problem with the love. He doesn't love you. Is that it?"

Mito's head moved from side to side. "Not necessarily. I know he likes me. He's always very nice to me."

Aleria frowned. "Likes you. Nice to you. Nothing romantic, but better than nothing. There's more than that, isn't there? Of course there is."

"Aleria, I'd rather not talk about it."

"You wouldn't. You never do. But then we do talk about it, because I won't let it go until we do, and then it's fine again. Every time."

"Not this time."

Aleria stared into her friend's face for a moment. "You're pretty serious about this, aren't you? There must be a real problem with this love of yours. Well, if you won't tell me, I can't help, can I? Oh, that's right. Clue number one – Aleria can't help.

"I know. You've fallen in love with somebody who can't love you." She turned to her friend in shock. "It isn't a married man, is it?"

"Oh, Aleria, of course not."

"Aha. Then it's that old status thing again, isn't it? This fellow can't marry you because of your family. But I can help with that. I have been. Mother and Father have been. Even Duke anCanah has helped. So how can it be that I..."

Inspiration struck her. "You're in love with Raif!"

To her utter amazement, Mito burst into tears. Huge sobs tore from her, and she sat, her hands in her lap, her face streaming, eyes closed tight.

Aleria had never seen Mito cry before. Not a real cry, not like this, like a heartbroken child. She slid in beside her, put an arm around her shoulders, and used the other hand on her friend's cheek to gently turn her face.

"Mito, what's wrong? I realize it's pretty difficult, him being the Duke's son, and all that..."

"I...told you not to push me. I told...you I didn't want to talk about it." More sobs. Mito pounded both fists on the tabletop, slowly, twice, as if the pain somehow allowed her to keep a grasp on reality. "And now I've lost my best friend as well."

"Whatever are you talking about? You haven't lost me!"

Mito's face regained some composure. "Well, I can hardly hang around someone when she knows I'm in love with her husband. I don't think it will work, somehow."

"Husband? I'm not marrying Raif!"

A sudden shock passed across Mito's face. "You mean you didn't know?"

"I didn't know what? Mito, if you started out to set me off, as you sometimes do, you're doing a wonderful job of it." She sat beside the smaller girl, took her hands firmly, and pulled her straight. "Now you are not going to play any more games. Tell me all about it."

Mito's lips compressed for a moment, then she shrugged. "Raif and I were talking, the day before yesterday. He told me that his father was thinking of arranging a marriage for him. I asked him why he was telling me, and he said it was because the marriage was with you. Again, I asked him why he was telling me, and he said it was because he thought I should know, and what did I think of it?"

Mito's head ducked. "And then I told him there wasn't much point in my having an opinion one way or the other, and then I'm afraid I left, a bit more quickly than was strictly polite."

Aleria burst into laughter. "You mean you told him off and walked out on him? Mito that is beautiful. He needs that once in a while."

Mito smiled slightly. "He did seem a bit shocked."

Aleria lost her laughter. "But what a bone-headed stunt! He does that, sometimes. He gets it into his brain that he has to do something, and so he just goes and does it, no matter what the consequences to anybody else. I'm going to have a word with him. He can't just walk all over people's hearts like that!"

"Aleria, please don't."

Aleria stopped in the doorway and looked back at her friend. "Look, Mito, you didn't want me to pry into your last problem, and now look what's happened. Now you know I'm not marrying him, and you have a clear field."

"You're not? But you sound as if you haven't even been asked yet."

"I haven't, but if I am, I'm not marrying him. We fight all the time! What kind of life could you have with somebody you fight with?"

A thought struck her. "I know! Why don't you marry him, and then I can come and visit and have a good fight with him about once a week, and that'll put him back in tune for you! I like that idea."

Mito grimaced. "It sounds fine the way you say it, but I still wish you wouldn't meddle."

"Look, I'm not going to tell him you're in love with him, all right? I'm just going to tell him off for bothering you. Want to come along and watch, to see if I do it right?"

Mito gave one of her resigned sighs. "Oh, no. I'm not going to be anywhere near. In fact, I think I might just go back to Hymnos for a year or two until the smoke blows away."

"Don't you dare. If he's any kind of a gentleman, at least he'll come around and apologize. Then, when you've got him at a weak moment, you can sink your claws in him!" She made a sudden lunge at Mito, fingers crooked.

The dark girl laughed. "Well, Aleria, at least you cheered me up. Thanks for that."

"You're welcome. I told you I would. Now I'm off to meddle. I won't be back today, because I'm doing a training run with Master Ogima. See you tomorrow."

* * *

She found Raif easily, because the servants always knew where he was. He was, in fact, in deep discussion with his father. She quieted the servant, who was making anxious noises, and reached for the door handle.

Faced with this potential disaster, the servant made it to the door before she did and slipped it open. The two faces turned toward her as she entered. The Duke was the first to rise.

"Aleria, how opportune. We were just talking about you."

Aleria took his offered hand, dipped a quick curtsey. "That's good, your Grace. Now that I'm here, maybe we can straighten this out."

"Straighten what out?"

She raised her eyebrows, turned to stare at Raif. "And I have unpleasant things to say to your son."

"You do?"

"Yes, he has been very unfeeling and cruel to a friend of mine, and he should be rushing around right now to apologize."

"Raif?"

The poor man stumbled to his feet. "I don't know, Sir...I..."

"Yes, you do. Why don't you save me the trouble and you the embarrassment of having this out in front of your father? Just go and apologize like a gentleman should, and I'll stay and straighten this whole marriage mess out with the one in the family who has proper sensibilities."

Raif looked helplessly from Aleria to his father.

"Well, Raif, it sounds like Aleria is a bit ahead of us. If you have a gentlemanly duty, perhaps it would be best if you perform it at once." There was a chill in the old Duke's voice, and Raif straightened.

"Yes, Sir. I suppose Aleria is right. I acted hastily, though I had no intention of causing strife. If this person was injured by my action, I will go immediately and make my apologies."

He turned to Aleria, "But I really can't see why she should be so upset. I merely asked..."

She took his arm, propelled him towards the door. "You can think about it on the way over there. If you haven't figured it out by then, ask her."

Once Raif was on his way, she returned to his father. "I'm sorry, your Grace. I know I shouldn't have barged in like that, but I was so angry with him. He just does things like that, without considering other people's feelings."

"Other feminine people?"

"In this case, yes."

"Do I gather that means our little discussion about you is premature?"

"To put it bluntly, I think stillborn is a better term, your Grace."

He nodded slowly. "Ah. So there is no thought of marriage?"

"We fight all the time, your Grace. Can you imagine being married to someone you fight with?"

"With due deference, Aleria, I have observed you two together on numerous occasions and I had the impression that you found considerable pleasure in each other's company. I would never have put this idea forward, had I not felt this."

"Oh, I like Raif a lot. He's a good friend. But I couldn't marry him. Besides, there's another impediment. As we just mentioned."

"Ah, and who is this impediment?"

She thought a moment. "Your Grace, I find myself in a difficult position. It is not my intention to meddle in the affairs of the Canah family, except where they involve myself and my friends.

Since this whole situation is...problematic...I don't know if it is my place..."

The duke sat, and motioned her to do the same. "My dear, we could play guessing games, and I could get this information from you. Or I could use my rank to force it from you." He raised his hands defensively. "Perhaps, perhaps not. Why don't we avoid all that, and you just tell me what information you know is true. You know I will act as I see fit, whether now, on your word, or later, on Raif's."

She sighed. "You know how to appeal to me, your Grace. I hate the playing around as much as you do."

He smiled. "I didn't say I hated it. I just prefer to dispense with it in this case."

"All right. The problem, your Grace, is that I think Raif is a bit sweet on Mito anTrus. He can't marry her, so...he's got a problem."

"Ah, Mito. She was helping you in some way with that business in Taine, wasn't she?"

"Exactly. And as a reward, he went and asked for her opinion on whether he should marry me."

"He did that?"

"He did."

"Ah. I hope he finds a very acceptable way to make apology." The Duke frowned, looked at her. "And he can't marry her?"

"I know you are aware of her family's situation, Sir."

"Yes, I am probably more aware of it than most. A serious miscarriage of justice, in my opinion. I am doing what I can to right the wrong, but it is difficult, after fifteen years."

"A miscarriage of justice?"

"Very much so. It is a familiar tale these days. Business deals are becoming far more complicated than they used to be. It is possible for a sharp dealer to involve a lot of people in some scheme or other, then duck out when it fails, leaving someone else to clean up the mess. In this case, the Trus family didn't have the reserves to cover the losses."

"But they used those Mechanical bearings or whatever."

He shook his head. "Time moves on. Today every mill in the realm is using Mechanical bearings. No, I think fifteen years in purgatory is enough to pay for their errors."

"Does Raif know you think this way?"

"I suppose so. I haven't discussed it with him, but he is aware of my business dealings. He has to be."

"Business dealings?"

"Yes. We are expanding some of our enterprises into that area, and we are negotiating with anTrus. He could be very useful to us. He was right from the first, you know. Hymnos is the ideal spot in the realm for a sawmill, and he holds the rights to it. The plan is to rebuild their mill with the proper Mechanics, use Dennal's raftsmen to take our logs down to Hymnos to be cut, and Dalmyn wagons to bring the planks back to the markets. It's a very neat plan. You can ask your father about it."

"Well, your Grace, I think you are about to make up for fifteen years of injustice."

"I thought it would help."

"It will, but if I know your son, he is in the process of making it up in a more practical way as we speak."

The duke smiled. "Is that your considered opinion?"

"Knowing what your opponent will do next is a technique we practise in Battle Arts classes, your Grace."

"And you consider my son an opponent?"

"In a way. If I don't keep him in line, who will? Oh. Of course I won't need to any more, will I?"

"You think this young lady can? She seems quite meek. Enchanting, though. I remember finding her very attractive, in her quiet sort of way. Very...composed." He nodded slowly. "Yes...while perhaps not the alliance I had been hoping for, she might be the right type for a Duke's lady..."

Aleria laughed. "Sir, she has been practising 'meek' for fifteen years. I think she has tempered into fine steel underneath."

She looked up at the clock on the mantelpiece. "And now, your Grace, I think I have meddled enough. I have a special training session this afternoon, and Master Ogima has little patience for latecomers."

"Ah, yes. I had been meaning to ask you about that. You have been training in the Battle Arts quite seriously."

"Yes. It started as a solution to my fears after my experience in Slathe's rebellion. However, I find I enjoy it immensely."

"I see. And did it stop the dreams?"

"No, reality did that. The training allowed me to deal with the situation afterwards."

"Ah..."

"Don't worry, your Grace. It's no problem for me to talk about it. I usually don't, because it bothers other people."

He smiled, that faint twist of the lips. "Thoughtful of you."

"If I go around talking about it all the time, it looks like I'm trying to attract attention or sympathy. Besides being very boring after a while."

The Duke rose. "Again, Aleria, I find myself in the unfortunate position of expressing regret that you will not be joining my family. May I assume your friendship with Raif will continue?"

"If he marries Mito...she is my best friend. One of the few including Raif, I guess. I am also taking a more active role in my father's business, so you might find me at meetings also."

He nodded. "Good. I will enjoy that."

"I find that marriage has rather retreated from my mind these days. Other interests seem more important."

"I gather so. Have a good practice."

"Oh, I'm sure I will, your Grace. Thank you for being so understanding."

"Thank you for meddling, Aleria. Do you ever get the impression that most people wouldn't be able to function if you didn't give them a nudge once in a while?"

"Yes, your Grace, I do. And every time it happens, I slap myself across the head with something heavy. I doubt if it helps, but at least it seems that I'm trying."

His laughter followed her down the hallway.

* * *

The marriage of Raif, heir of anCanah, to Mito, of the recently ascendant anTrus family, was the wonder of the season. Aleria stayed in the background as much as possible, determined that no act of hers would spoil the wedding of her friends. She was aware of the speculation that brushed by her occasionally, but she wasn't interested. She allowed the ceremony to flow over and around her, enjoying the colour, the lights, the music and the obvious joy of her two friends.

It was late in the evening of the wedding day when she had a final word with the bride before her new husband whisked her off to honeymoon at his rustic country seat, to bask in the autumn colours of the mighty forests of the Northwest. Aleria sat for a moment, regarding her friend, until Mito put a hand to her hair.

"Is something wrong? Why are you smiling like that?"

"How could anything be wrong? I'm smiling because I like to be proved right."

Mito sat back, lowered her brows. "And in which instance have you discovered yourself right, this time?"

Aleria laughed. "A year or so ago, at our graduation, I told you that you were beautiful. You ducked the compliment with your usual blend of modesty and good sense, but nonetheless, you disagreed. Now, finally, my opinion has been corroborated by at least a thousand people. Read the newspapers tomorrow, if you manage to find enough interest in the outside world."

Her friend cocked her head to one side, wrinkled her brow. "No, it's more than that."

"Are you changing the subject?"

"Not at all. I'm trying to figure out why you look the way you do. It's not an expression I have seen a lot of, especially recently."

Aleria shrugged, leaned back, and allowed the other girl - no, woman - to regard her. Then Mito snapped her fingers. "I've got it!"

"Have you? You must tell me what immediately. I can barely contain myself."

"That's it exactly. It isn't what I see. It's what I don't see."

Aleria raised her eyebrows. "Brides are allowed all sorts of latitude to be irrational at their weddings, but you're going to have to explain that one."

"It's simple. You don't look like you're about to do something rash."

Aleria shook her head. "That's easy. I decided, long before your wedding, that I wouldn't do anything in the slightest to spoil your day or take the attention away from you. It was the least I could do."

Her friend smiled. "That's very gracious of you, I'm sure, but that's not what I mean. What I see on your face is...not that you won't do one of your old stunts. No. What I see is that you don't want to."

"Ah! Deep analysis. Isn't that what I just said?"

"Not at all. You not only don't want to, you don't need to. You're happy, Aleria. That's what it is."

"Why shouldn't I be? I can say honestly that I only have four friends, and two of them are getting married today. I had some small part in bringing that event about. I have also just been through a difficult time, and I have proved capable of handling a great deal of trouble. I'm not so naive as to think I'm free of the consequences, but I have proved myself able to handle those as well.

"Of course, I haven't yet found the ideal circumstances that suit me perfectly, but I have proved myself capable of coping in many situations, so I am optimistic that I will soon be able to find a place, or at least be successful until I do. Yes, I think you're right. I'm happy." She regarded her friend. "How about you?"

"Do you have to ask?"

"No. It stands out all over you. I was just being polite."

"If it weren't beneath my dignity as a newly-married lady on her wedding day, I would throw several large and heavy pillows at you."

"I consider myself chastised."

"Good. Then you'll be in proper form to greet my new husband and his father. I see them coming this way."

Aleria rose. "You know, I take that back, about having only four friends. I think Duke anCanah is a very interesting man. He never did marry after his wife died. I wonder why?"

Mito turned to her in horror. "Aleria! You aren't thinking..."

Aleria burst into peals of laughter. When she could finally speak, she choked out, "You didn't think you were going to get through the day unscathed, did you?"

Gordon A. Long

Mito smiled weakly. "For a brief moment, I pictured having you for a mother-in-law..." She shook her head and shuddered briefly. "It doesn't bear thinking of."

Aleria smiled. "Well, if it was any other day I'd keep you in suspense, but I'll let you off the hook. The duke, rich, powerful, and stimulating as he may be, is not on my list of possible candidates."

"Oh, thank you, Aleria. That's the best wedding present you could give me."

The groom approached, and the ceremonies of the wedding swept the two friends apart.

26.   Master Ogima

Late the next afternoon Aleria was feeling quite ready for a bit of good, clean exercise, so she headed off to Master Ogima's training rooms.

Where a different sort of reception awaited her.

"You are early for practice, Aleria."

"Yes, Master Ogima, though not as early as I planned. I had hoped to work by myself for a while, just to blow out the cobwebs from the week of celebration."

"Just time for a chat, then."

She lowered her head, looked up at him. "I know about your little chats."

"Good. Follow me, please."

When she was seated on a cushion in his private reception room, he also sat, and looked at her for a moment. "You have had an eventful year."

"I have, Master."

"Have you had time to think about these events, time enough to get them straight?"

"Yes and no. Time, yes. Enough time, no."

He nodded, a faint smile quirking his lip. "Some would say there is never enough time for that."

She waited for him to make his point.

"Have you any thoughts on the rightness of your actions?"

"Yes. Some were appropriate, some less so. One, in retrospect, was unnecessary."

"Four deaths, only one in error?"

"I believe so. One was necessary for survival. One was necessary for the protection of all. Of one I am still unsure, but under the law, it was destined. The fourth served no purpose other than the gratification of my anger."

"The last will be the important one, then."

"It will?"

"Actions that are justified require little scrutiny. Actions spurred by emotion, unaffected by reason, require much more reflection. Thus, in a future situation of the sort, you will act on different principles and be more pleased at the outcome."

Gordon A. Long

"I sincerely hope I will not be in a situation of the sort at any time in the future."

He shrugged, his head tilting to the side. "However...?"

"What do you mean, 'however?' I don't plan to ever place myself into that kind of danger again."

"Yet you are here."

She thought of that for a moment. "I enjoy practising."

"Why?"

"Because..." His stare stopped her, caused her to think again. "I see what you mean."

He nodded. "Good. If I may be allowed to make an observation...?"

She suppressed a smile. "Your observations are always welcome, Master."

"You have perhaps made progress in that area, as well."

Was that a small quirk to his lip? She nodded slowly.

"My observation, Aleria, is one that applies to myself and all who work with me. Once you have made your life dependent on the use of violent means, you can never go back."

"Never?"

He shook his head firmly. "It is not possible. Once you have demonstrated to yourself that a violent act may achieve your ends, you will always consider the use of another violent act."

"But what's wrong with that?"

Now he did smile. "Did I speak of right or wrong? If you look at my avocation, you must realize my belief on that subject."

"Of course."

"The fact remains. You made a decision the moment you started your practices with me. The option of violence had already become part of your thoughts."

"Damn right it had! It was slapped in my face often enough while I was with Slathe's rebels."

He raised a calming hand. "Once again, we do not speak of right or wrong. We speak of factors which influence your life and how you should live it from now on."

"And how should that be?"

"Once again..."

"...we do not speak of right or wrong. Fine. What does this factor mean for my future life?"

He shrugged. "Who knows the future?"

"Oh, don't give me that mystic pap. What you mean is that once I have taken all this training, there is no way I can ever go back to being a pampered and protected lady. I will continue to put myself in positions where it is necessary to use my training, perhaps only to justify it."

"It is true that our society has made progress in that respect."

She shook her head, not following this sudden change of subject.

"There was a time when even the noble women of our society were expected to consider the possibility of the violent act. Hence the barehand training and the Quest at your Academy. As you have been known to opine, this time is passing. However, you discovered that it has not run its course completely. Our people have made progress, but that gives us new problems to solve."

"Are you saying that you think I was right?"

"I assumed you knew that. I did accept you for further training, did I not? Your parents agreed." He lowered his brows. "You don't think you got your way through the strength of your will, do you?"

She laughed. "Perhaps, at the time. When you put it in that perspective, I feel rather foolish."

"Good. Perhaps that is the best learning of all."

She shook her head ruefully. "Oh, I've had plenty of time to think about the foolishness of my actions."

"We all need to be reminded of our human failings. And our failings as a society."

"You mean the unrest that allows people like Fauvé the chance for success."

"I do. Perhaps some day you will work on that."

"Me?"

"The first step is to know the problem exists. Many are aware of it, now. You are as far ahead as any of us in the second step: knowing why."

"I am? That is a frightening thought."

223

"It is. Perhaps you should keep thinking on it." He rose. "I hear the others coming."

She began to precede him from the room, but his hand on her arm stopped her. "Remember, this, Aleria. In every situation fate has placed you, your actions have been completely consistent with your training."

His other hand took her left arm, grasped tightly. "We are all fiercely proud of you."

He left her there, her face burning, and strode out to meet the rest of his students.

Epilogue

The merchant's hand was on his sword before he came fully awake. Reassured, he opened his eyes. Light, shuffling footsteps outside the tent. In some kind of pattern. Step-step pause, step-step pause. Curious but not alarmed, he rose and slipped open the door flap. Aleria was working through her routines: punch, kick, block, spin. He watched in appreciation, enjoying the precision of her movement, the play of moonlight and sweat on her skin. Finally, when she paused, breathing rapidly, he spoke.

"A little late for practice, isn't it?"

"Just working off a bad dream, Arnaud. Nothing serious."

"You said you only get nightmares when you're worried."

"That's right. It's how my brain tells me that something's wrong."

He lifted his sword. "What does your brain think is wrong?"

"The wagons are too heavily loaded, the cargo is too valuable…"

"…and that marshal, or whatever he called himself, in the last town asked way too many questions."

"That bothered me, too. I just doubled the sentries."

"So what will your men think, when they pull extra duty because you had a bad dream?"

"It wouldn't occur to them to ask. They know I don't do anything without a reason."

The merchant nodded. "A loyal bunch."

"They are, and everybody knows it. Nobody bothers a Dalmyn caravan, even this far from home."

They stood in silence for a moment, enjoying the moonlit scene.

"Can I ask a question?"

She shrugged. "If it seems the right moment."

"I was honoured to join this enterprise."

"You're a good man for this sort of thing."

"But your first trip to Aesmark, you used the Cloet family."

"You have been asking questions."

"It can be useful. What I find interesting is that the pattern is backwards. Usually a merchant decides to risk a new trade route, and he hires someone to transport him and guard him. Not in this case. You start out with Roeble Cloet. The next trip, the merchant is Girard, but the wagons are Dalmyn again. Now it seems to be my turn. What's happening?"

She considered the question. "Roeble came on the first trip as a personal favour. We needed him for his experience, and we made it worth his while. For the second trip, we looked to another partner, and the Cloets went back to their farther-reaching routes."

"I see..."

"Girard didn't work out. You don't need to know why. You were next on the list. I think you've done pretty well."

"Yes, I think I have. The prices we got for...wait a moment, that's not what you meant, is it? You're not talking about my profits." He turned to face her. "You've been testing me! You brought me out here on speculation, to see if I could handle it. Your father trusts you to make that kind of decision?"

"Not only my father."

That set him to thinking. She waited.

"The Canah connection. I wondered at that. Everyone knows that young anCanah has been making powerful contacts, but nobody knows what he's doing with them. Does this route have diplomatic repercussions?"

"We'll be home in a couple of weeks, and you'll be told the rest by those who know much more than I do. That is if you want to join us."

He chuckled. "Oh, I want to, that's certain. As I said, I've done well on this trip, and I can see ways of doing better."

"That's another reason I'll be recommending you."

He turned away, speaking to the world in general. "Here I am, worried that my chief partner on the expedition is only a young girl, and it turns out she's been assigned to keep watch on me, to see if I'm worthy." He swung back to her. "I apologize for any slight, however unstated. I should have known I was in good hands. You don't think we're going to be attacked?"

"I don't expect it, although we will take extra precautions until we cross the border, and a while after that. Don't worry. We'll handle anything that comes up."

"I have no doubts. Good night, Aleria."

"Sleep well, Arnaud."

"I think I will."

She stood regarding the campsite, every sense alert. All was calm. She slipped back into her tent and stretched out on the blankets. The terror of the dream had faded as it always did, and she composed herself to sleep. She wasn't that worried. Her men were loyal, well trained, and alert. All they needed was a bit more stiff action to form them into a fine unit. Arnaud was a level head, not the type to panic, with firm control over his drivers.

Her fingers strayed to the sword slung by her head, caressed the hilt lightly. Comforted, she slept.

The End

If you enjoyed this book, please do the author and other readers a favour. Go to Amazon or another online retailer and give it a review. Even a star rating would be nice.

About the Author

Brought up in a logging camp with no electricity, Gordon Long learned his storytelling in the traditional way: at his father's knee. He now spends his time editing, publishing, travelling, blogging and writing fantasy and social commentary, although sometimes the boundaries blur.

Gordon lives in Tsawwassen, British Columbia, with his wife, Linda. When he is not writing and publishing, he works on projects with the Surrey Seniors' Planning Table and is a staff writer for <indiesunlimited.com>

More from Gordon A. Long

Other Titles by Gordon A. Long available at
<amazon.com>

Science Fiction

"Factory 4-80" Freighty 1
"Outback Rebellion" Freighty 2
"Asimov's Laws" Freighty 3
"Occam's Razor" Freighty 4
"Slivership" Freighty 5
"Centauri Triangle" Freighty 6

Coming Soon
"Plague Jumper" Space Opera

Fantasy

"Ocean of Grass" Petrellan Saga 1
"Waves of Stone" Petrellan Saga 2
"Path of Water" Petrellan Saga 3
"Zoysana's Choice" The Petrellan Saga 4
"The Innkeeper's Husband" Petrellan Saga 5
"Mercenary's Dream" Petrellan Saga 6

"Out of Mischief" World of Change 1
"Into Trouble" World of Change 2
"Mountains of Mischief" World of Change 3
"The Trouble with Tents" World of Change 4
"Queen of Mischief" World of Change 5

"A Sword Called...Kitten?" Romantic Comedy with
an Edge
"The Cat with Many Claws" Sword Called Kitten 2
"Cloud Cat" Sword Called Kitten 3

229

Gordon A. Long

Other Genres

"Storm Over Savournon" (A Novel of the French Revolution)

"Why Are People So Stupid?" Social Humour with a Point

Online

Look for Gordon's books, selected reviews, poetry and short stories: <airbornpress.ca>
Gordon's opinions on humanity "Are People Really That Stupid?" blog:
<http://airbornpress.ca/arepeoplestupid/>
Find all his reviews and his ideas on writing at "Renaissance Writer:"
<http://airbornpress.ca/newdir/>

www.ingramcontent.com/pod-product-compliance
Lightning Source LLC
Chambersburg PA
CBHW060317260626
47160CB00007B/2642